Clarity's Doom

by

C.L. Scholey

Ancient Origins Book 1

Clarity's Doom

Contact Information: info@thewildrosepress.com

Cover Art by *Kristian Norris*

The Wild Rose Press, Inc.
PO Box 708
Adams Basin, NY 14410-0708

Visit us at www.thewilderroses.com

Publishing History
First Scarlet Rose Edition, 2016
Print ISBN 978-1-5092-0989-7
Digital ISBN 978-1-5092-0990-3

Published in the United States of America

**Sinkholes have never been more dangerous…
love has never been more explosive.**

Clarity was certain she heard someone talking, someone close by. The hairs on her nape stood tall, her body chilled just as the oppressive heat consumed her again. Someone was inside her home. A fine line of sweat dripped at her temple.

Resisting the urge to call out, Clarity moved toward the source. Her computer table was dark. There was no battery, it died, and she had been too busy for a replacement. It ran on electricity alone. Her hand moved toward the headphones she recently plugged in to blare music and not have the neighbors complain. She lifted the set to her ears and held her breath.

There was a voice on the other end. A strong male voice. She tried to concentrate on the language being spoken but it was no use; she couldn't make it out. Not one word was familiar which surprised her. With the AC not running, the room was immediately engulfed in heat. The sudden chill vanished, and sweat began to drip from more than just Clarity's temples. Her hands shook.

"Hello?" she whispered.

The words stopped. Quiet in the room made the pounding of her heart that much clearer.

"Hello, female."

"Who is this?"

"You will find out soon enough."

Clarity dropped the headset, the purse slipped to the crook of her elbow. She backed up a step when she heard the voice again. "…*we are coming for you."*

Dedication

This story is dedicated to those of us who have had to pull ourselves up and begin again.

Chapter One

"There are no answers as yet to the devastating sinkhole in Newfoundland."
Click.
"Deer Lake images of Viking village, recent sighting of massive sinkhole."
Click.
"Scientists have no indication as yet to how deep the enormous sinkhole is…"
Click.
"When ocean and land collide to form a sinkhole, sightings of sharks and horses create strange bedfellows…"
Clarity reached to turn off the radio, punching the button with an annoyed finger. The static from the airwaves lingered in the confined space, taunting with numbing quiet. Every channel broadcast the same thing. Massive sinkholes erupting or eroding in places stretching across the planet. The frequency at which the anomalies appeared was growing in consistency. So much so, some people were too afraid to venture from their homes, until homes started disappearing. Entire towns slipped into mass voids, claiming the lives of thousands. Gone without a trace. Video and cell phones caught terrifying glimpses of strange abnormalities, sending graphic images to news stations or the web.

Speculation was rampant. Aliens, to government

conspiracy on handling overpopulation. Some people insisted government officials weren't what or whom they appeared to be. Drastic images, real or photoshopped showed certain members of parliament hovering over the ground. Pictures that were immediately blown off by authorities or openly revered by naysayers had many up in arms. Many more were certain the return of Christ was forthcoming.

Disaster lurked in every corner of the Earth. Eyes were everywhere. No longer was a person's last breath sacred. Each new picture or footage more gruesome than the last. Every scenario replayed in the minds and hearts of anyone watching. The scenes were next to impossible to avoid, and in Clarity's line of work she couldn't look away. Science wasn't for the faint of heart; it was for truth seekers.

The images assaulting her mind made Clarity shudder. It was impossible to turn off the pictures of one's cognizance—a damning revelation. People, cars, malls, villages one moment there, the next vanished into the earth. Screams of terror cut short as individuals and families were swallowed whole into the bowels of Hell. People's faces became set in masks of forlorn desperation to the lost and grieving.

Sinkholes, though not rare in entirety, gave birth to a new breed of panic. The holes were never ending, leading where no one knew. No traces of bodies were found over the course of two years. On rare occasions, there was the odd vehicle spotted on a sinkhole's cliff. Embedded metal rooftops formed seals against the sometimes smooth, sometimes banked hole sides.

Fracking was blamed, but there were some scientists, Clarity included, almost included, as she hadn't finished her studies in geology, with unorthodox ideas. There were so many new ideas in the world, and science was growing by leaps and bounds. Shade balls and thirsty concrete were invented, to name only a couple, to explain how the sinkholes could be caused. There were many farfetched ideas.

Many children vanished. Sucked into unforgiving holes. The sad gravesites boasted a sea of wreaths and flowers, stuffed animals and other childhood paraphernalia to mourn a senseless, unexplained loss. So heart wrenching were the losses, families set up an endless stream of nonstop videos of loved ones to play and replay mounted on screens near the devastating sites. Videos of Christmases past, birthdays, holidays. Tributes to the dead. Tattered papers of hand-written poetry curled in the air. Expressions of grief, as though words could find their way into the unknown where whispering souls now treaded.

Governments denied any allegations of human blame and imposed strict bans on photos leaning toward environmental disasters. A battle they were fast losing in today's technological society. Clarity understood the idea behind the government concept: Mind your own fucking business, and if we want your opinion we'll give it to you. The ostrich effect wouldn't work in a society fueled by zealous curiosity—and outrage. Politicians weren't always the smartest; they were often the biggest bullies. When the masses stood up to the bullies, they were put in jail, their assets frozen, stolen because asking informed questions came at a price. Political temper tantrums.

One theory Clarity couldn't pinpoint in the beginning was the lack of identifying marks of smallpox inoculations on a certain age group, if records were correct. She tried to wrap her mind around the idea as to why none of the victims possessed the one tiny mark. Of those lost to sinkholes the age group indicated forty-seven years and younger. As well as seventy-three years and older.

Stages of the development of the shot could have been different in the older generation. Problems developed when touching the mark—as the inability to open the eyes for a short period—hospitalization was required. Mass inoculations were reintroduced for children from the late '60s to early '70s, eradicating the disease in developed countries, then stopped once the threat appeared to have passed.

Bodies were also lost in third world countries, and there was no proof of actual age groups. But it was a theory that gnawed consistently, as those missing appeared to be within the same age groups. Lack of records was a huge hindrance when trying to discover if the theory proved correct. One single age group seemed untouchable if medical records could be believed. An undying question nagged Clarity. Just over a decade after discovering Area 51, mass inoculations went global. Clarity wondered if there was something in those doses people didn't know about.

When she broached her question to higher powers years earlier, the reintroduction of a new inoculation appeared almost overnight. Mass amounts of children and adults were targeted. The plan included all except seniors and those already marked with the smallpox vaccine. Newer records hinted any unable to seek medical aid were at risk, as well as those who refused the shot. Clarity was still trying to figure out exactly what risk the others were exposed to.

Unconsciously, Clarity touched the moon shaped indentation on her upper left arm. The shot was mandatory in her line of work. There were those in the public who refused the needle. Some suspected tiny tracking devices or microchips were inserted under the skin. Clarity had no clue, she remembered being ill for four days after the shot, and in fact many experienced the same problem, but not all. There was a roundish small pink mole where the shot had punctured, but the smallpox inoculation left a mark as well. Some like Clarity became feverish to the point of delirium. Strange dreams followed Clarity after she recovered. Many she didn't want to dwell on.

Clarity groaned. "Work day is over. Leave it at work. It belongs at work. It stays at work." Her mantra. One day Clarity planned on getting married and having children. When she was at home, she wanted only to be a mother and a wife. As with everything else in her life worth achieving, Clarity began with practice.

She turned her little silver Jetta on to her street and swung into her driveway. The townhouse was small, clean, in a quiet neighborhood, bought and paid for with her own money. Clarity worked hard, continuing to make a name for herself in her career. Even if it was only a small name, it was a start. Nothing was given to her in the beginning of her profession—the Mrs. Ingalls of the woods—until a different company snapped her up.

Clarity was in possession of an elevated IQ and because of her expansive knowledge and aptitude, the company she now worked for kept her happy. Her boss, an older gentleman, developed an interest in her aptitude early. His special interest wasn't physical and there was nothing she could put a finger on, but he seemed to be grooming her for bigger and better. His persona seemed different in a way that nagged at her. His mannerism was beyond worldly, more universal in nature. The idea made her shudder sometimes, smile at other times.

Pushing the door handle of the car, the blast of warm, heady summer outside air assaulted Clarity as she swung her legs to the ground. The skirt she wore was hiked to her upper thighs. Her shades slipped down her nose as she ducked back in for her purse on the passenger side floor. Ass in the air for a mere moment, she felt her skirt settle to cover her revealing panties. The driveway was sticky under her heels; the pavement sweating. The accompanying sucking sounds irritating as she moved to the porch. Three steps up, she punched in her lock code, twisted the knob, and she was inside away from the sweltering heat of the day. Entering into the solid wall of stale air made her groan.

Oppressive ominous, blah.

She tossed her large leather purse onto a blue easy chair and the multitude of contents clanked before settling. Clarity strode for the kitchen, heels clicking across the hardwood floor. There was a bottle of Blue Light waiting for her in the fridge. When she cracked the seal, a spiral of smoky air wafted when hitting the heat, and she lifted the opening to her lips, closing her mouth around the sleek coolness. A fine drop of wetness slid from the bottle to land on her throat, and she shivered when the liquid dripped between her breasts, her warm skin already heating the moistness. The black microwave caught her image and she saw the heat of the kitchen was curling tendrils of her hair, moistening her temples with sweat.

Half the bottle drained, chugging like a pro, she sauntered to the ancient AC in the living room and switched a button. The cool air was a relief, and she lifted her shirt to cool her belly. Regardless, she would be happy when the central air was installed next week. Central air hadn't really been a concern when she bought her home in the cold winter month of February. It was now the blistering heat of what was appearing to be a long stifling summer. Her cell phone chimed the song of her choice and Clarity sighed as she read who the caller was. She put her beer down and took off her earrings before answering.

"Hi, Edward."

"Hey babe, I can't make it tonight. I'm still crunching numbers."

She knew he would be. Edward was married to his job. She slid off her heels, a balancing act with the cell pressed to her ear.

"Not a problem, Edward. I'm beat. It was a long day. It's too hot to eat anyway."

Clarity flopped into her favorite chair, reached down and deftly undid the top three buttons of her shirt, shrugged and stripped it off. Her curtains were closed to the blazing sun. She decided the furniture wouldn't be offended if she tossed her bra. She glanced down at her white, high, firm breasts with dusty rose nipples showing the outer glow of a tan she was working on when possible. For a second, she smiled cheekily thinking to tell Edward she and her naked body were headed for a cold shower, then decided against it. No doubt he would tell her 'that's nice' in the indifferent tone he used when consumed with a project. Not flattering.

"Rain check?" Edward asked.

"Sure."

"Talk to you soon."

Silence. Edward was no doubt working on his task before he hung up with her. Clarity tossed her phone beside her and chugged the rest of her beer. Half-naked, she walked to the kitchen, ditching her heels to clatter to the floor. Barefoot now, she reached her hand into the fridge and grabbed another bottle of beer and headed to the shower, losing her skirt to the tile bathroom floor followed by lace panties. She placed the beer bottle on an empty square shelf meant for soap. Clarity gave her head a quick shake—*who the hell uses hard soap anymore?*

She shivered with the first blast of icy water as she turned only the cold handle, her fingers wiggling under the spray, then she leisurely added a tiny touch of warmth. Arctic tundra was too much but frigid was good. She stepped under the cascade gasping and groaning with relief. The cold pounding water cleared her muggy thoughts.

She stood still, hands splayed against the wall as she felt the water sluice over her face, breasts, and belly, running deliciously between and down her legs to pool for a few moments at her feet. Water, always the demanding lover as skin everywhere was touched at once.

Women should be so lucky with a man.

Clarity turned, eyes closed, fumbling, she found and gripped her beer and sucked lazily at the contents. She set the icy bottle between her tits for a moment, head back, and let the water massage her shoulders and back and drip between her ass cheeks.

When finished, she dried and dressed in a blue tank top, bra, clean panties, and jean cut-offs. Her beer empty, the edge taken off the oppressing heat, Clarity decided she wanted a decent dinner. Alcohol always stimulated her appetite. A marinating chicken breast was in the fridge calling to her stomach. She put the frozen piece in this morning as an afterthought knowing there was a ninety percent chance of Edward canceling dinner out. He was always unpredictable when he was engrossed in a new project. She doubted he would remember to eat. It wouldn't take much to toss a small salad to go with her meal.

The kitchen was hot and she reached to flick the switch of a fan knowing the AC would take a while to reach the back of her house. She opened the freezer and stood close looking for ice, thinking a tall glass of water would go great with dinner, and basking in the coolness offered. The fan came to life for all of six seconds before the power went out darkening the shadowed corners of her home. The freezer became a frozen silent cave. She sighed and closed the door. Peeking out her window she saw signs of a block-wide power outage.

Clarity groaned. "Damn it."

She retrieved the small battery-operated radio she kept handy and switched it on. Wondering if the outage was restricted to her area. Dinner out in an air-conditioned restaurant wouldn't break her budget, but she was loath to go back outside into the oppressive heat and then realized it would soon be as hot indoors. Barbequing was a no. Nothing like standing out in the tyrannical heat leaning over fire. That was an appetite killer.

Static from the radio filled her ears until she was able to maneuver the dial onto a channel without a life/death, of its own. The anchor was frustrated; it was in the tone of his voice. Clarity turned up the volume. She felt her brows furrow.

"Some say the bodies appearing are from two years ago. All intact but deceased. Time of death no more than forty-eight hours ago. Where did they go, and why are they suddenly reappearing? The government is being extremely closed mouthed about this, and we have to question the motives behind the secrecy and..."

The radio freaked out again, the anchor suddenly sounded alien, and Clarity growled and shook the device near her face.

"Where, damn you, where are the bodies reappearing?"

Silence. Clarity slammed the radio down onto the table hard enough to dislodge the backing and pop the battery free. She ran a frustrated hand through her damp hair and took a deep breath trying to maintain control. A few simple sentences left unsaid, and said, were enough to cause a stir of emotions. The disturbing sinkholes had many feeling uneasy. A significant enough number of lost lives and missing civilians were on the mind-numbing side as of late. But a find of this magnitude was relevant; the government couldn't be allowed to conceal vital news.

Clarity slipped on her runners determined to find out where this development was occurring. Somewhere out there someone had to have power or a generator. Her cell still sat perched precariously where she set it down. There was no reception.

"Damn it. What the hell is going on?"

She snatched up her purse, used to the weight of a seasoned fast traveler, and tossed the cell inside. If she had to, she was ready to board a plane. She spun to race to the door, her purse slung over a shoulder. A small sound reached her ears, stopping her. Talking, a voice growing in intensity. Clarity was certain she heard someone talking, someone close by. The hairs on her nape stood tall, her body chilled just as the oppressive heat consumed her again. Someone was inside her home. A fine line of sweat dripped at her temple.

Resisting the urge to call out, Clarity moved toward the source. Her computer table was dark. There was no battery, it died, and she had been too busy for a replacement. It ran on electricity alone. Her hand moved toward the headphones she recently plugged in to blare music and not have the neighbors complain. She lifted the set to her ears and held her breath.

There was a voice on the other end. A strong male voice. She tried to concentrate on the language being spoken, but it was no use. She couldn't make it out. Not one word was familiar, which surprised her. With the AC not running, the room was almost immediately engulfed in heat. The sudden chill vanished, and sweat began to drip from more than just Clarity's temples. Her hands shook.

"Hello?" she whispered.

The words stopped. Quiet in the room made the pounding of her heart that much clearer.

"Hello, female."

"Who is this?"

"You will find out soon enough."

Clarity dropped the headset, the purse slipped to the crook of her elbow. She backed up a step when she heard the voice again. "*...we are coming for you.*"

Clarity was about to race to her room to lock herself in. Loud undeniable havoc reigned outside her front door, stopping her. With one hand, she grabbed her curtains and yanked them apart. Sunlight crashed in, blinding her momentarily. Blinking, her vision clearing, Clarity watched horrified as the pavement along the townhouses split. A fine line ran an ominous race to a destination, then stopped as quickly at a huge tree base. Silence. Clarity's breath expelled in a whoosh as her breathing grew rapid. Her home rumbled when the ground gave way, the tree exploded, and fifteen homes dropped into a chasm vanishing from sight with a *boom*. The line on the pavement began again, heading toward her home. Clarity dropped her curtains and ran.

****

"Holy fuck it's hotter than hell's whores out here."

"Will you please watch your language when the kids are around?" The woman lifted her shades slightly to give him a scowl.

The man sent his wife a scathing glance in return. Three children were screaming and splashing in the deep end of the half-sunk, oval, semi-above ground pool, while their parents sat under an umbrella on a large deck in Zero gravity chairs, slathered in sunscreen and wearing baseball caps.

"They can't hear a damned thing we say," he said. "They don't even notice we exist."

"You'd be surprised what they hear."

"I'm their father. I'm under no delusions. They're kids. I could have a heart attack, and they'd be oblivious." He then grumbled, "Yet, a fucking ice cream truck drives by and all hell will break loose. Little monsters would shove their grimy hands in my pockets for a few bucks while I turn cold."

His wife grinned and tilted her head in agreement. She lazily sucked back on the vodka cooler she was drinking then paused. Her brows narrowed.

"Jackson, when did you change the pool liner?"

The man's beer bottle hesitated at his lips. "I didn't." He shifted slightly forward.

Both the man and woman rose slowly to their feet setting their drinks off to the side, to gaze at the bottom of the pool. Pitch black stared back. The children continued to laugh and play, oblivious.

"Jackson," the woman said, her tone anxious.

"Easy," he responded and he reached to grip her hand, noting she was two seconds from diving in. "The kids are fine. If it was a sinkhole they'd be gone." Then to the children. "Come on guys, out of the pool, daddy's gonna get you ice cream."

"Dean can't have ice cream. He pulled my hair. You said so." A girl of twelve called back.

"Did not." Her twin brother howled.

"Out. *Now*," Jackson demanded as the inky blackness began a slow creeping up the sides of the pool, covering the light blue and tropical fish pattern in an ominous ebony inch by inch.

Grumbling, the children began swimming back toward their parents. When the oldest, a boy of fourteen, reached the side he put his feet down and floundered, then gasped in air.

"Dad, where's the bottom?"

The twins stopped to look down. The young boy

swam in a tight circle. The girl began screaming. "*Daddy,* something's got me."

Her father dove in, yanked his daughter into his arms, and grabbed her twin by the hand, or so he thought. When he pulled on the limp, large hand he gaped as he dragged a black man near his chest and released him. The body tumbled in a lazy fashion to reveal a face then turned again. The young girl, mouth agape, buried her face against her father. A few feet away a head and arms broke the surface, followed by another. One by one, corpses began appearing in the pool surrounding the man and three kids. Soon the entire pool filled with dead bodies until they spilled over the sides, thudding to the ground. The woman on deck covered her mouth as more bodies slipped onto the deck and she lost sight of her husband and children in the mass. Fists now clenched at her sides, one by one she screamed out their names, and screamed, and screamed, and screamed….

****

"There must be a hole in the kiddie pool."

The man held the hose and glanced at his wife while she chased after their toddler. Not a fan of tub water, the child could always be coerced into the plastic backyard pool decorated with mermaids and sea horses. Her father was seriously considering painting their tub. The little girl was covered in sand from head to toe, her diaper sagging, and her father was losing his patience with the pool.

"Honey I just bought it. Thank heaven the store has a surplus for the summer. Which reminds me, maybe we should invest in a few or two dozen before the fall hits." The woman grabbed the struggling child up into her arms. The toddler was soon hanging upside down laughing uproariously. His wife was grinning cheekily at him, but the impish pair did nothing to alleviate the tension.

"It seems to drain almost as fast as it goes in." His frustration was growing. The pool held water, then didn't, disappearing in an odd way. "Damn it, I want nothing more than to cuddle my daughter, my *clean* daughter, before her nap time."

His wife giggled and pulled the toddler upright. Finally the man stepped into the kiddie pool. The water washed over his feet. He tossed his arms up in agitation. He spun in a tight circle checking for any signs of bubbling.

"I can't make heads or tails of this."

Baffled, he stood for a second more, wiggled his toes, and scratched his head. He sighed and took a step to vacate the pool. The ground beneath his feet gave way and down he went. The bottom of the pool closed over his head. His arms and legs thrashed creating a whirlwind of bubbles. Screaming from under water he beat at the solid purple plastic, smashing his splayed hands repeatedly. The material wouldn't give. It wasn't plastic at all. The substance was harder than metal.

"This isn't the child," a voice sounded.

"Get rid of him."

Screaming, the man was washed away into a tube-like duct. His horror grew as his body was sucked down into an abyss. He was going to die, and something wanted his baby.

****

The vast foliage surrounding the vacationing couple was breathtaking. Greenery as far as the eye could see—ultimate, intimate, seclusion. The hot tub frothy and bubbly added to the sensual moment. The high sun peeked a few rays through the woody ceiling of forest, casting just the right ambiance of dim light. Champagne glasses tinkled as the couple touched, pressing chest against chest in a teasing fashion. The young woman giggled, and her new groom smiled at her. The woman giggled again.

"What's so funny?" he finally asked, his gaze filling with a bemused expression.

"You know."

"You're happy. I can tell."

"With your hand where it is why wouldn't I be?"

The young man frowned in confusion. "I have one hand on my glass and the other is stretched out on the surface of the side of the tub. See?"

The young woman took note of both his hands in plain view; he wiggled his fingers in a wave and smiled at her.

"Then what…?"

She set her glass down then reached between her legs into the water. Both she and her husband began screaming and struggling to get out of the water when her search produced a deceased elderly woman.

The chaos was only beginning…

****

Warm summer wind swept across the park's vast play area. Blue skies overhead set the stage for a ruling blazing sun. The toddlers laughed while they played in the large wading pool, knee deep or lower to most adults. High enough for a small hint of danger to the young adventurous ones. Parents conversed near the edges, keeping close watch over their precious little ones; many giving in to scoops of water drizzled over exposed body parts. Pails and shovels floated in a lazy fashion until scooped up for use. A small squabble over a pink ball ended in tears, and the promise of treats was soon in effect. A Ziploc bag of seedless purple grapes was produced, another of raisins and tiny carrots. Sunscreen was slathered while children remained stationary for all of two seconds. The young seemed oblivious to the heat. Hats pulled off by a small hand and a giggle, tugged back on by a larger one and a groan.

A bare-bummed two year old raced back into the water when her mother let her go for a mere second. The mother, exasperated, raced after her, grabbing her laughing daughter into her arms and then watched horrified as the water swirled and went black. The pair dropped like a stone. The youngsters in the wading pool, aged eight months to three years, began slipping under the water as the ominous inky darkness covered one end of the pool to the next in a sinister creeping fashion. One by one they floundered, coughing and choking.

Parents howling and yelling raced to dive into the blackness to save their children, while all around the black abyss began filling with zoo animals. A rhino thundered to the surface, its legs smashing into the back of a man who reached for his son and tossed him to safety last second as his back snapped. A giraffe slipped and skidded its spindly legs trying to free itself of the pandemonium. A tiger, soaked and snarling in fury lunged off the shoulders and heads of humans to the pavement leaving jagged bloody scratches in its wake.

The water was a rolling wave of mass confusion

surrounded in death. The tumbling choppy waves grew to eight feet in height in the thirty-foot length rectangular wading pool. White caps crashed over heads. Other adults within the park area raced to aid the flailing children and parents as elephants appeared, gorillas broke free to the surface after dragging those in their way back under. Platypuses, polar bears, camels, all emerged until the grassed area became a refuge for the dazed and confused.

A sea of life and death muddled together as police and fire fighters arrived with first aid and paramedics. Among those to offer help were animal shelters. Wild life workers moved in as shots were fired, *and fired*.

****

The chopper hovered over the massive black circular hole over the ocean. The humming whoop-whoop of the blades was the only sound in the silence. The pilot and three vacationing passengers stared in stunned surprise.

"Oh my God."

Humanoid and not so humanoid alien life forms began appearing on the surface. Blue and green faces bobbed and rolled. A single horn protruding from large-chested, bald beings. Smaller beings void of horns, thinner, curvy, long webby hair, twisted as the black mass filled. All looked dead. Aquatic animals never seen before came next. Grotesque blobs with hundreds of three toed legs, mouths open to reveal purple innards. Long-necked gooey substances rolled within the waves.

"What are they?"

"Not from this world," the pilot said.

"Black holes?" another asked, speaking in awed

undertones.

"Sinkholes maybe, linking our planet to theirs," the pilot speculated.

"Get me out of here," a woman demanded and began to hyperventilate, her hands waving in agitation.

The pilot took the chopper higher. The woman screamed as a massive soggy furred being shot from the hole upward. Twenty feet in height it lunged with jagged teeth hitting the underside of the craft. Talons scraped the metal. Squealing protests of fiery sparks flickered as the underside exploded with the contact, flashes dancing across the air. The chopper surged up; a man out of his seatbelt for better pictures flew from the chopper, last moment grabbing the landing gear. Another grabbed for him as the pilot sped off for safety and the monster plunged back into the mass below bellowing.

The black hole began to grow, so too did the number of alien creatures appearing. Not all were dead, and many were decidedly enraged.

****

Outside, everywhere Clarity gazed the ground crumbled. Long gaping splits in the asphalt ran dozens of feet separating streets. Across lawns, ornaments were sucked into oblivion. Gnomes, birdbaths, rock gardens, nothing was sacred or spared. People were running, screaming, others stood still, their feet frozen with horror. Women, children, men, parents with babes in strollers, ran when there was nowhere to run. Each direction blocked with sudden rising slabs of concrete and broken water mains. Downed hydro lines crackled against the surface, dancing sparks of death. Dogs barked, snapped, snarled, others whined. Bright, endless, innocuous blue skies overhead taunted existence. A horrific rumbling within the earth bubbled to the surface, as though starved for human sacrifices.

A small sinkhole opened and people began screaming as creatures the likes never seen before emerged, grabbed a human, and plunged back down into inky darkness. Clarity stood gasping as a humanoid creature, muscles bulging, grabbed a young woman, eyed Clarity, and jumped back into a sinkhole.

The sinkholes remained but Clarity knew from a look the portal or whatever opened was gone, the ebony now a mist of dark earth. A sick feeling in her guts built as she guesstimated the ages of humans disappearing in front of her eyes. The forecaster said people were returning, dead, after years of being lost. What were the ages? There was no mention of children returning, but the broadcast was cut short too fast. A boulder thundered into her chest with her thoughts. What purpose did these alien creatures have?

For whatever reason, people of all ages were disappearing in front of her. Some must have been inoculated as was she. Especially the children. Was her theory too farfetched? It couldn't be considering the inoculations had begun again. *Why?* her mind screamed. Did any human now appear to be fair game? There was too much pandemonium for much speculation about inoculations when other pressing thoughts bombarded her. The ground shuddered as the water tower in the distance crashed to the ground. A giant wind turbine was next. Nothing was spared.

There were confirmation reports of sinkholes opening in basements. Though Clarity turned off the radio, she didn't escape a few sordid details. There was gossip in her building at work. The government couldn't hide everything from everyone. Sinkholes popped up wherever people resided. Now it was plain to see. Humans *were* being stolen. If they were returned dead, there was no hope for survival where they went.

Squealing tires caught her attention. A massive black object descended on her. Clarity dodged the rolling vehicle where it crashed over a tree trunk and screeched to a halt, teetering on the edge of oblivion. Children pounded on the darkened window of the backseat of the SUV. Calling out to her. Clarity could make out their expressions vaguely. She raced to help, but the blacktop rose up splitting the yellow line on the road and the car slipped downward. She knew it was useless, but Clarity grabbed the bumper yanking with her entire being. Little faces, tears trailing their way down pale cheeks pressed to the window.

The pain in her arms was too much, even in her desperation Clarity couldn't lift a five-thousand plus piece of tin. The car toppled forward as she fell back on her ass, then she scrambled to peer over the edge. The children were still pounding on the window as they disappeared into an ominous ebony darkness. Clarity howled her rage, smashing her palm onto the pavement. She turned to scream at someone, anyone. Why didn't someone else try to help her? She gazed left, then right. There was no one. The street was deserted.

Her teeth began clicking together as she remembered the words spoken across the airwaves. Someone was coming for her. She was alone. Clarity swallowed hard. The ground beneath her was too hot to remain where she was as the sun beat down mercilessly. Her exposed flesh was burning as the blackened pavement absorbed the sun's rays.

On shaky feet Clarity rose; her legs trembled as she settled her purse back onto her shoulder in an unconscious action. Slowly she turned. Eerie quiet assaulted her. There were no people, no animals, no aliens. *Nothing*. Her breath resounded in her ears, throat constricting. Heart pounding, she took in the devastation. Her once warm flesh was now saturated in sweat and goose bumps. A small gust of wind ruffled her hair then settled. Her jaw clenched to stop the clacking noise as she cocked her head to listen—for anything. Trees once covered in the lush foliage of summer were bare. Petals from flowers fluttered then slipped into holes. Everything but Clarity had been sucked beneath the surface. Only a few homes remained. The ground a slice of Swiss cheese, pock marked and riddled with destruction.

One foot in front of the other, Clarity drifted, glancing at smaller holes. Ice filled one, long jagged icicles dangled down, plummeting into nothing. Another caused her body to shake as steam wafted to her nose, the scent of fire and brimstone threatened to bring bile to her throat. Another hole filled with bubbling green goo, boiling and popping; the sides of dirt eroding as it expanded. Certain hell awaited unlucky humans.

Dazed, Clarity roamed the broken street. Beneath her the ground grumbled then stilled. A tiny gasp tore from her throat when to her left a small stone statue succumbed to the green goo hole. A movement caught her eye and she stopped, noticing a man in a window. For a second, they stood gazing at one another. She lifted her hand to wave. The ground suddenly shook.

Clarity's body weaved. Her wave turned into a desperate plea for help but the curtains snapped closed. The terrain opened up beneath her feet. Clarity was falling, screaming. There was nothing to hold onto. Down she went into the bowels of the Earth. Her world turned black. Air rushed up, her breath caught and held. The smooth surface of the hole caught her attention when her ass and hips collided with a bump, another bump, then settled.

Clarity tried to breathe but couldn't. The air was racing by too fast in her freefall. She pulled her arm around her nose and mouth to filter the air. She could feel the sides of her shorts hike as the assault to her ass cheeks scratched further exposed skin. The heels of her runners scraped and she almost tumbled head over heels until she bent her knees. Her back was the next to connect to the hard surface. She was sliding in a curve. Both arms lifted to cover her face as she tried not to let terror consume her. A painful sucking began to her left, and Clarity was thrown sideways. The movement rattled her brains.

A tiny light grew in velocity beneath her. The end was near; her end was near. Clarity braced for impact. She screamed when she became airborne. The sudden shift made her belly flip. The light hurt her eyes after seeing nothing but darkness. Her arms still wrapped around her head, knees tucked to her chest, she curled into a tight ball waiting for the inevitable.

Chapter Two

The tingling of his skin told Doom when it was time to leave the safety of the village and venture to his fate. *Has it been a month already?* Each time there was a harvest of innocents, Doom walked to the cave of sadness, named as such by him, and sat quietly while the etching on his body drew a path of despair on his flesh. Each line, each mark engraved on his soul. Their faces and other beloved images blurred, there were so many. The darkness offered a single comfort. There was nowhere to show his reflection as two single tears made their way down his cheeks. There was nowhere his damning gaze could reflect to condemn him, confront him.

Eyes squeezed tight against the pain, he waited where he knew the brilliance of life would sluice across his skin. There would be no blood, but his flesh was stained with suffering. His sharp breath was the only indication of when the assault started. He swallowed hard once, twice, then settled. Over the course of a year, he tried to connect with each individual he would lead to the slaughter. Not all images were faces. A coveted item, a hammer, or other tool the victim created intertwined across his skin to mix and mingle with the others. The marks were loathed and welcomed. An image of death on his skin meant life for his people, at least for another year.

When the movement across his skin stopped, Doom opened his eyes. He hadn't moved; yet, his limbs were heavy from exhaustion. Each passing year, the etching took longer as the quota for the hybrids increased. The beasts were insatiable, their need for humans snowballing. With a small shift, he took a deep breath and turned toward the hint of light he had hidden from. He didn't want to look and at times refused to see the markings. His will wasn't great enough this time for one reason: he owed his victims that glance.

There she was, her beautiful face etched into his body, a remembrance for eternity. Doom knew it would be her face to haunt him. The only thing she'd coveted was him. Her sweet infatuation would have been his undoing, if he had let her in. He kept his distance to a degree, never letting her close enough to consume his soul. There was time for that after she was gone. If he had spared her, one of his people would have died. If he went in her place, every soul he promised to release would be damned. He must die whole, not ripped to shreds. The images must remain intact. Doom would know when it was his turn for death. Wishing his demise didn't bring the end any swifter.

He lifted his fingers to gently caress the tattoo. Smooth flesh a deceit when every inch was a dagger to his soul. That one face stood out, bolder than the rest— the one he struggled with. If she had only been a year younger, if not blossomed, if only a child in the hybrids' minds…. Doom's entire life was filled with 'if only'.

"Fear not, young one. When I die, you will come with me into the valley of souls where you will be free."

The idea was his salvation. The first time the markings appeared, he knew somehow they were his penance and his saving grace. A day would come when the victims would find peace and happiness. Doom swore it on his life, on their deaths. For now, the mark was his solace. He would carry her reflection forever. As long as he remembered her, the Seers would also. The Seers would know of her sacrifice to save his people. The Seers saw everything, how could they not? They shone from the skies, giant hearths, the moon and sun but mostly the stars. Each ancestor blinking down on him and his people were revered.

Rising, Doom strode to the clear pond. The light green of the water reflected his appearance. He hated his image. His hair gone, from stress, he had no doubt. Six foot six, two hundred and eighty pounds, a mighty and powerful male. Helpless. His chiseled features gazed back, mirrored in his glare. Stone cold brown eyes filled with fury as he took in each one of his tattoos. At least, those he could see. Mercifully, the ones he couldn't see were the marks of his own people when their quota came up short. Each mark one of fury, sorrow, and hope.

"You will all be reborn. You have the word of a warrior, a doomed warrior, a warrior who no longer battles, but my word can't be taken from me. Only a liar and a coward breaks his word. I swear, if I have nothing else, no one can steal my oath. In life, I could not save you. In death, I will make it my mission to free you."

When that death would come he had no clue, but he had a gut instinct. While there was room for a single image to adorn his body he would breathe life. The bare glimpses of tanned skin left gave him hope and dread. For now, his people were safe…for another year. Another year to hope their sorry existence would lead to substance. Doom was allowed to dream. But he did so in private. After years of dreaming the same dream, the images drifted further into the abyss of his mind. When dreams turned to fables, dreams became less as hope died. Reality, though harsh, was what ultimately defined existence.

The new collection already begun for the next harvest, sacrifices would be found not only for his tribe but for others. The Neandersauri were settled into their small slumber after their feast of death, or perhaps they celebrated. Perhaps they danced on the moon. Speculation made his head throb. The possibilities were endless. The longer he deliberated, the further his mind was assaulted.

Let it go.

Once the humans were released on their own in the forested jungle, they no longer belonged to Doom. Not that they ever belonged to him, merely kept in trust. A broken trust. No villager was allowed to leave the safety of home until the writing had been cast. It wasn't safe in the jungle this time of year; other animals were on edge. Doom was lucky the hybrid creatures were satiated for so long. The creatures ate other beings, but he had no idea why they wanted the beings from Earth and had for some time. Sacrifices? Food? The conundrum kept him awake nights. For now, it was time to return to his people and see how they fared.

Fog infiltrated the surrounding foliage. Wispy tendrils of smoke from the village fires rose off in the distance. The scent of cooler air filtered through his nostrils, nothing more. Scent was everything on his planet. Normally, once the unsuspecting caught a whiff of a creature before seeing it there was hell to pay. By the time a dinosaur was visible, you were dead. Not far from where Doom walked, he heard the unmistakable cry of a child. A dangerous noise if not heeded quickly. No child in his village was left unattended, and every child from his village knew sound was deadly in the open. The voice had to be from a recent gathering from the dark holes. Children were never sacrificed, not from any village. Doom moved toward the weeping. He heard the stumble of little feet on the few old leaves. Children tended to look at everything at once, except where they were going, when afraid and sometimes when they weren't.

The child Doom stumbled across brought a smile to his lips. Black tousled hair and cornflower blue eyes were a charming mix on the tiny imp. He was spindly as Earth children usually were, thin arms and legs, dressed in the material others called pajamas. His small blue shirt was filthy, but there was a cute pattern of a large smiling green creature with antennae on the front. His feet were bare. A human boy could be spared. The Neandersauri were only after mature individuals, and a child could be given to a waiting couple.

The little one, perhaps five, stopped motionless and gazed way up. A warrior was a daunting figure, but Doom learned some of the little Earth humans had imposing fathers, warriors of sorts who fought for their country. Some young ones he came across would dry their eyes and ask him if he was their daddy. The childish wondering words led him to believe Earth soldiers were away fighting their own battles. He wished the holes would offer over their warrior fathers instead of their weak, their old men, frightened men, or helpless women and children. Doom wanted to rage to the skies to send him someone who could help his people fight before it was too late. Instead, he assessed the boy. This boy appeared dazed. He must have recently exited a sinkhole.

Doom dropped to a knee. "Don't be afraid, little one. I won't hurt you. It's scary out here alone, isn't it?"

The boy nodded. "Yes."

"How old are you?"

The boy held up a hand with all five fingers splayed. "I was sleepin', am I dreamin'?"

"No, this is no dream."

"Then I'm lost."

Doom smiled. "How can you be lost when I've found you? I know a couple who have been waiting a long time for you. They will be pleased you have finally arrived."

The child cocked his head. "I want my mommy and daddy."

"The couple *are* your mommy and daddy and waiting in my village and will be happy to see you."

Doom never mentioned a child's old family. Parents would never find a child here. There was no way to search for them. This was the boy's home now. Like all of his people, Doom was responsible for him. Doom scooped him up and the child sobbed in his grasp; he weighed nothing. Little arms wrapped around his neck. He smelled of fresh soap even though covered in dirt. His clothing was damp, not wet, but Doom wondered if he had recently been bathed and perhaps put to bed. His parents were either dead or wandering elsewhere. There had never been an incident where a child came through a sinkhole with parents. Doom held the boy to his chest and soothed him.

"You're safe now. I won't let anything hurt you, sweetheart."

Doom rose and began walking. The ones he could save didn't haunt him. Even when they cried in fear, they were safe. The children were welcomed into the fold. The child was lucky Doom found him. The boy was early. Normally, a harvest didn't begin this soon on this part of the planet. Doom wasn't positive, but he thought some older hybrids migrated to a warmer climate. Some stayed, watched, and waited. When the harvest of humans began, it customarily started with the young ones. With the hybrids sated, the children were safe from them, but not from everything. The forest was no place for the vulnerable. Other creatures resided here besides the hybrids. Many carnivores could make a meal of one so young and tender.

From the foliage Doom saw a creature. To others, the creature might appear camouflaged. Not to Doom. His father once told him Doom's vision was a gift passed from leader to son. The fact he was also ambidextrous where most of his warriors were right handed aided the hunt. Doom stooped to pick up a rock and pitched it at the carnivore. The beast yelped and fled on two long legs with its tail stretched back and waving. There would be no sneaking up on unsuspecting prey for that beast at this moment.

As Doom approached his village, the child gasped and buried his head deeper into Doom's chest. This was something the warrior understood. People of Earth had a strange history of a meteor and ice age. Doom's planet had suffered through neither. As a result the humans were in terrified awe of the beasts they called dinosaurs. Creatures that were and were not like those of the ancient bones archeologists on Earth found. The subject was a favorite discussion of Doom's when humans began arriving. After time, the strongest and fastest animals thrived on his planet. That didn't always mean the largest. Many of the massive dinosaurs of old were hunted and killed, their brains too small for survival. Other creatures bred and mixed to create the beings now waking the planet. Dinosaur life evolved as did the land's people.

Of those dinosaur beings was the malevolent bulwark, a mixture of cave bear and dire wolf with the intensity of a wolverine. Alone, unevolved those creatures wouldn't survive much longer, all three species were almost extinct, but as hybrids they were strong. Four of the guardians roamed his clan. They kept other dinosaurs from entering. They kept humans from escaping. Their love of Hell pigs was a boon and often his people roasted the carcasses of the huge beasts.

As always the hesitant, long faces of his people greeted him. Doom wasn't the only one to develop relationships with the humans. Why deprive a damned people of humanity for an entire year? The cruelty inflicted, the betrayal, was kept from their victims until they were released into the forest. The Nendersauri waited, and the humans were snatched. It took a month before the slaughter and during that time Doom had no clue what the beasts did with their sacrifices. He presumed they had their own ritual. Bred into Doom was the need to keep his distance from the creatures who almost hunted his kind to death. The tingling of his skin began early morning, informing him it was time to leave the village and prepare for the marks of death. The hybrids would allow him safe passage.

The upright hybrid dinosaur had developed growing intelligence. Somewhere there was a means to an end but Doom and the other leaders had no idea what they were after with the humans. What could an animal be thinking? And they did think. It was a question to ponder. *Later*. Doom grinned as he approached a couple. The woman's face lit with a joyous smile. Doom gave her the boy.

"Congratulations. You have a son," Doom said.

"You're not my mommy," the boy said.

"Yes, I am." She cuddled him close to her chest; a huge smile split her lips. "Edge, we have a son."

The new father pulled Doom aside away from the woman who fussed over the child. "Do what you must to keep my son safe."

Doom nodded. The child was safe, until he was full grown. If the quota couldn't be met, they must use grown villagers. The agony of his clan when that happened was almost too much to bear. Doom's responsibility slouched his shoulders. The weight of the world dragging him into misery permeated every step he took to the holding place where humans would be kept until their time was up. Touching the stone door warmed it under his hand and the door slid back for him to peer below the earth's surface. A pit in his guts, Doom surveyed the open, empty confined darkened space. He wasn't certain if he was happier when it was vacant or full.

****

Clarity's ass connected with the lush foliage as she skidded down a sodden hill. Huge leafy plants smacked her in the face and chest. Slick massive roots grazed her bare thighs. The almost vertical position eased as she plummeted downhill. Plant life slowed her descent until she came to a stop. Her breathing ragged Clarity sat still, groaning, legs stretched before her, elbows bent, rapidly blinking, waiting for any sign of pain to emanate from the filth that was now her entire being. Aside from small aches and scratches, she was fine. Small bits of vegetation covered her shorts and shirt. Green skid marks on her bare flesh would no doubt bruise. Muck coated her shoes. She leaned to her side to do up a loose shoelace caught and tugging on twigs. On shaky feet, she stood and turned in a tight circle. Nothing looked familiar yet other things did in a disturbing way.

Clarity stared hard at the vegetation. Not a paleontologist by any means, she loved archeology and was certain the plant life she was seeing was extinct. Nilssonia, Williamsonia, plants from the Triassic, Jurassic and Cretaceous period slapped her in the face. The air was clear. Void of any pollutants reminding her of home. *Ancient and new at the same time.* Massive trees with long vines loomed, eerily silent of birds or squirrels. She slapped an insect from her arm.

The sky overhead rolled with clouds forming odd shapes and sizes. Clarity made out one moon and one sun. The moon was huge even in daylight, a massive round crater-riddled phenomenon, so close in appearance even while the sun was high. She stretched her hand for a moment certain it could be touched. It couldn't. An illusion.

She was chilled; her sweat left her damp. The air was warm when she slipped into the sinkhole. Her body shook from her experience. Everywhere she turned, strange images assaulted her. Prehistoric plant life run amok. Odd scents mugged her system. The ground was solid beneath her feet; she knew that too could change. She wrapped her arms over her breasts. Her damp shirt clung as a second skin. She took a tentative step, and her foot collided with her purse. Clarity snapped it up, not bothering with the strap, tucking it under her arm. A sharp whistle caught her attention. There was something peculiar in the tone, foreboding and unhuman. She heard something moving in her direction. A massive behemoth of a tree sporting a hole big enough to crawl into was in her line of vision and Clarity raced to it, huddling inside. The whistling increased.

Her breath caught and, wide-eyed, Clarity peeked at the creature which came into view not fifteen feet from her hideout. Eight feet in height, standing upright, Clarity had never seen anything like it. An erect light grey-green dinosaur walking on two long legs with huge thighs tapering to five-toed feet. The toes were clawed with white hooks resembling ivory. The beast wore a wrap around its waist. *A dinosaur with clothes?* When the creature turned, Clarity covered her mouth, her bones shaking. Long arms with five-fingered claws, all ivory in color, were wide as the creature ducked down to sniff where Clarity landed after her harrowing ride downhill.

The frill of a triceratops wrapped round the back of its bulbous bald head from ear to ear, giving the beast the impression of having no neck. Long florescent veins lit and traveled the length of the semicircle from top to bottom, fine lines of pulsing molten lava. Round rainbow eyes, set on either side of its face gave it a 3D perspective, where the piercing white pupil dilated, then shrunk as its head cocked. A ridged forehead protruded giving the creature a distinct Neanderthal impression. Oblong jaw thrust forward pushing its four dull white fangs past its upper lip. Covering its flattened nose. The dinosaur had a man's chest with bulbous muscular arms.

For a second, she swore it grinned showing huge square teeth in a crooked row along the top and bottom. Solid high cheekbones tapered to small flaps where ears might sit. As she stared, the ear flap bent forward then back careening as though concentrating on catching sound. It blinked. Over its reptilian skin were patches of feathery fur down the massive trunk-like upper thighs to the feet. As the creature moved against the mass foliage the fluttering wisps changed color, browns, greens, whites and reds; a chameleon, blending in with every change of position to camouflage its appearance. The same spattering of feather fur coated the shoulders down each arm to the wrist. The creature gazed in her direction. Clarity crept back further into her hideout. Sweat dripped from her temples, her flesh turned icy cold.

A human dinosaur? No.

Her breathing ragged, Clarity pressed as far back into the tree as was possible. The rotted damp, sponge-like insides gave way when flesh connected, sinking her deeper into the tree. Earthy scents assaulted her as she tried to become one with the behemoth. The walking dinosaur whistled again. Not a sharp pierce but a call as it cocked its head to one side then the other. The noise was compelling, a come hither, but not enough for her to risk her life. Not an animal person by nature, Clarity was terrified of big dogs. This creature was too much.

An answering whistle and Clarity heard two separate calls. There were at least two of them; she knew it. Each new whistle was distinct. Not unlike a dog's bark but further developed. Every new tone had a change in pitch, a complex word perhaps, a variety of onomatopoeia as unbelievable as it sounded. Each note different, and yet familiar. The creatures were communicating with each other, answering each other.

Talking to each other.

Above her head were small indents. The tree was hollow higher up. The leather of her purse strap was slung over her head and a shoulder. Clarity would need her hands free for the climb. She reached up and began to pull her way deeper into the high tree using the slippery indents to crawl upward. The higher she rose, the darker the inside became until she could only see with her hands and the touch of fingertips. Every second her concern grew she might inadvertently touch some hidden unsuspecting creature. Her body hugged the smooth dampness as her heart pounded and handholds became less frequent. She was terrified she could slip and slide down to land in a heap and give herself away.

At a small ledge she stopped. The bottoms of her shoes and calves were still visible when she peered down, and she was covered with tiny tree bits and moss which added to her bedraggled appearance. Her clothing and flesh wore spatters of sticky sap and mud.

A massive head poked into the hollow from below and Clarity froze when the beast growled showing off the protruding fang teeth. A scream caught in her throat. The creature sniffed the air, face raised and she was positive it could see her and she could see it. Hard human features became distinct. The white teeth amidst the fangs were visible. Closer, she determined they looked like overlarge human teeth. Intelligent eyes blinked. The nose was broad and flat the eyes tucked under heavy brow ridges. A spatter of coal dark hair covered its head in places. But there was no mistaking the creature beneath her wasn't human, and yet it wasn't a dinosaur. It was decidedly both. The idea made Clarity shudder.

It could enter no farther as it was too large. The bulk of its rounded frill caught on the bark. The massively muscled back filled the entry. The hollow was deprived of light, except for two bright rainbow eyes softly glowing. The eyes blinked, everything went dark. Clarity was certain her heart stopped beating. When the eyes opened the beast had moved a fraction closer. Eyes blinked, darkness. Opened, it had moved no further. The eerie lights turned as it tilted its head. The creature stopped growling and whistled a soft tune. Each sound rolled with undeniable words. Nothing she understood except it was trying to communicate.

Clarity couldn't breathe, she didn't remember how to. The creature pulled from the tree, the soft sunlight was welcome. The unmistakable sound of razor talons slicing into the bark caught her attention and she crept higher, reaching, stretching, above her head, her fingers a tenacious grip on the last moist, slick, hardened protrusion. Another head poked under to stop her. Her ass pressed against the back of the tree; her hands and feet rested on small indents.

The whistle from this creature was demanding. Its hands made odd gestures. The thing was interacting with her, or trying to. It wasn't possible. Clarity closed her eyes. As unreal as it seemed the creature signaled for her to come down.

'Come down so we can eat you' just isn't working for me.

Her head shook slightly, a quick no. Though she didn't have a hope it would understand the gesture. The creature snorted and ducked back out. From a tiny crack higher up Clarity struggled to press her eye against the incoming light. The creatures were moving away, strolling as huge men would on a summer day. Their loincloths swayed with each step, giving her a slight visual of hard ass cheeks, humanoid ass cheeks. They whistled and gestured to each other. Each tone, every pitch different and similar. Clarity tensed when she was positive one laughed and shoved the other against its shoulder.

Laughed?

Soon the foliage swallowed them. Only then did her jaw relax so her teeth could clack together. Her breath expelled in a whoosh. She placed a hand over her thundering heart. She wasn't on Earth, of that she was certain. The urge to cover her eyes and sob was hard to resist, but the sappy substance on her fingers and palms gave her pause.

She couldn't stay where she was. As frightening as the idea was she had to leave the relative safety of the tree. There was nowhere to sit comfortably and if she fell asleep, she'd fall. Eventually, she would need water and food. There could be stranger, larger creatures that might find her and knock the tree down to get to her. *Just move.* Her climb down was hesitant, what if the creatures backtracked or were hiding? Clarity clutched each individual handhold for leverage as her knuckles turned whiter in the reappearing light. Fingers aching, she poked her head out of the opening and pulled back, poked out, pulled back. The bushes were unmoving. The directions she could see were clear.

With trepidation she crawled on all fours from her hideout. The sun was low, evening approached. As she stood, Clarity leaned back against the trunk, the surface a deceptive safe haven. The creatures could reach in after her if she stayed inside on the ground. Her heart pounding, her first step was the hardest. Soon one foot followed the other as she walked, half-crouched, wary, her gaze traveling everywhere. Each breath escaping her tortured lungs sounded ominous in the quiet.

Clarity came to the indentation, the outline of the walking creature's footprint and placed her foot next to it. The footprint was massive and clawed, but on further inspection she narrowed her eyes. Within the outline was another outline…of a human foot. Five toes, a heel, and the ball of the foot were unmistakable. The human foot size was close to fourteen inches. For a moment her heart skipped a beat wondering who else was here. The human foot went deep into the surface; whoever it was must weigh hundreds of pounds. Clarity had seen impressions when on nature walks with her father. Something strange stared back at her. Clarity realized the two impressions were in fact one. The human bones made up part of the erect dinosaur's feet. A foot within a foot.

How is that possible?

Not a fan of horror stories, Clarity decided it was worse to live one. If erect dinosaurs wandered the place she landed on there could be far worse creatures living here. Scientists hinted the numerous sinkholes appearing might lead to a different planet or dimension. The rumors were brushed off, quieted. Clarity knew the doomsday sayers were correct. But if she was taken, where were the others who fell with her? Shouldn't they all end up in the same area? The children in the car, did they land here? Where was the car, the kids? On impulse she glanced left then right but saw no other signs of life. Her mind raced to the last seconds of her fall. She had been snatched from a strong pull. Was it possible time stood still in sinkholes?

The idea of traveling to other galaxies in one year and sent back taking another year to return boggled her mind. Was that how the dead had returned? Some humans might never have set foot here. Was her destination fate? More than likely something else played a factor. Whatever the reason, here she was. Here she'd stay if she didn't get moving.

The gloom of the overcast sky made Clarity look up. The wind whistled through the trees making her gasp, wondering if for a second it was a creature. The air filled with the scent of a shower. The way she looked and felt, Clarity wouldn't mind being wet. The sticky substance of the sap covered her, and her hair was pinned to parts of her forehead. Her fingers fused together and she despised the tug as she separated each digit, stretching her skin.

Clarity stood, waiting for the first spatters of rain to fall. Arms out at her sides, palms up, watching the heavens, she frowned when the wetness hit the back of her hands. She stood there, now staring down as her runners became saturated. Her palms turned down and the coolness of each drop hit her skin with a *pat pat pat* and slipped through her fingers.

Single droplets floated up as she watched wide-eyed with wonder. Water bubbles stretched, separated, again elongated, and continued their ascent. Eerie, massive clouds, gray and unwelcoming overhead moved in. Sharp thunder, rocking Clarity to the core, commanded the grounds to release the moisture in words unheard but heeded. The sogginess dampened her ankles, then calves, snaking up her thighs, over her hips. Tickling lines of wetness caressed her. Swirling, rising, her shirt blew up to her midriff. Her hands swayed as her neck twisted to see the rain rise *up* to the sky, left and right. Foliage ruffled, puddles emptied. The scene surreal to the human eye. Drops trailed their way up her skin, against her inner thighs disappearing to stop at her panty line.

Dripping could be heard as the rain spattered the underside of leaves. The storm grew in intensity. Ground lightning, a sizzling zigzag, toppled trees making Clarity jump. Thunder roared overhead. Precipitation from a pond rose into the heavens. Huge black-gold frogs climbed down trees to slither into dark holes as snakes. Clarity blinked hard wondering if her eyes were deceiving her.

A frog snake?

A roaring filled her ears as she became saturated. The novelty of the strange happenstance quickly turned to panic. Rain flew up with intensity to fill her nostrils until she thought she might drown. Covering her nose and mouth she began to run. The ground grew slick beneath her feet, tripping her, covering her knees in small red marks she knew would bruise later.

Clarity raced terror stricken through the forest looking for shelter. Any opening exposed to the sky gave up its water supply. The gray sky overhead swirled with massive amounts of rain, hovering, swarming. She was at the mercy of the wind. Her arms pressed against her head trying desperately to shield her face. The intense foliage she battled through, now crawling on a hand and knees, dragging her purse behind her, dumped sheets of water to run in rivulets first down her body then changed haphazard in their direction to race upward.

The vulnerability of being assaulted from beneath and sideways dropped Clarity to her belly where she remained. Lightning crackled and zipped over her, racing through the trees. A sharp explosion sounded when a bolt hit a target, the tree shattered. To add to her fear, the rain mixed as droplets landed from the sky as the heavens opened to return rain to ponds. Bombarded from both land and sky, Clarity screamed and choked as water flushed her mouth. Condensation and infiltration run amok. She was drowning on land.

"Help," she screamed, then choked.

Strong hands on her shoulders made her cringe and cry out. She peered up under an arm, gasping, her face sodden with rain and tears. A beast didn't have her. It was a man. The biggest man she had ever seen. He pulled her into his arms and ran. The pounding deluge continued from under them, above them. She didn't know how the man could see where he was going. She pressed her face into his bare chest, her arm snaked up to clasp around his neck. She cupped her hand against her mouth and nose trying to form an air pocket to breathe. When it didn't work, she muscled her purse up to her cheek to try the same. His powerful grip crushed her to his warm skin. Strong legs pumped beneath him as his feet flew across the terrain.

Nature's assault stopped and Clarity heard the man's deep intake of breath when he stood motionless for a moment. Instinctively, she knew they were no longer outside. With a few long strides, he settled her down atop a lush mound of leaves within a shelter of rock and moss. Her purse slipped under a leg. With his warmth and protection now gone, the chill in the air brought goosebumps to her arms. Blinking, she gazed at her surroundings. The blowing of wind beyond the entrance scattered more leaves in her direction. Foliage wasn't placed strategically for comfort; it was a natural occurrence.

The man squatted on the balls of his feet before her. The heavens no longer a daunting force, the rain dripped down his features. Fine moisture drizzled from his forehead to slip from the tip of his nose. He wore earthy, rugged-looking moccasins hugging his feet and ankles to below mid-calf, and tanned hide pants covered him to his knees. The simple garment had numerous strange deep pockets which bulged with their secret contents. A thick, braided woven rope strung round his hips held simple tools, a crude hand axe, the handle made of beautiful deep purple quartz, a long ivory-handled stone knife, and a rustic leather pouch.

Rugged, powerful, intricately tattooed, he gazed at her. She would have expected a cocky glance from a man of his size but he seemed thoughtful. Sad and hopeful. Clarity wiped her face with her hand and pushed strands of hair behind her ears. It took effort to settle her clattering teeth. He continued to stare at her, study her.

She knew her hair when dry was so blonde it looked white when wet. Edward claimed her eyes were a mad hazel of all colors. The man before her dwarfed her five foot five. Many men did, but she had never encountered the sheer beauty of one so well proportioned. There was something prehistoric in his features in a fascinating way. Ancient, his gaze was primeval as though he'd lived a thousand lives over a million years. If he were primitive man, he would be considered the epitome of the best there was, the alpha male. This man hadn't fallen in a sinkhole to get here. He belonged. The surroundings complemented the man and vice versa.

"My name is Clarity." The moment of truth. She doubted he'd eat her, she doubted he'd understand her, but a name was a simple place to start. "Clarity." She pointed at her chest then motioned to him.

"Doom."

It occurred to her that although his tone wasn't that of the voice in her living room, the word was as frightening. Was he Clarity's *Doom?* Would she die here in this cave filled with green vegetation, with a man who saved her life only to take it?

"I'm afraid," she whispered.

He reached to cup her chin. His hand, though callused was gentle, his look sincere, his tender smile earnest. He gave her chills.

"You should be."

Chapter Three

Doom's voice was deep, his words clear and not threatening. Clarity could have been knocked over by a feather.

"You speak English."

"I speak talk."

"No I mean you talk like me."

"No, you talk like me."

Clarity wondered at the evolution of speech. Where, how did it originate? Ancient origins? Scientists would have a field day here. First, communicating dinosaurs, and now a male who spoke English. What other languages were here? Clarity didn't know where she was, but she definitely knew she wasn't anywhere near home.

"This isn't Earth is it?"

"No. Not your Earth, this planet is my Earth."

"How do you even know what Earth is? What do you mean *your* Earth?" He didn't by any means look stupid but his primitive weapons suggested the lack of space flight.

"Others come. Like you. Through holes."

Clarity rose to her knees. "You mean there are others from an Earth like mine here, now?"

"They leave."

It was the way his gaze shifted, the sudden tension in his shoulders. He was lying or omitting a part of the truth. Doom looked human, but there was something more.

"What is this place, this planet?"

"Your planet and this one are similar I've learned, except we never experienced an ice age. Or a meteor never landed. Your kind speculates what Earth might look like today if those things never occurred. We, my people and I, live it."

Clarity's mind was in a somersault. Languages developed over time, why not here? Of course speech would find a way, people needed to communicate. She urged Doom to continue.

"Your Earth is a tumultuous planet of natural and manmade disasters I'm told by some. We have no climate issues. No global warming. I've never in my life felt our planet shake except in a certain place, but it's a natural occurrence. I've traveled far across the globe and have never seen a mountain filled with burning liquid. Our ocean waves behave. We experience all four seasons, and all four are extreme but many creatures migrate. Many creatures on this planet are dangerous. Many mammals. Many of the beasts are dinosaurs, many different breeds."

"Dinosaurs," she whispered and wondered how many he was talking about and what kind. The single word dinosaur was a broad scope. Her heart began to pound. "There were dinosaurs walking erect, like a human but strange. They sounded like they were calling me. Whistles, hand gestures were used."

"Neandersauri. Long ago the different species on this planet fought for dominance. Including humanoid types. From evolution each humanoid form fought for supremacy, evolving, changing to survive. A walking relative to my people were Neanderthals. Our cousins were larger boned, bigger everywhere. There were certain dinosaurs that continued to evolve. They were thinking creatures. Their brains were larger, smart. Somehow they evolved and created man-dinosaur hybrids. Accident or not the changes gave them an edge and they began to evolve faster.

"A species that can manipulate its bones—the ones appearing on its outward skeletal structure and the one within—by dislocating the outer bones when necessary. It gives the hybrid advantages: making weapons, fire, cooking, the sheer strength and muscle mass in battle. Its outer structure keeps the internal one safe. The hybrid species almost destroyed my people. They don't like the mixture of them and us, and will not breed with us, nor us with them, it would be impossible. They are as smart, but stronger. At one time, their goal was to annihilate my people. If we are gone, they rule the planet. They almost succeeded. I'm surprised they tried to interact with you. Normally they leave humans alone until…. Well normally, they leave humans alone."

"Do you communicate with them?"

"Their leader, he calls himself DaV-nin, leads all of his kind." Clarity shuddered at the name, his tone was guttural, animalistic, almost a growl. Clarity could understand a Neanderthal being named but a dinosaur with a name, calling itself by name, was unconventional and too strange.

"DaV-nin," she whispered.

"DaV-nin," he repeated, rolling the words in a growl. "Their number is many and growing. Far outnumbering my own kind. We understand each other well enough. They use little words, mostly whistles and hand gestures, grunts and growls. They adapt to any weather, heat, cold, rain. And they make use of skins and furs as do my people. I'm uncertain where they live, or what their home structures are, but I think they dwell deep within caves. Dinosaur and man. When they need to they switch to the use of the bones which will aid their environment necessities best."

"So they wear clothes. Like the Neanderthal their flat nose and added mucus warms cold air, so maybe they don't migrate. The feather fur is a bit of a surprise, must be the dinosaur aspect. They think, problem solve. Brilliant, really." Clarity sat pondering; the scientist in her couldn't help but be impressed.

"Deadly, more so." His tone again suggested an evasion of truths. He turned and sat beside her as the torrential rains rose from beyond the stone opening.

"Why does it rain up?" Clarity asked.

"Why wouldn't it?"

"The clouds release the rain."

"Yes, so does the ground."

"That is the most extreme sense of evaporation I've ever witnessed. So, do I just wait for a sinkhole to come pick me up?"

He cast her a fast glance before looking away. "No, you will come with me. I've explained the hybrids to you for a reason. This planet is dangerous to those who don't know it. You are safe with me and my people. There are few rules. You will be happy. We have simple lives, no currency. We trade expertise. It takes about a year before you will be welcomed home."

Clarity groaned. A year to be here, a year to go home and die, that had to be why the scientists found the bodies. Or had she already traveled a year? There would be no way this man could know to return was certain death. What would be worse, here or dead? Maybe not all died on re-entry, maybe. Living with dinosaurs on a strange planet wasn't on her bucket list—at twenty-eight she didn't have a bucket list.

Crap.

"I can't stay a year. I have no clue how to survive here. I have no home or job. If your kind has no currency, I have nothing to trade." She was mortified; she couldn't keep the wail from her tone. The three hundred and ten dollars and eighty-five cents in her wallet was useless. The same with her credit and debit cards. All she had was her purse and the ripped and stained clothing on her back.

Doom reached to clutch her hand. His features tightened. "There is no one better than me to take care of you during your time here. Entrust your life to me. I promise to keep you safe."

"You don't know me."

"I will."

****

Doom meant what he said to the human female. *Clarity, her name is Clarity. What a beautiful name.* There was nothing more precious than her life to him. Her life meant the salvation of one of his people, his family. Doom's family survived for decades together; there was no one more important than the people he cared for. For a year, Clarity was his to feed, clothe, and care for. The first of many, he hoped. Eventually, she would be moved from the protected area to aid another family through the rough winter approaching.

During the time of the great sleep, the human children in the village would need to rely on human adults. He learned humans thought it odd he and the villagers hibernated for a short time, the coldest time; Doom thought it odd humans didn't.

Keeping the truth from humans was imperative, especially when the villagers slumbered. The snow was deep and humans would freeze to death if they left the safety of their homes. There was no escape. The bulwarks hibernated as well, but the snowdrifts were brutal. If the humans ventured out, sank into the snow, and died, Doom's people would die. Humans brought to the village were made to feel safe and wanted. Each was coveted. Everything was provided for them. Locking them all together with the human children in the safe area was impossible for six weeks. The humans needed to be able to roam the entire shelter, to access food supplies and water. Keeping them in the village at all times was paramount.

The humans he met were happy to stay in the safety of the village. From the village, they could see certain dinosaurs that helped prove his point. Many times Doom had come across a human fleeing from a dinosaur. Their flight for life into his arms made trusting him easy. He wished it was.

The storm stopped and Doom took the opportunity to guide Clarity from the cave. He needed to see her safely to his people. Glancing at her as she watched every moving leaf, he wondered if he should keep her for the duration. The Neandersauri coveted human females the most. Doom didn't know why the females were killed, as were males. If the beasts who discovered her tried to interact with her, Doom wondered if it was to send her in his direction or kill her. The beasts had never kept humans on their own. They wouldn't take the time to feed and house them, to keep them safe. It was rumored the hybrids hibernated, but Doom wasn't certain. The hybrids wouldn't keep humans close when vulnerable. Unless they were never vulnerable as was also rumored. To date, Doom knew of no one who had killed a hybrid, the theory was too much to grasp.

Clarity grabbed his hand at a shrill noise. Humans always behaved in this fearful fashion at first. Doom could only imagine their terror, especially after hearing how docile their planet was. It was hard for Doom to imagine a world without dinosaurs and hybrids. At first when the harvest of humans began, Doom guiltily sent them to their demise, and though the guilt was raw and real, learning their planet was home to billions of humans made the sacrifice easier. A planet that harbored billions could afford to miss a few each year. Doom wasn't greedy; he wanted only to meet his quota. The villagers of Dooms' kind counted in the hundreds, or small thousands, if that, spread over the planet. It was hard to tell when gatherings of clans ceased so long ago, before Doom was born.

Humans who came through the sinkholes spoke of countries and States or Provinces. Doom had traveled often on his planet before the village was created. He couldn't fathom a world where people were cut off from one another by oceans. His kind were kept apart by hybrids.

The female's small hand was warm and sticky. With bits of tree and sap covering her, he could only guess at where she sought shelter from the beasts. Her earthy smell could have been what put them off, perhaps questioning if their scent was right. This little human was smart. For a second his heart raced, he had to hand the humans over by setting them loose in the forest of loss, the villagers aptly named the area. If the offerings escaped the beasts, it wasn't his fault. His breath expelled in a sigh, *no* human ever escaped. The beasts were too efficient, the humans too afraid. The hybrids learned sweet whistles would draw a human to their fate. It's why no villager ever whistled, and human children were reprimanded if they did.

The males of his tribe had a hard time letting go of the beautiful humans found. Letting this one go would be difficult for them all. But when a protest was made, the ultimate question was would they be willing to sacrifice someone from their own family. It was rare, but there had been a few occasions his people gathered more than their quota of humans, and then a nearby tribe would trade for a human if they were short.

Doom's people were more important than the humans. So were the other tribes fighting for existence. It was a race to find any humans, many perished moments after landing on the planet, the other creatures of this world made no deal with the Neandersauri. They wouldn't know how. Sometimes Doom damned his people's ability to think. Even humans used the term "ignorance is bliss."

Doom's people had an uncanny life span compared to humans, so he was told. He supposed it was part of their ancient breeding with other humanoid types. He never really questioned the amount of time for his existence before. Doom learned humans were obsessed with the concept. As the animals of his planet evolved, mixed, and the strong prevailed, so too did Doom's kind, and unfortunately so did the hybrids. His people had stopped breeding, and as far as Doom knew only his kind and the hybrids were left of the known thinkers. For every new birth, DaV-nin wanted another sacrifice. In a way, Doom's people saved as many of the humans as possible, sacrificing the joy of having their own children to spare suffering. Human children found wouldn't add to the quota. The evil beasts considered them offerings sooner or later.

At Clarity's gasp, and the pressure on his hand increased, Doom watched as a dinosaur crept by. Humans told him it was a mix of a turtle and alligator. Doom had never seen either species as a whole and was surprised when humans informed him their creatures were mixed. He should have known earlier in his planet's history animals bred for supremacy. It was that or extinction, but the knowledge was a revelation when he first learned. The creature lumbering before them was massive and would attack if cornered or challenged, Doom did neither.

Clarity pressed against him, eyes wide. Culture shock apparent. Doom had no doubt if he went to Earth the culture shock would be his. Humans spoke of strange inventions, artilleries, but none were capable of recreating such weaponry. Strange lightning that zipped across the heavens instead of weaving through tree trunks. One human was able to develop matches. For a while, Doom had optimism that one human would be the one to save them, but it didn't happen. There was always hope in the back of his mind a human would come to help them with the hybrids. Each sacrifice dimmed his hope.

The beauty beside him was timid, small. She would be among the first captured when the time came. It was a shame; she was the first female in a long time to stir his loins until he quashed his ardor. There would never be anyone for him. Some human men lasted longer during the hunt, when they possessed brute strength. It wasn't morbid curiosity that led him to watch the gathering on one occasion. A human man, powerful yet weak with kindness had fought back. He was brought to his knees by a hybrid, thrown over a shoulder, and taken away. Doom watched no more gatherings after that, hope was too elusive.

There was nothing strong about Clarity. Her dainty hand lifted to brush a lock of hair from her face. She was what humans called Caucasian, but something about her features nagged him. She was human there was no doubt; he'd seen many humans of varying colors and races. His mind shrugged, her looks didn't matter; she was a sacrifice. For the next year, Doom planned to make certain her life was happy. She deserved that. Her hair was damp from the storm, her eyes a whirlwind of mystery waiting to unfold. He hoped she had many stories to tell. Humans were fun during the long winter months before the deep sleep of the most brutal of weather, swapping tales of their adventures.

She's cute…so were many.

The first thing she needed was a bath, then clothes, then food. He debated whether he should put her alone in the protection chamber. When they entered his camp, she decided for him when she gripped his hand in a way it would take a T-rex of old to pry her off. He chuckled at the image conjured. The T-rex was said to be formidable at one time. Folklore.

Curious about the newcomer, the villagers came forward. Some of the older women wiped tears away or ducked heads to avoid a direct glance, welcomed Clarity, and moved off. The men eyed her. Some looked hostile but they were of an age to want a mate; the anger came from frustration. Trading for mates with other villagers became scarce as time went on. Doom's race was destined to suffer alone.

"Good God what is that?" Clarity asked.

A lumbering malevolent bulwark slowed as they passed it. The beast sniffed at her and Doom was certain she'd climb into his arms. The female beast was taller than Clarity while on all fours. Dark shaggy brown in color. The beast's head was massive, her shoulders broad. Huge feet sunk into the moist ground leaving the impression of her five three-inch claws. As the beast sniffed, her lips curled back exposing sharp teeth. Doom always imagined it was her way of smiling. Even Doom could smell Clarity's fear. To Clarity's credit, she stood still until he realized she was frozen to the spot in terror. This was her first exposure to such a creature. The idea of a race losing their heritage to a meteor or the environment was something unfathomable. Then again, the humans didn't suffer from hybrid dinosaurs.

"The beast won't hurt you, Clarity. There are four who protect the village and villagers. Including you, now that it has your scent. It's an evolved creature, a cave bear wolf mix. A human called them mutts. This one is female."

"I died and went to *Jurassic World*," she whispered.

The beast ambled off grunting and Doom turned her, placing his hands on her shoulders. "You are alive. Trust me."

"I may need new underwear," she mumbled.

Doom chuckled. He enjoyed spirit; he'd have to reassess her. Doom could learn to care for this human, in a small way. "Come with me. I will show you a place to bathe. I need your clothes, I will provide more."

"Why my clothes?"

"Other animals, dinosaurs might come if they scent the strangeness of your garments. The satchel you carry must be burned as well. The animals on this planet are a curious lot. Nosy-ass things."

Clarity gripped her leather pouch to her chest surprising him. Her features twisted into an unpleasant scowl. Feet spread her stance was rigid.

"On my planet, a man knows better than to mess with a woman's purse."

Doom blinked. No other humans had ever come through the sinkhole with anything but the clothes on their backs, some not even with that. He admitted to being curious as to what the sack contained. He thought he would look through it and dispose of it while she washed.

"Give me the item," Doom said, holding out his hand.

Her scowl deepened. "No way. It's all I have of home."

"I will not argue in front of my people; you will do as I say. It's best you start now."

"No."

Doom heard chuckling from behind him. A small group of men was watching. Soon everyone would be talking. He wasn't about to battle a female in public. It was beneath him to engage in a tug-of-war. *In public.* Shaking his head, Doom dipped down and tossed her over his shoulder. She howled as though being eaten. Doom had no clue what was in her sack but he cringed when it connected to his ass repeatedly.

"Hell, female. What the fuck is in there, a T-rex?"

"Only things I need and I'm keeping it," she bellowed.

She whacked him again. Then again. Doom growled.

Something tells me this will be the longest fucking year of my life.

Chapter Four

Clarity sat naked in a cove of water, clutching her sodden purse to her chest. Both she and Doom were snarling and gasping in air. He was as saturated as she was. The wet hide knee-length pants he wore pooled liquid at his moccasin feet. Eerie droplets of water dripped from faces tattooed on his body as though the images wept. Doom tried wrestling the purse away while she fought like a wildcat; he bore the assault of a perfect French manicure. He managed to strip her, but she felt victorious as she held onto her purse. He stood outside of the large pool soaked, fists balled, a hand squeezing lace panties, looking as though he may lunge for her. Clarity leveled her best evil glare, the one that made Edward run for cover, onto Doom.

"You're going to have to bust my arms before you pull this purse from my cold dead chest. *If* you live." The words were controlled menace.

Doom roared in fury, clutched the rest of her clothing up off the floor and left, stomping from the hut-like structure inside a larger cave.

"Damn," she grumbled. "A three-hundred-dollar purse and he acts like it's Pandora's box."

Searching her surroundings Clarity placed the purse on a natural rock shelf. The ceiling overhead was that of the cave. Four large hide walls made inside the interior were for privacy and warmth as added protection from any breeze. Further, she could see other steaming pools. She wondered at hot springs. The light in the room emanated from strategically placed rocks. A fire outside the cave entrance kept predators away, so Doom managed to inform her as they fought. He seemed under the impression her small weak self should be terrified without him. She admitted part of her was when a bulwark nudged the hide aside to peer at her. Clarity wondered if the beast could smell the food in her purse.

The people seemed ancient and uncouth, but the landscaping of the pool was solid, beautiful, and breathtaking. The pool she sat in was smoothed stone. She shifted and noted where her behind sat was lit with a bright light, not hot. Curious, she touched the side of the pool. When she pulled her hand away, the rock glowed a soft blue, further lighting the area.

Reaching, she lifted the purse and scrambled to her knees in the waist-high water. There was no light where the purse had sat. Clarity touched the rock. Warmth tingled her fingers, and soon the rock lit with her handprint.

Florescent minerals. Extreme thermoluminesence.

"Weird and yet mildly entertaining."

Clarity rifled through the contents of her purse and pulled out a wet wipe to wash her body with. She used her small containers of soap, shampoo, and conditioner to get rid of the sticky sap and places where rain hadn't washed away the mud. When finished, she pulled out her scarf, frowned at the lace, and decided she could dry it off. After patting down her skin until she was less wet she wrapped her hair in the scarf after combing the tangles, donned an extra pair of clean silk panties tucked away in a side pocket, and sat on a polished chair of wood and waited with her purse in her lap.

Doom entered the bathing area and seemed surprised. "Give me the sack," he demanded.

"It's the only thing between you, my boobs and hoochy."

"Your what?"

"If that is clothing in your hand for me, I'll take it. *Now*."

"I'll trade you for the sack."

"Nope."

"Damn it, you have no idea what the creatures on my planet are like."

"This happens to be real leather and since you are in leather I think the creatures can survive this simple culture shock even though it's not shaped in the form of pants."

And I highly doubt silk panties from China's silkworms will kill a stegosaurus or bring a hybrid to its knees.

"Clarity, let's be clear on this," his voice was dripping in sarcasm.

Well, I'm the queen of sarcasm. "Yes, let's be clear. My purse is mine. It stays with me. If you want your balls to stay with you, heed this warning; touch my sack and yours will suffer the same fate."

Doom's eyes widened. His fingers twitched. "If one of my people threatened their leader there would be harsh consequences."

"If you want to see consequences try getting your hands on my tampons or Midol."

Doom threw the clothing at her. "Until you hand that sack over willingly I have no choice but to place you in the protected area. For my people's safety."

Clarity struggled into the clothing glaring at him, the purse slipping while her breasts jiggled. The hide halter-top was loose and she needed the leather drawstring at the top tied in a bow to keep the garment on. He growled when he glimpsed her flimsy undergarment as she stuffed each leg into a pair of hide pants identical to his. She struggled with the finely woven leather belt. She scowled and leveled a deadly gaze on him.

"By all means. I wouldn't want anyone killed over a band aid and hemorrhoid cream. God forbid you come into contact with toothpaste and a toothbrush."

"I am the only protection against the beasts out there." He pitched two round surprisingly heavy flat leather objects at her and glowered. "They're for your feet. Put the fur side on the inside and tighten the leather thong around your ankles."

"Booties? Cripes almighty." She drew the leather together securing the footwear and stood feeling ridiculous in her new round feet. *Protection* from a man who obviously wore his own booties, they had conformed to his feet, was less than desirous. "Obviously your people have never benefited with the discovery of mace."

Doom grabbed her arm and dragged her outside. She didn't struggle. They approached a large domed mound. Doom stood before a massive quartz-type door. The rock was the same as the glowing rock in the cave bathing room. There was no way she could think to open it; the door looked to be too heavy even for a man of Doom's power. Doom placed his hand on the door. The rock began to glow immediately and the door slid sideways. She gazed up at Doom in stunned surprise.

"Only a villager's hand can open the door to my holding. This is why we are safe from the hybrids and dinosaurs. You can't open it from within. Any other door may be activated by a human touch, but not this one. We are like you, human, but there are subtle differences occurring over hundreds of thousands of years. This door detects the differences."

She understood the threat. Clarity could see the mound was deceptive, the area beneath appeared huge and dug several feet underground. There were polished quartz steps leading into the vast darkness all a foot high and disappeared on either side. She counted ten before they were swallowed by gloom. Doom shoved her forward.

"The rock is of different quality. It will not light with a touch. I'll think about bringing you a lantern or torch to light the others inside when I bring food," he glared as he said this.

Clarity smiled, dug into her purse, and pulled out a flashlight attached to her keychain. She switched it on and thought for a moment Doom would expire. She almost chuckled thinking if he had hair, every strand would be standing on end.

"No problem."

Doom growled as she made her way below. "I'll think about bringing food," he bellowed.

When the door slid closed behind him Clarity went to sit on a raised mound of furs. She fished into her purse and pulled out a bag of trail mix. She chewed a mouthful erratically and swallowed.

"No fucking problem."

She cast the light about the room and noticed

torches high off the ground. She fished in her bag and pulled out a lighter. She went and deftly lit all six torches until her surroundings blazed. All around her were giant furs—on the floors, the walls, and ceiling. Some looked old and worn, others fresh. Small bags of water dripped in an area covered by stone. On further inspection, she determined the water bags were the stomachs of creatures.

Even the Flintstones had running water, even if it was from a mammoth trunk.

Her discoveries were far from over as she crept through her surroundings. Never a believer in psychometry, Clarity was certain as she fingered the fur beneath her from a raised bed, a wash of icy water down her spine made her fingers tingle. Emptiness assaulted her. There were many other raised beds making her wonder.

Doom said humans came to stay for a while and then left. He was evasive and she suspected lying. If humans once filled this chamber, where had they gone? Really? And if there were to be no more, why were the beds all aired out and waiting? How could humans suddenly appear and disappear? A sinkhole wasn't a bus. There was more to her situation, something scary, she could feel it. She had no doubt she was standing in a cell, a beautiful cell, but she was a prisoner. Unconsciously her palm caressed the side pocket of her purse holding her mace. Her situation *was* a *huge* problem.

****

Doom was pacing in his home, a common occurrence and the worn hybrid mammoth mastodon mix fur beneath his feet showed the proof. Within the confines of his domain, Doom could be curious, angry, afraid, and any other emotion he chose not to share with the villagers. His mind a whirlwind of tumultuous thoughts. Inside, a special soothing wind chime tinkled, the man-made flow of air aiding in the virtuoso sound. Each note meant to engage the soul and center emotions. Today, the melody was no help. Doom blocked the notes, it was no use; he could only concentrate on one thought.

"How is it possible to have fire inside the small tube and project it—with no heat?" Doom's people had glowing rocks earthlings marveled over, but Doom was used to the phenomenon. It took warmth to ignite the light of warmth within the stone. Clarity clicked a switch. Could the touch of something so small be so powerful, or was there more to it?

His heart pounding, he wondered what other magic Clarity could pull out of her sack. Humans who came before her told a good tale. Flying birds that ate people only to spit them out at a new destination unharmed. How could the insides of a giant bird serve refreshments? The idea was laughable and he scoffed off the notion. But seeing a flashlight, he had heard of flashlights, actually work the way described was amazing. The pitter-patter of his heart skipped a beat. No wonder she guarded the bag. A purse she called it. A human female treasure possessing magic. Doom loved magic, especially scary as hell magic.

He battled his thoughts. She must learn to obey him. She must listen to his every whim. Doom commanded here. He was leader; he knew what was best. Until he had to hand humans over. That wasn't for the best; it was a necessary evil. Every sacrifice broke him further until his emotional bones were shards. He was as desensitized as possible, but it was never enough. For all his size and power, he wished with all his heart his life was different, wished he wasn't leader. Doom stood clenching his fists.

Turn off the emotion.

Clarity was too compelling with her small stature and huge rebellious streak. Their physical confrontation intrigued him. There were women who would actually confront him? *Unbelievable*. Having her in his arms was torture. She was the first woman he ever clung to for so long—even if they were battling. His cock still twitched from desire. He couldn't turn off his emotions; they tumbled through him, around him, over him.

Doom couldn't stand it; he had to go to her. She must show him the contents of her sack. To learn about something new was fascinating. If she shared her knowledge with his people for a year it was possible to take a step closer to freedom. Doom sucked in his breath. Freedom was an elusive word never spoken aloud. Why had he thought such a thing? Hope was a better word. Still, freedom nagged his insides.

Racing from his home, Doom crashed through the door of the protective shelter startling her, not waiting for it to slide back completely before muscling his way in. Clarity was sitting on the last step up and he came close to tripping over her. She screamed, jumped up, and aimed something at him. Suddenly, Doom's eyes were on fire. He couldn't see. She wounded his eyes from a distance. Groaning, he lost his balance and rolled heavily down the steps where he landed on his knees, his fisted hands digging at his eyes.

"Doom? You startled me. Oops."

"Oops. All you can say is *oops*. I'm blinded."

"Calm down, the pain won't last forever. I'm sorry. I thought you might be one of those beasts, what did you call them, erectasaurus? Or something."

"There is *nothing* remotely erect right now, trust me."

Doom could feel her hand on his shoulder, and she shoved a skin of water into his hands. He dumped the flask over his face to soothe his eyes. He blinked. The pain was still there but he could see her through blurred vision.

"What the fuck did you do to me?"

"It's mace. Very effective."

"You think?"

Clarity helped him to his feet and guided him to a bed. "I see you brought no food. You're still not getting my purse."

"I wanted to see what was inside, not take it from you. Humans have never brought anything through the sinkholes. You're the first. Damn, I don't know what hurts worse my eyes or my ass." That fall would leave bruises. Tag-teamed by a woman and stairs. It occurred to him the torches were lit. He wondered if she understood the magic of matches.

"Maybe I shouldn't show you what I have. You live in a primitive time. Too much knowledge too fast can be dangerous."

"From what I hear Earth was primitive, too. Over the last two-hundred years it's come even farther. Some of the humans here speculated alien interference. They don't know why. Maybe aliens are cultivating you. Making you smarter for a new colony."

"You just pulled that out of your ass."

"No." Doom poured more water over his eyes. "Humans have only been coming here for the last few decades. Each human has a point of view. I think about all of their points. Maybe you were sent here to give us the aid we need." He wasn't lying. Every individual was listened to for any clue of survival. Doom remembered everything. There had to be a reason humans began appearing. Doom devoured every morsel and crumb of knowledge.

"Your people coexist with dinosaurs. I have no clue what help I could give you. I'm a fish out of water here."

"We adapted. You humans coexist with deadly Earth creatures, maybe not as overwhelming as dinosaurs but I have heard the 'terrorist' beast is formidable and unpredictable, though some call it cowardly. Most animals have some form of defense."

"Yep, those terrorist animals are a piece of work."

"The dinosaurs you are used to hearing about aren't like the ones now. They were at one time long ago. I have seen skeletal remains. Everything evolved. Everything will continue to evolve until nature's plan is perfect."

"It won't if you're given technology to make weapons of mass destruction. You will slaughter the animals and kill your world."

Doom squinted at her; his heart began to race. "Mass destruction. I've heard that term before."

Clarity rose and paced. "I don't belong in your world. When the hole opened I was headed somewhere and yanked onto your planet. I'm positive."

Doom jumped up and gripped her hands. "How can you be so sure?"

"I was given a message before I fell. Someone was coming for me. The voice wasn't yours. And from what little I saw and see, you don't have the means to send any message to other tribes let alone across galaxies." She made a point of casting her gaze onto furs and water bags.

"I'm not stupid or simple minded."

"You survive with dinosaurs," she sounded surprised. "Of course you're not stupid. As for simple I'd use the term complacent. You know how to survive and since there are children here you adapt."

Doom winced. Not one child had been born to his people in a long time. He was the last. Her eyes were bright and earnest. An untold lie was still a lie. A lie told to yourself was a lie. Doom reached to tuck a strand of her silky hair behind her ear.

"I have food in my home. This place is too empty for you to stay all alone. You're safe with me." He gave her a wry smile. "Okay you're safe with your purse. I'll watch you both."

Clarity smiled. "This place is scary as heck but I would like to see more of your planet."

She was never allowed to leave the village. Perhaps showing her the dinosaurs beyond the perimeter would change her mind as it had all the others. One glimpse and she would be too afraid to go anywhere.

"I will show you more after I tell you of the dangers. That could take a while."

"Gee I never imagined."

****

As Clarity moved through the village following Doom, she noted the grass-covered mounds. Sixteen in all, all various sizes, all incorporated into the landscape.

Nothing appeared out of the ordinary. The range appeared a vision of gently rolling hills with massive rock formations. There were caves as well, many with panels of hide, and she wondered at their contents.

Doom explained their dwellings. Each home was dug out of the ground. Huge stones were cut and placed inside to form the floor and walls. Cement was used as a filler. He took her to an open door where she peered inside a villager's home. She didn't venture down. The structure was brightly lit inside. Though Doom used the word cement, the ebony substance was very fine and at a touch it heated and glowed. Not exactly tar either, as the thick substance was neither wet nor dry. When pushed it held tight.

As they moved on, Doom explained the ebony mass also held an undetectable odor to humans and his people but repelled reptiles. For the ceiling, large mammoth tusks made a dome which was covered in grass. They were in the process of making another home. Clarity examined the mammoth tusks. She couldn't be certain, but something nagged the mammoths might be a hybrid of mastodons and perhaps another large creature.

There was something odd about the bones—massive and whole, none broken or chipped, all smooth perfection. Clarity wondered if the bones were unbreakable. Doom said they could cut the stone; nothing was mentioned about the bones. Every home had a tunnel connecting it with the others underground. The village outside was situated in a circle, inside the circle were blazing fires and smaller fires.

For a people who dealt with dinosaurs on a day-to-day basis, no one appeared afraid. A woman played with a small boy who seemed quiet. All villagers dressed in the same short pants. The men went shirtless; the women wore small leather tops. There were few children, perhaps five, of various ages all in different forms of dress depending on age. Everything looked primitive to Clarity. The people wore skins and furs. Almost everyone seemed happy, except for the little boy of perhaps five.

Clarity could see there was a difference in this child. A woman gave up trying to encourage him to play with others and held him while tears streamed down his wan face. She was joined by a huge man, his father perhaps. The child resembled neither parent. He was healthy but thin. Every person in the village was big boned except the children. All the men were massive and bald. Some men wore tattoos but none as intricate as Doom.

The women all stood over five nine, all less than six feet. They were muscular. They all wore their white hair in braids or a bun. Doom's people were beautiful, but ancient suffering flooded the depths of their eyes. Hopelessness filled the atmosphere. The lush beauty of the parts of the planet Clarity had seen was breathtaking. Except for the creepy bear wolves, there wasn't a single threat she could see. And when Clarity saw one of the beasts drop to the ground to roll in a playful manner, she couldn't help but smile.

Off in the distance Clarity saw a sauropod. The huge beast lumbered along, stripping trees as it went. The beast was magnificent. Never in her life had she thought to dream she would see such a sight. The dinosaur was beyond massive. She had a thought.

"How do you keep the larger dinosaurs from

stepping on your homes? I'm sure the bones are strong but a mammoth tusk couldn't hold one of those." She pointed as she spoke.

"It's not only bone protecting the homes, although yes the tusks are strong enough. Nothing can break them. The hides are thick and useful for many of our needs and the meat is succulent. Every so often, small rocks from the sky fall in strange pieces. They're amazing for reinforcing the bones as a precaution. They are placed near the tops of the mounds, when anything large comes close the rock will glow through the dirt and grass and the bright light scares the dinosaurs."

"I thought meteors never landed here."

"Not in large sizes. I'm certain Earth had small meteors land that didn't cause damage. The ones we use were already near here, so we took advantage. The material is like nothing on our planet and doesn't break. We could only incorporate the substance and build around it. The bulwarks aren't our only defense. You see, in the trees over there? Those devices make a noise the dinosaurs don't like. Many dinosaurs have a set path when they migrate as well. All of the meat-eaters are too small to break through the numerous layers of bone covering our homes. For the larger ones, we have tar pits that surround the back of the village where you're gazing. Those beasts are too big to avoid the hazard. They have learned to fear the smell of man. We hunt them, especially if they get too close."

"You hunt those?"

"Yes, the meat is good and feeds many for a long period of time. We have massive trees sharpened at a certain height to hamstring a beast. Once they are down, it's easy enough to slit a throat. Their own weight can crush their organs when they fall. We normally hunt one before they migrate. It takes all of us working together to slaughter and retrieve the choice parts we need. The blood draws too many predators after a while. But by then we have our packs loaded."

"Amazing," she whispered as they continued to walk.

A powerful man stopped chopping wood to stare at Clarity and her smile died on her lips. He was in his prime with many tattoos. His gaze wasn't hostile, exactly. He was intense as he studied her. Finally, he shook his head and she could see his lips move as though he muttered under his breath. He attacked the wood before him with a vengeance.

"Are your people angry I'm here?" Clarity asked.

Doom followed her gaze and took a deep breath. "There are times my men ask to keep a human safe until it's time for them to leave. The humans always go, and the men are left bereaved. Menace is the last of his tribe, near my age. Salvation came too late for his people."

"Salvation?"

Taking her arm Doom encouraged her forward. "The Neandersauri are relentless."

"Your people have survived."

"It's taken time to rebuild, we were hunted almost to extinction. Others from neighboring tribes joined with me after losing their leaders. Few leaders joined with me after losing their tribes. I lead all here."

"A human's greatest asset is their ability to think, to reason and solve conflict. What are these hybrids capable of?"

"Death."

"Reproduction?"

"Yes."

"Why don't you hunt them?"

"With what? Our weapons are useless against them. We have nothing to pierce their hides. Our spears aren't enough. They are built for death, toned over thousands of years when all humanoid-type species realized in order to survive we must adapt and integrate with stronger species. Their bodies are massive; their claws rip our flesh to shreds. They think; they're stronger. It's impossible to hunt the hybrids as animals. When last they attacked my tribe they went after leaders. My father fell when I was still a boy on the verge of manhood. Many leaders were slaughtered across the planet. Their assault was systematic and strategic."

"Are they smarter than you?"

Doom glanced away. Clearly he was uncomfortable. "They want something."

"What?"

"I don't know. Earth humans haven't always come here. It's only been a while."

"When did humans start coming here?"

Doom shifted his feet. "In the last few decades. The hybrids have grown smarter. They hunt in numbers no less than two."

Clarity stopped. "Since humans started coming here."

"It's a theory."

She grew angry. "What happens to the humans on this planet?"

"They go home."

Doom released her arm and strode forward; she

had no choice except to follow. He led her to a mound of grass, domed, twenty feet in a circular diameter. He gripped the solid rock door with both hands. The places he touched lit with pink and blue light but he was too impatient and dragged the door open. Clarity knew from the bulging of his muscles she'd never in a million years budge the door. They stepped down sixteen steps—she guessed the height from floor to ground to be twenty feet.

Doom's home was different from the protected human area. A dwelling the likes she'd never seen. Tools, benches, and furniture were placed strategically. Cupboards were cut into rock faces. There was only one raised platform where he slept; his bed was massive, the headboard made of polished yellow obsidian. Clarity blinked at the splendor. She never would have imagined stepping into another world under a mound of dirt.

The furs everywhere were brightly colored, and she wondered what animal they were from. Whatever it was it was large, perhaps the mammoth hybrid. She wondered at the animal's size. Doom's people could hunt things of this magnitude but not the hybrids, intelligence had to factor in. Beautiful furs on the walls delighted her. A mixture of fur and feathers interwoven. His home was the same as the protected area for humans, minus the splendor. She saw a tunnel leading underground, branching out, until with a touch Doom sealed it off. There was no tunnel in the place they kept humans.

Protected area or jail?

Clarity's mind was racing as she fingered the furs on the bed then strolled over to a place with what looked to be huge bamboo shoots. A wooden sprocket could be twisted, and water flowed into the smoothed rock sink. At a sectioned off area were another sink and huge bathtub, both made from large amethysts. A million-dollar bathroom with polished rock flooring, but no toilet.

"Where does the water come from?" Clarity asked.

"One handle turn comes from the cave where you bathed. There are many hot springs inside. The other is from pools we created."

"Where do you, um, poop?"

Doom gave her a disgusted gaze. "Why on earth do humans feel the need to make waste right in their own home?"

"Because outside our asses would freeze or get eaten, at least here."

"We have a shelter in another cave. Your ass is safe."

"Good to know."

Beautiful fossils hung from the walls. The air was fresh and she wondered at the ventilation. It was strange seeing a place where ancient collided with new age. Doom's people had knowledge, limited, but it was there. If two types of species survived so far she wondered if the hybrids might be that much more intelligent. Two having merged to be stronger, but who was smarter? Or rather when did *who* become smarter?

Clarity knew there was a connection between the hybrids and humans. She didn't need to be a rocket scientist to wonder if the Neandersauri found a way to breed with humans. If they did, what happened to the human? The few pieces were falling into disturbing places.

Lost in thought, Clarity slumped onto a wooden

chair to eat at a smooth rock table. She accepted the bread Doom gave her and chewed small pieces methodically. The hybrids were too big for a human to carry offspring. Dinosaurs laid eggs. Human females produced eggs but gave birth to flesh and blood. Was it possible for a woman to have an egg birth? The tug of a frown made her forehead hurt for a second. What resources would an egg deplete if a human female actually gave birth to one?

"Not possible," she whispered aloud.

"What isn't possible?"

Clarity jumped, she forgot Doom was near her. "Tell me the truth. How long have you been harvesting humans for those hybrids?"

Doom looked guilty as hell and surprised—he looked surprised. "Humans go home."

Clarity rolled her tongue on the inside of her cheek, a gesture when she was pissed. Edward called it her duck and run like hell move. She slipped her hand into her purse and pulled out her taser. For a moment she rolled it in her hand letting Doom get a good look.

"Mace is nasty."

Doom nodded. "Yeah sure is." His eyes were still red.

Clarity leaned forward. "This little device will make mace seem like a child's toy."

"I have no doubt you're lying."

"Try me."

"Your fate is sealed."

"I make my own destiny. Fate is for fools."

"You will spend a year here. Why would you want to spend it in fear?"

"So you do hand humans over. To save your own

76

neck."

Doom jumped up to pace. "I keep my people safe. I pay for every sacrifice." He stopped abruptly then growling, he continued. "Do you know the agony I suffer or that Menace suffered? I keep humans innocent of harmful thoughts or actions from others for as long as possible. Not only are the hybrids out there. Some humans don't even make it to me. I save them. Then they go home."

Clarity watched him pace for a moment, a telltale groove in the fur rug suggested the act was habit. "Has there never been another who questioned your actions?"

He paled visibly. "Some question, perhaps some guess. Many say nothing. They are gentle humans who don't come to me with a satchel of weapons. The first human didn't. But if she had a purse she might have."

Clarity wondered if there was more to the selection of humans harvested from sinkholes. Human lambs was a theory.

"Are the humans you have known weak? Or ill?"

"Some yes. They are different than you."

An odd thought occurred to Clarity. This planet was like Earth. What if there were more Earth-like planets in different stages of advancement. Why not? Science fiction didn't have to be made up of freaky alien planets with strange alien-type creatures. Earth was crazy enough in its infant stages. No one could tell her a dinosaur wasn't a wacky creature.

"Will you tell me about the first human?"

Doom continued to pace casting her periodic glances. She could tell he wasn't a liar by nature. Why was it so hard to realize large powerful men had hearts and hurts? That was the look in his gaze—hurt, remorse, anger, fear, all bundled together—making the largest man she'd ever seen appear as vulnerable as a small boy. His tone, when he spoke, was soft.

"One by one my people died, hunted to the brink of extinction. We were always running, hiding, crying with our fear. I spent many a night huddled in my mother's arms wishing I was as big as my father, until I realized he was helpless. The agony of that notion terrified me. We were doomed. But not as yet, there were still many different types of humans. The smaller were killed first, and one by one the races died. The hybrids are systematic creatures. Kill the weak first. My people are the strongest of the humanoids left.

"We were clever and learned to hide. There was danger when we left our hideouts to hunt, but my own village remained strong in numbers, or so I thought. Until one year, many years ago after my parents died a human appeared. Her name was Alice. We were happy to have her, thrilled. Alice was fun and full of life. She was kept safe and welcomed into our midst. I adored her and her stories; I was young then. She was a number of years older. She wasn't old enough to be my mother but she was smart like her. I learned a great many things.

"We were nomads; all humanoids had to be with existing cultures. Our people, our type of humanoid, were considered the hierarchy. There were still a number of us in my tribe, and we didn't need to integrate with anyone, especially a lesser form of human. We avoided other humans and looked the other way when the hybrids killed off the others. As I grew older and cockier, I was adept at keeping my villagers safe. Little did I know it was a matter of time before we were next. Perhaps our arrogance, my arrogance, almost killed us. My people began to fall. When she, Alice, found the rocks and the way they glowed, she designed the homes we have now. Alice was right, the time had come to stand our ground and lay roots. The crude implements she devised seemed so sophisticated to us.

"The homes couldn't be built fast enough. More people joined us, and I allowed it, welcomed them. I should have seen the safety in numbers. The tragedy is our ideas came too late for too many. We soon discovered only our kind and the hybrids walked the planet. The hybrids hunted wherever whenever, no one was safe. The work was tedious and backbreaking, but all could see the value, how smart the human was. She taught us to harvest and store food for more than just the big sleep. You remind me of her in a way, but you are much younger. We warned her of the hybrids, to keep her distance. I wanted her safe. Alice was always wandering, always looking for new ideas."

"Or maybe the sinkhole that brought her here."

Doom stopped pacing to sit. He ran a hand over his face and took a small sip from a wooden cup before continuing.

"The attack of the hybrids on our village was swift, we were given no warning, everything was chaos when they hit from every direction. Alice was so loving. She helped whomever she could. The last time I saw her, she faced off with a hybrid. He was going to kill me and I was injured. The tiny little thing holding a weapon was only trying to protect me, but for some reason the hybrid didn't strike her dead, at least not at first, he took her away."

There was pain in his voice; Clarity could tell the

images haunted him. He must have loved her more than he let on. Alice must have loved him to face such an opponent. Again the wheels were turning in her mind. She wondered at Doom's kindness. If he handed humans over, he had to remain aloof.

"We lost so many, it was the single home the human female that had us build that saved our lives. I was dragged into the home. A hybrid couldn't open the door, even with their hybrid human-type hand bones. The solid rock is impenetrable. Other tribes were destroyed and scattered having no such safe-haven. After the attack brought us to our knees, tribes joined tribes to unite, but it was almost too late. We were almost hunted to extinction. That was the hybrids' goal, to annihilate us. The human female was right. The hybrids wanted us dead. We were a threat. We could think. We were the last humans to stand in their way of owning the entire planet.

"Then something changed. It was the first time I met DaV-nin, a new leader of the hybrids. He was the only hybrid who wanted to speak to me. Hybrids are so dangerous because of their accelerated growth. They are adult by the end of their first year. The first time we were raided by the hybrids after the human came, the hybrids promised a truce. My people were spared. They would leave my people and the people of the other tribes alone as long as we gave them a human quota."

"Didn't you question why?"

"No," he shouted and jumped to his feet. "Yes," quieter. "But it was the first time since my father's demise I saw hope. As long as we meet the hybrids' needs we are left alone."

Doom sat, he buried his face in his hands, then

lowered them. The tortured glance he cast in her direction told her his pain.

"Our number is so little on this planet. Perhaps a few thousand of us. Some I think are hiding out there. It seems every year the quota gets bigger. Some of our people can't make the number and the hybrids take our people."

Clarity's mind was racing. "They went from wanting your people dead to trading with them. They must need you. Maybe to keep the humans alive for a certain period. Or to capture humans. The hybrids are scary as shit; I sure wouldn't go near them. Mixing with a human from Earth might have caused a change. Depending on how fast the hybrids grow it might even be DaV-nin was a product of the first Earth human. The offspring might have been more intelligent, enough to trigger the idea in the hybrid. The more humans they captured the smarter they would become. Even a hundred years ago humans were learning in leaps and bounds, now with the intelligence today. My God."

"What?"

"In the last fifty years we have moved well into space travel. What if the hybrids know this? What if that's their goal. If the hybrids are multiplying, it means they will need a new source of knowledge, space, food. Eventually your people and humans won't be enough. Do they breed with their own? Breeding with humans seems so farfetched. Even if their internal skeletal structure is close to human, the outer dinosaur hybrid is too big."

"After the first human was taken we noticed a drop in hybrid females. I've come across the little corpses as though they were crushed after birth. Why they would kill their own is baffling."

"It's scary as shit. If they feel their females are inferior for some reason, this isn't good. A mass army of killer males. Or maybe only males are compatible, or maybe there isn't enough of the humans for all, and they have selected their females for extinction. What kind of species has no compassion for their own?"

Clarity had to stop the annihilation. The 'what if's' were endless. If the hybrids wanted to branch out and head to Earth, they might have figured out bombs and ways to use other weapons. If a single hybrid could somehow mate a human female to produce offspring, the scenarios were endless. But what did they need human males for? For a second, the idea of a hybrid eating the human brain to absorb knowledge made her want to gag.

"Do you ever find the humans' remains?"

"No."

"How many offspring do the hybrids have at a time?"

"Three. I came across an enclosed nest once. They had burrowed their way out. The little ones were small, the female crushed, the two males were already deadly though waist high. I'm not sure if it was the siblings or an adult who killed the female offspring. I barely escaped with my life. A grown hybrid had come to collect them and called them off. It's death to harm a hybrid."

"What happens to the humans you collect?"

"They go home."

"Damn you, you better tell me or so help me I'll shove this taser up your ass."

"I don't know. I saw no trace. There is never any

trace. After they are released, we never see them again. Maybe they do eventually find a way home."

"You send them to their death and you don't know?" Clarity was outraged.

Doom stood and spread his hands wide. "They die, they go home. They will go home. I will take every last soul with me and set them free. I swear. Can you not see I speak the truth, how can you not see what's in front of you?"

He spread his arms wide. Scowling Clarity stood to study the tattoos. They were no ordinary markings. Each line, each face was personal. Symbols of intricate articles were carved in his flesh. He was beautiful, and frightening. Clarity was beginning to understand what those tattoos represented.

"Who draws those on you?"

"I don't know. After the humans began being sacrificed, the images appeared. I carry the mark of each individual and when I die, they will walk with me and be free."

"What do you do with the humans?"

"I don't hurt them in any way. We all walk into the forest."

"And only you ever walk out."

"My people are all I have."

Clarity felt her eyes prick with unshed tears. There were thousands of tattoos. All flowing in beautiful designs. The best of the humans was etched on his soul. When she glanced up at Doom she watched as a single tear trailed down his cheek. Clarity placed her hand on his arm. She was gazing into the face of defeat.

"It's time to take you and your people out of the killing field of the dark ages."

Chapter Five

"At one time the ashes of our dead were so deep we trudged through them. The hybrids killed for sport, leaving bodies where they dropped for disease. Other animals feasted on my kind's flesh and so we burned the dead. Once an animal gets a taste for a certain meat it can become their favorite. We killed off many dinosaur species, because we were always hunted. It was easier to kill the animals. The killing of our own had to stop. Women refused to give birth until they were no longer able. Mental or physical condition we don't know. Maybe they're simply too old now."

Clarity lay beside Doom in bed, having no other option. There were furs she could have tossed on the floor to curl up in but she wanted to talk. Doom left his short pants on but removed his belt. His tone was desolate as he spoke. They lay side by side, a fur between them and another covering them. Her day was long and stressful to begin with, it appeared night wouldn't be any better. The image he painted shimmered her groggy sleep into induced nightmares. She could hear the drone of his voice as he invaded her mind. A young boy, long black flowing hair walked hand in hand with a massive man. Clarity looked up seeing both man and child through her eyes and the boy's.

She thought for a moment the man was Doom but

not one tattoo adorned his body. Looking down, she saw they were ankle deep in ash. Clarity knew it was the ash of their people. A frightened woman raced to the pair where she flung herself against the man who caught her.

"Where? Where do we go from here? Our home is gone. Again we're being chased into the unknown where stranger beasts live."

The man ran a shaky hand down her long white hair. "I don't know, my love. Our tribe is almost gone. Our men are depleted to skin and bone; our hair is gone. Our women waste away, their hair gone or white as snow. No children since Doom have been born. The hybrids have almost destroyed us."

"We should have had a girl and named her Hope," was the woman's bitter reply.

The man cupped her face between her palms. "No, my love, her name would have been Destiny." He turned her in his arms, locking her in his embrace. "Look around. There is our destiny."

Sheets of ash dripped from tree branches, oozing its way to the ground in plops. Languishing amidst the rotted foliage. Their village was a killing field. Nothing looked familiar to Clarity. The smoke spiraled from the ground and she inhaled its rancid odor.

"Take a good look, my son. This is why you were named Doom. The last born of our kind. I saw it in a vision. True as clarity. Because there is nothing clearer than this."

The smell of dankness hovered. The scent of despair. A grayness was in the air, steaming from the ground.

"The ashes of the ones who have nothing left to

give litter the ground. We walk on our fathers and mothers, our sisters and brothers, cousins, aunts and uncles. Every relative we had is gone. Once we are gone, the hybrids will have nothing left except the dinosaurs. Their race will inherit this earth. Like other races before us, the hybrids have almost annihilated everyone."

The villagers went into hiding, but the hybrids were relentless. Bloodlust ran too high. The only way to appease them was to ask for any willing to sacrifice themselves so others could live. The occasional villager appeased the hybrids and kept them from hunting everyone. Doom's father knew the people were being toyed with; their demise was simply a matter of time. The hybrids were in a game of annihilation. The leader kept the others as safe as possible until one day there was a choice. Doom's father gave his life for his son.

Clarity saw Doom's vision through his words as dreams of his reality flooded her thoughts. After Doom's father was taken, a known warrior for his people, the hybrids became a systematic breed. For a time, Doom and his people were left alone. A feeling nagged at Clarity's guts. The hybrids were after something of importance. Doom's father may have been the first to change the thinking process, until the slaughter began with renewed vigor. The hybrids approached Doom after a last attack on the leaders.

She could envision the single human female who had stayed with Doom, trying to help. He had been so young, so few of his people were left, living hand to mouth as nomads, collecting the stragglers. The human woman made a stand; she taught them to use the materials around them. She taught Doom and his people how to think. Alice gave them new ideas to expand their minds. There was hope, until she was taken.

DaV-nin appeared not long after and demanded the exchange of humans for the tribe's life. There were so few people left, all battered and broken, to refuse would be death. Clarity wanted the images he painted to stop the assault on her mind, but she couldn't wake. Doom's father made him promise that until he could stop the hybrids from killing, there would be no more of his people to sacrifice.

Doom kept the promise but it came with a price. None even knew if more humans could be found, but they were. Soon after, Doom began finding more humans, keeping them safe until the time of reckoning. Sadness consumed him. Handing over innocents hurt his entire being. The pain was unbearable and he couldn't make it stop; he needed some way to make his actions right.

After the first sacrifice, a strange thing happened to Doom as he stumbled into a dark cave. A place to hide his tears, a place where he didn't need to look at his stricken features. A place where he screamed his frustration, begging aloud for damnation and salvation. The cave was dark, but Clarity saw his agony in her thoughts. Doom was consumed with self-loathing. A tug to his skin began, then another. He sat on a rock where he felt the pinpricks, wondering if an animal was consuming him as the pain increased. For a long while he didn't move, even after the sensation stopped. His breath ragged, he struggled to his feet knowing he had to face his people.

Pausing only moments to wipe his face with water, he gazed into the pond at his exposed flesh. Images were on his body. Doom wiped at them but they wouldn't come off. Realization struck a blow to his guts. He was gifted, guilted, with the protection of human souls tattooed onto his body. There was no explanation. Only acceptance of a great responsibility and a small sense of relief that he hadn't really lost them. And after a time, he came to learn such was the fate of each leader, to bear the mark of their kills.

Doom rolled toward Clarity, the fur between them. He gripped the fur and pulled it away. Clarity was awake instantly, or maybe it was her mind that had slipped into thought. Her heart thundering, she was soon settled into his embrace. Doom did nothing more than hold her. The images lingered, the smells, the clarity. His pain was in her soul.

"How old are you?" Clarity whispered.

"I don't know. My parents died long ago. The foliage once more turned lush in the places villagers were killed. The land returned to its former state. The animals breathed easier. One single woman saved us and damned us. She unknowingly killed her own kind. My people live in agony. We are a peaceful people if left alone, warriors only to defend. The hybrids made us killers. She couldn't have known; none of us did."

"Did you love her?"

"I was too young for Alice, but yes I loved her in my own special way. We all did."

His breathing slowed and Clarity knew he slept. For her, sleep remained elusive as her mind began some detective work. She knew a human would problem solve. If the hybrids were given the ability to problem solve, they would be wondering at their best recourse. By destroying their own hybrid female offspring, it gave the males a chance to have smarter children by only being with humans. It stood to reason a human male would never copulate with a hybrid. A human female could be forced, but Clarity didn't think that was the case. Something was missing. What that was remained to be seen.

After his father was taken, the hybrids changed the way they thought, like a warrior would think. Then again, when Alice was taken. An icy finger slid down her spine. What were these creatures doing and what were they after? It was high time someone found out.

****

Clarity wasn't in bed when Doom woke. He wasn't concerned. The beasts that kept the other dinosaurs at bay wouldn't allow her to leave. She would be too afraid of them not to heed a warning snarl. Leisurely, he washed his face and rinsed his mouth. Clarity seemed surprised when last night he brushed his teeth. He and his people weren't primitives. They knew the importance of cleanliness. It's why they slaved to bring the underground water source to each home.

Doom was informed by other humans their plumbing was crude but effective. Over time, humans aided in bringing greater luxuries. It wasn't as though he and his people weren't intelligent—they were different. When running from dangers was paramount, that was the focus. Running water wasn't even a close second. Simply existing was tiring on his planet. Ideas were fine as long as raptors weren't attacking.

Humans had so many ideas Doom was surprised they could keep up. For a moment, Doom wondered again if mating a human and keeping the child a secret would advance his people. Then he realized his kind and the hybrids developed differently. Doom and his people could learn if taught, but they needed teachers. The hybrids advanced simply from having humans. But did they mate with them? The idea was disturbing and not something he wanted to consider. He wondered if it was the dinosaur DNA always striving over the millennia to produce smarter and stronger offspring. Whatever they did with the humans, the hybrids were advancing.

At a bang on his door, Doom went to open it. Menace stood there, his normal scowl plastered to his face. He held a tray loaded with food in one hand, his bloodied spear in the other. A fresh kill. Doom sighed, wishing it were as easy to kill the hybrids. Their flesh seemed impenetrable. A thrown spear was useless, and by the time any villagers could get close enough to stab a spear into a hybrid with more power, they were sliced to pieces.

The man was a warrior, volatile from the time the first human appeared until she was gone. For precisely a month Menace relaxed, pretending life was normal. Once the first human arrived, he made it his mission to kill prey. His reprieve hadn't been long enough. The meat looked shredded. So did Menace. The gaze in his haggard angry glare was always the same. No man should ever lose everything and everyone to tragedy.

"Thank you, Menace. I'm surprised Aba didn't bring the meal."

"She's busy with her new son. The boy's insisting they help find paper so he can make planes. I know the humans speak of flying machines but it appears his father was an actual peelot."

"I believe the term is pilot."

Menace looked past him. "Where's the female?"

"Outside roaming the village I guess."

"You guess?"

"She can't go anywhere."

"You better make certain. I noticed one of the bulwarks are gone. I guessed she was hunting, but you better be sure."

"You worry like an old woman."

"If I was smart I'd take the female and run like shit to a place the hybrids can't find us. I'd have a hundred children and form an army and fight."

"We are outnumbered."

"We only need better weapons. We need a male human with battle smarts. The female is small and defenseless. At least she seems healthy."

Doom sighed. He wasn't in the mood for this conversation. A wry smile tugged at his lips. "Defenseless my ass. I'd like to see you get past her mace and purse of tortures. "

Chuckling at Menace's confused expression, Doom set the tray on the table. He grabbed his spear and followed Menace out. The village was alive with work. He could hear Ada's pleas of 'stop that' and 'come down'. The human boy had his arms spread wide standing on top of a home. If he jumped, the fall wouldn't kill him but he might be injured. Before Doom could react, the impulsive boy leapt into the air. Menace was already on the move and captured him in his arms while Ada swooned.

"You see," the boy said. "You do it like that."

Menace lifted the boy under his arms dangling him in the air. "If you're going to jump make sure you have a soft bed of grass to land on."

"Good idea, Captain," the boy said, and made an odd gesture with an open hand near his forehead.

"Captain?" Menace glanced at Doom who shrugged.

Menace set the child on his feet where he raced away into the tall grass. Doom glanced around. Every person was engaged in different chores, the necessity of community effort. In the evening, the villagers gathered in a huge underground hall to talk, eat, and swap stories. If there was a recent kill, the stews would be bubbling already. The boy's arrival would be celebrated. So would Clarity's. The boy would be welcomed into their lives; the woman would be welcome for a different reason. Her life spared the life of one of his people. In fact, her life spared Doom's. After, any other humans who came would be given to the person whose life they would spare. Humans were guarded closely.

The village wasn't huge. Mostly everything was built underground, but the perimeters were watched. There was nowhere a hybrid or any animal could lay in wait while everything was open concept. Menace was right, only three of the bulwarks were present. The two males were tussling. Clarity was nowhere to be seen. Doom scratched his head. He wondered if she befriended someone already and was in having a warm morning drink. He had noticed her purse was gone; he hoped to find everyone on their feet.

"Ada have you seen the human female?" Doom asked.

Ada, white hair askew, winded, and sweaty from running after her new son, stopped for a moment.

"You had to find me the child with no off switch,"

she complained. Doom chuckled at her Earth human reference. "I swear I lose a few pounds when he opens his mouth. He rambles on and on. I have to race to keep up with his words. Damn, there he goes again."

Doom watched as the boy jumped from another home, into Menace's arms. Menace directed the child to find more grass.

"He thinks he's a blasted bird. I swear when he sleeps I'll check him for feathers."

"Ada, the female?"

"What? Oh, no, can't say I've seen her. I can't take my eyes off the boy."

"We can name him tonight. That is if you want to keep him," Doom said.

"Well, of course I want him. Look over there. Old Nada is eyeing him like a prize treat. That woman would steal him in a heartbeat. My Edge is thinking on names."

Ada went running off when the boy started further into the brush. He was still small enough to be carried away by a bird. Menace was watching with a spear. If any bird came close they would be eating fowl for dinner. Menace claimed he would sacrifice himself over a human, but they needed the powerful warrior. And only a human could die in another's place. His sacrifice would be for nothing. Doom's position was no different and without him his people would fall.

Doom continued to search for Clarity until it became frighteningly clear she was gone. The woods were dangerous anytime but after a gathering frenzy of the humans, blood lust ran high in other animals. He wouldn't risk any of his people. Alone, he entered the danger zone.

"Clarity," he boomed.

Further into the foliage he traipsed, his heart falling at each passing moment. No doubt she was dead. At a scuffle, he ran to a small clearing. The female bulwark was fighting with a raptor. The furry, feathered raptors traveled in pairs and Doom cast his glance around wondering if the dinosaur's mate was making a meal of Clarity. To his dismay and surprise Clarity was in a pond up to her waist holding her small weapon she claimed was frightening.

The beast was flailing, screaming, and instead of moving away, Clarity moved closer and rammed a white piece of cotton past its razor teeth and down its throat. She leapt away, tossing the weapon to dry land and kicked water into its face for all she was worth. Doom bellowed and jumped in after her. He grabbed her into his arms and yanked her out of the water.

The raptor clawed at his throat. The bulwark's long two front fangs ripped into the underbelly of the other raptor on land. Both creatures died. Clarity was snarling.

"Ha, you ugly bastard," she yelled, waving a fist. "Choke on that." She turned to gaze up at Doom who was surprised as hell. "Tampons, the necessary evil you love to hate. Extra absorbent."

Doom didn't know whether to hug her, shake her, or laugh. "How the hell did you get out of the village?"

"I used a neat method, called my feet."

Now he wanted to shake her. "I mean how did you get this bulwark to allow you past her and to follow you?"

Clarity sloshed back into the water to rip out strange barbs from the raptor with an odd-looking pair of pinchers. She then fiddled with her weapon and stuck it into a satchel at her hip. Doom eyed the satchel warily.

"It wasn't hard."

"In all the time we've had humans, no one has ever gotten past any of the animals guarding the village."

"I'm guessing none of them had a Mars bar. You'd be surprised what a female will do for chocolate."

Clarity went to the beast and ruffled her fur, crooning to her. "Thank you, Muffin."

"Muffin?"

"Well, she kinda looks like a muffin, all brown and round and cute. Poofy, but poofy would be a silly name."

"Why did you leave the village? It's too dangerous out here."

"You said you'd take me out, but you were sleeping. I didn't want to disturb you. You drool in your sleep."

"I do not," he bellowed.

"Yeah, you do. It's pretty gross, too."

She began walking toward the village with the bulwark following her. Her sodden feet clomped; her clothes dripped but started to dry already in a warm breeze. The beast nudged her and she rose on her toes to drape an arm around her neck. The pair rested their heads together for a moment. If Doom didn't know better, he would swear the beast loved her. The beast growled as the foliage ahead ruffled, but settled when a herbivore came into view. Clarity squealed in delight.

"Oh my God, cuteness wrapped in cute."

The beast was small; humans said it looked like a pony and a bat got busy and they described the colors they saw. It was ebony except for a flowing white tail. Black bat wings, red eyes with multiple black streaks in the retina. The mane was a surprise to humans. It wasn't fur. A fin went from wither to elongated nose, becoming smaller as it traveled the face.

"It looks like a dragon baby."

Doom stopped her from getting close. "That's no baby. It may be an herbivore but it can still kill. Look at its feet."

"Whoa. I've never seen two claws on a pony hoof before. That's badass."

The creature moved off. The bulwark made it antsy. "They taste pretty badass, too."

Clarity glanced at him. "You eat those adorable little things? I think I'd cry watching one killed."

"No part of them is wasted. And you will never see one killed. My men hunt and skin everything in the forest. Blood attracts too many carnivores. With winter coming we need to catch and butcher as many animals as we can. Winter can be dangerous. The hybrids have learned to make wraps for clothes. They can utilize fire. We stay underground until the thaw. Just because they have a quota doesn't mean they won't try for humans when pickings are slim."

"Your choice?"

"What do you mean?"

"Do you stay underground because you need to, want to, or because the hybrids dictate to you?"

"We have furs to wear for warmth but the snow is too high. You sound angry with me. You left the village; I should be pissed with you."

"You plan on using me as a sacrifice. What part of that should I be grateful for?"

"I'm saving my people. We don't all have that interesting weapon."

She glared at him. "Your people are dead already unless you do something. When those creatures breed they become smarter if what you say is true. I don't know how yet, but I plan on finding out. They're after something, and I think it's something big. Did it occur to you they might want space flight?"

"That's not possible. You mentioned that before."

"It's possible all right."

Doom shifted his feet. "How could they learn about something we don't even know of?"

Clarity seemed stumped for a moment. "Doom, space flight is when you create a vessel and send people or animals into the skies overhead. These vessels can go to different planets."

"Can you make a vessel to take us away?"

"It would take me years."

Doom's heart fell. For a moment, he wondered if he could keep her safe for years. "How many years?"

"I don't know. I'd need help. Materials. The point is I know how. Humans crave knowledge. If the hybrids learn from humans they might want smarter humans. Are you going to be the one who gives them the knowledge to make it happen? When they can go anywhere in the universe they want, you become moot."

"If they leave then my people will be free."

"No, your people will be a nesting ground. They won't need you. They'll find their own humans and bring them here to your nice little village. You won't need it when you're dead. The humans can be kept as prisoners and fed like dogs. They no longer need your people except to fill a quota. Once they fill their own quota, they'll cut loose the middleman. This planet will be theirs."

Doom was devastated. What if she was right? All along had they been aiding in a means toward their death? Why was this human so different from the others? Then he realized no other human had guessed the hybrids' intentions. Clarity had been quick to figure it out. She poked a finger into his chest.

"I know space flight. In fact I know a lot of things. If the hybrids get a hold of me, it could be game over. I've been learning about sinkholes. What if these hybrids discover the holes might be able to gain access to Earth? When I left, there were signs of people suddenly showing up, after being gone for two years."

Doom had a sudden thought. She came out here to look for a way home. If she left, she would tell Earth what was happening to their people. Humans would double their precautions. Doom's people didn't steal humans, but they counted on them for life. If she returned home, her people would arm themselves, all of them, every last one of them. If Clarity could come through the hole with her purse maybe others would. Maybe their weapons would make Clarity's look like children's toys. What if they used their weapons on his people instead of the hybrids?

"You must never leave my village." His tone was urgent.

"You have a choice. Fight these hybrids or die. Today, tomorrow, next week it will happen. Do you really want these hybrids to get a hold of me? I got past your sentry. Hell, I bribed Muffin. You said I'm the first. What other talents would you like me to pass on to these creatures you're so scared of? Because at the risk of sounding full of myself, I'm smart as hell."

She was right. The idea of a secret child might be their salvation. "Give me a baby."

Clarity scoffed at him. "In this world? No way. I don't even like children."

That was a surprise. "How can you not like children?"

"Simple. They're barf machines, poop terminators, and they throw tantrums. Gee, what's not to love?"

Something in her stance made him wonder if she was lying. Her shoulders were tense. Her jaw clamped shut. She appeared sad. Doom glanced around. She would be afraid to have a child here. So was he. His planet was a scary place to be. His father gave his life for Doom. An idea whacked him soundly: his father must have been terrified to leave Doom alone. What would he do if he had to give his own life for his child? Who would take care of his child if he were gone?

"I'm sorry," Doom said. "That wasn't fair. I take care of my people; I don't have time for children of my own. It's a stupid…"

"Dream?"

"I don't dream. Dreaming is for fools."

"You and I have different ideas about dreaming and what makes us fools."

They strolled together for a moment before Doom took her hand and led her away in a different direction. Not everything on his planet was deadly, for some reason he wanted to show her. He shooed Muffin toward home then groaned, realizing he'd never get that name out of his mind now.

Muffin. Crap.

What's worse, the beast seemed hesitant. Was every female on the planet now going to challenge him?

"Go on, beast. You have a job to do."

With a low growl, Muffin ambled away with a last look at Clarity.

"Where are we going?" she asked.

"Not far."

The beach was empty when they parted the foliage and entered the clearing. As they walked along the sand he could hear it singing. Clarity was smiling. She was beautiful and the corners of his lips tugged for a second wanting to return the smile. You never smile at someone who will be gone soon.

"I've heard of singing sand. This is stunning." She stood still and cocked her head to the side.

She leaned to pick up a striking blue stone, but Doom stopped her. "No don't. The rock is deceptive. They wash up on shore once in a while. A victim touches it and the numbing agent freezes them, they fall and are unable to escape. When the tide comes in, they're easy prey for the creature who uses it. Unless another gets them before that. Either way, it isn't a pleasant way to go. The freezing lasts for hours, and you can feel everything done to you. You can't fight back, scream, cry, nothing."

As he spoke, another blue rock was tossed onto the shoreline. Doom pulled her away from the water's edge. In the distance, he could see a massive head surface for a second. Huge eyes gazed at them. Doom considered these creatures the sloths of the seas.

"That thing is creepy smart. Amazing, fishing on dry land. That would be a weapon of choice. Why not throw these gems at the hybrids?"

"You can't pick them up."

She stared open-mouthed at him. "Use something to pick them up."

"Like what?"

"Good God you are in the Jurassic period. Why not leather? A sack. My purse."

"When the rock touches something, it turns to liquid and seeps into its victim. Depending on the size of the rock, it immobilizes quickly. A mammoth could be stopped by a few. You would only need to touch this small one to be in trouble. A man my size would need to touch two at least, perhaps three. A perfect weapon, but untouchable."

"It's touching the sand. We need something to scoop it up from beneath it and put sand in my purse, now there's a nasty thought."

Doom stared hard at her. Scoop up the sand to put it in sand. "Then we need to throw it in sand."

"That's not a problem. A catapult is the least of your worries."

"Cat-a-pult?"

"A device you use to throw objects a farther distance."

"Why would anyone throw a cat? Felines are vicious when pissed."

She leveled an undetermined gaze at him. Her teeth worried her bottom lip for a moment. Doom could almost smell the ideas forming. "I wonder if I could make glass here. Glass is made from sand. If I can get my hands on the right materials."

"Glass?"

"Glass is a substance made from components and heat…"

Doom knew he was standing there looking stupid, he felt stupid. "Um."

"Come on, we have work to do, I'm starving and these stupid booties are drowning my toes."

Clarity gripped his hand and pulled him toward the village.

Chapter Six

Clarity sat munching on a hand-sized juicy piece of meat, cut in interesting slices. Hacked, it looked hacked; it was unlike anything she ever tasted. She was surprised it was so flavorful. Clarity loved seasonings, and she knew these flavors weren't in her world. The meal before her was made up of two types of bannock; the one bread was flat and hard but tasty. The other rounded and roll shaped, no doubt cooked in animal fat, served with berries with honey. A salad of greens she wasn't certain of had a drizzling of dressing. Three pancakes that tasted surprisingly like potato were silver-dollar-sized and smothered in the most wonderful butter she'd ever eaten. A cream sauce for dipping lay between her and Doom.

"This is good."

"We can cook," he drawled.

The cold fruity drink she sipped had bits of floating vegetation, flowers she was certain. Her next bite of meat yielded a hint of the slightly sweet pink flower as well as salt and black pepper. Anything could be growing on the planet if dinosaurs walked the earth with humans. Any extinct plant or flower on Earth could be thriving here. She was anxious to discover more of her new world. Doom watched her while he put pieces of fruit into his mouth and chewed mechanically, honey dripped over his fingers.

"What are you thinking?" he asked.

"I'm wondering about a lot of things. What meat is this?"

"Dinosaur. If you want specifics, I'm guessing a carnivore. We can use ourselves as bait when we hunt the meat eaters. They're cocky and not as cautious when they think they're hunting us. The herbivores are sweeter tasting and most are huge, so we need many hunters to bring one down. I'm certain Menace took a group to hunt a woolly rhino. Dangerous beasts but exciting to bait. This was a recent kill and cooked over an open flame so it's not as tender. Tonight, after it's been boiled for a few hours, it will fall off the bone. We make a bread substance to drop in a stew and another bread to dip in it. The other humans said the one bread is much like dumplings."

"Do you grow this stuff? The vegetables."

"Growing anything would attract animals. Why would we bring attention to ourselves?"

Good point.

"Then you forage?"

"These certain vegetables grow not far from our village. They mostly attract herbivores. Some are nasty, some dumb as dirt, and others who think a human might make an interesting new toy. A hunting party goes out with women and keeps a close eye out. We collect what we can and dry what we're able. Herbivores move fast, we need to move faster. Do you like the meat?"

Clarity took a bite of the chunk in her hand, charbroiled on the outside, pink on the inside. "Doesn't exactly taste like chicken. It's heavier with a gamey taste, not too strong, different. Your planet evolved over time to create new species as did ours. Your planet seems to have avoided every disaster Earth battled through. Why? It's like some creepy experiment of what ifs. Without the extreme heat you shouldn't have needed to make your way onto land and develop legs, but you did. Or maybe some elements stayed the same except for huge disasters. Maybe humans were just meant to be. The meteor, the ice age, and volcanic eruptions shaped the earth, I wonder if your planet is one big continent. I wonder if you have icebergs. You don't have dogs but you have the cave bear wolf mix. So humans would have sought out aid from animals regardless. Do you have any history?"

"Just what our parents tell us. Long ago there were different types of humans such as myself but different. They died out until only us and the hybrids remained. Our past suggests groups of females once roamed alone as did males. During our long years of wandering, we discovered deep caves where only the bones of either sex were found. I guess after a while our kind discovered males and females together; working as a team we survive longer. It came as a surprise when I found the destroyed hybrid offspring."

"You say there are other tribes, do you all speak the same language?"

"What other language would we speak?"

"Do you read or write?"

"What's read or write?"

"My people create symbols. Wait a second." Clarity went to her purse and rummaged through. She pulled out a book and handed it to him. Doom reluctant to take it at first and eyed it warily until she shoved it into his hand. "It won't kill you I promise."

With caution he opened it and scrunched his eyebrows.

"What are those funny marks? It looks like small birds danced over the material."

"They're letters on paper that make up words that we read."

"We make pictures of strong events. Pictures are better; our pictures last forever. Pa-p-er? This paper would fade, I'm guessing. This doesn't look waterproof, and it will rip. It's exposed, not covered by a cave. The imagery is boring. What would entice you to take a second glance at this?"

Put like that, he had a point. Clarity tried to look at it from his perspective. No doubt he'd never seen paper before. The material was flimsy and the marks were scribbles as far as he was concerned. He wasn't exactly clueless, or stupid, he and his people never needed to develop written words. They were too busy trying to stay alive.

"These hybrids. How long have they been around?"

"They've hunted us and we hunted them for as long as our history goes back. Thousands of years ago. Before we outnumbered them. My ancestors and the Neanderthal tried to cohabitate, they seemed the sturdier of any other human species. Our ideas were different, but we never hunted one another. We never hunted any species we felt was like us. Then one day a hybrid was in our midst. A dinosaur, so it was thought. It was killed, but wasn't eaten. Then more hybrids came and my people noticed the difference, the human quality cocooned in a killing machine. My people finally cut into one. At one time, they had a weakness; their skin wasn't as hard. They didn't hunt in groups so they may have been outcasts to start. It was then our ancestors discovered the human skeleton within. They've adapted and grown stronger over time. These beasts learned quickly that there was safety in numbers, preferably their own kind."

"I wonder if when each new species evolved they used them to procreate, and after each encounter learned." Clarity was speculating. "When the Neanderthal came, they became a single thriving species. My mind is working at a million miles an hour trying to wrap my head around the theory. You're a large man, the people in your village are huge, but Neanderthal bones are exceptionally big and strong. I wonder if the hybrids evolved enough to know your bone structure wouldn't support theirs. But neither would humans."

"Maybe they're just eating the humans."

"Then why not find them all year?"

"I don't know."

"Didn't they hunt your people all year?"

"In the beginning. Then certain times."

"When they needed to breed. Maybe these hybrids aren't eating humans at all. Or maybe they are. It's all so frustrating. Why didn't any other human think about this? Question this?"

"We never told them. We fed them and kept them safe. Humans are not allowed to leave the village. The others accepted this. They were too afraid of the dinosaurs. You can't tell any human we find what will happen, they will be terrified."

"I'm going to scream it from the rooftops. If we all put our heads together maybe we can figure out how to beat these hybrids. You need to find more people. More humans. Let's get this party started."

Doom sat open-mouthed. "Party?"

Clarity smiled at his confusion. "I'm guessing you've never partied in your life. Too bad, I bet you could be a real badass. Oh wait, you send people to their death, so that makes you more an asshole than a badass."

"I save my people."

"And now I'm saving mine." Clarity glared at him until he stood up and left. "I'm a bigger badass. And, apparently, I *do* eat dinosaurs for breakfast." Clarity ripped back into the meat, smiling.

****

Clarity busied herself with her thoughts during the day. She paced, sat, mulled over ideas, studied the vastness and thickness of furs and skins, and was surprised when Doom finally made an appearance. She could tell he was miffed; she hardly gave him a second thought when he left. Her mind filled with evasive maneuvers. She vowed not a single Earth human would be sacrificed and told Doom as much. She'd lead a rebellion against him and his people if she had to. They could be with her or against her, but she wouldn't go without a fight. Either way the sacrificing was at an end.

The pair squared off until her tummy rumbled. She learned a feast in her honor and another's was about to be served. Doom then spun on his heels in a different direction. The door Doom slid back at his touch and revealed a tunnel that surprised Clarity. She knew of the tunnel's existence, given a glimpse when she first entered Doom's home, but she wasn't prepared for the passageway itself. The walls and ceiling were amber, giving the channel warmth. As in Doom's home, soft light shone from within the stone. At a touch, it slid across the smooth surface, guiding their feet to the tunnel's end where another door awaited.

Once entering the room Clarity stopped in her tracks. The area was spacious, four times the size of Doom's home. The walls a masterpiece of beautiful rock. Many furs littered the floor, all thick and soft under her feet. She was tempted to remove her strange new booties that Doom produced while hers dried. Entire families were gathered for a feast. Leather pots were bubbling over rounded dirt holes filled with a burning substance. The aroma was delicious. Other areas void of the strange rock were filled with ovens. Within the ovens she could see loaves of bread cooking.

Doom handed her a bone cup filled with a darkish substance. Clarity sniffed at the contents. *Beer?* A tiny taste proved her suspicion. The taste wasn't the same as her preference but enjoyable. She began to wander when Doom left her alone standing stationary to speak to Menace. The man, dangerously handsome, intense, couldn't take his eyes off her. There was something predatory in his gaze, but more, there was possession, passion. There was a man who wanted love and no doubt would hold fast to the emotion if he possessed it.

Open bulging leather containers caught her attention. The scent was of the beer she drank. Chunks of bread floated in the largest satchel. The leather was double thick, the beast whose hide this came from must have been the devil's own to bring down and skin. Each satchel was filled with different stages of the fermenting beer. Other leather containers, most stoppered, held a liquid smelling of wine. Sniffing the contents of one Clarity was certain it was fermented plums. She uncorked the lid and dipped a finger in. The beverage was surprisingly sweet and palatable. With no one looking she drained her beer and poured a cup of wine, downed that, and poured another.

Booze, finally something tangible in this God forsaken hell.

Clarity shook her head. Her situation was dire but if she survived a sinkhole she would survive this mess. She needed to gain perspective on the positive.

Hmm, positive.

She again glanced at her surroundings and took a sip of her wine. Doom's people were so primitive and yet their creations so advanced with what they had to work with. Or perhaps they learned about what and how to create with human help. If, when, she found material she could work with, the villagers could be taught. The men and women clearly possessed the power and strength to wield weapons. They just needed better weapons. Clarity began roaming.

Adjoining rooms, their ancient smell preceding them, were filled with intricately woven baskets containing einkorn and emmer wheat, rye, and barley. The bins were half-full, and Clarity wondered if they went out to collect the staples in the fall. Other containers showed molasses. She dipped in a finger to find it bitter and wondered if it was made from or cooked with sugar beets. The idea made her head spin with marvel. These people functioned living with dinosaurs. Another bin was filled with small hard rocks. She picked one up and sniffed. With the tip of her tongue she took a taste. Salt. Clarity wondered if they were near the ocean or sea. Round stacks of hard cheese were in a cool corner. She scratched her head wondering where they got milk; there were no kept animals. Not even chickens. Then she wondered if there were eggs. Doom said they prepared for winter but the weather was more like spring.

In adjoining caverns were a multitude of drying herbs, for seasoning and medicines. Racks were laden with heavy burdens. In another area were rocks, flint, and bone in various stages of work for weapons and tools. Another area contained rolled furs set on shelves from floor to ceiling. Massive furs hides as long as the room itself. Strange gray leathers worked and stretched on triangular, rectangular, square, and circular frames. Long cordage was woven for types of rope displaying a variety of knots.

Dried fish, the likes she'd never seen, fresh and dried were tied to rows of racks. A number of circular domes were in another room. Clarity could smell the heat exuding from them. The smell of cedar was high and she wondered about sweat lodges. Rows further within the shelter held wood and coal.

How can they be so far behind?

Did the primitive era dictate the primitive people? Not one thing remotely resembled technology. Then again could dinosaurs walk the earth with man and a concrete jungle? Imagine a T-rex peeking in on your lunch break through a two-story window. Would raptors chase subways like dogs chased cars? The dinosaurs would need to be muzzled; you couldn't have a child eaten on the way to school. A disturbing image of a raptor holding a stop sign wearing a safety vest while people crossed a cross walk came to mind. At the end of the day someone would go missing. BBQ's would be an interesting affair. Dark meat, white meat, or dinosaur meat?

The special tonight on our menu is mammoth hybrid.

Clarity lumbered back to the main room shaking her head, sipping her drink, feeling a bit giddy. She was lightheaded and knew she needed to eat; the beverages were strong. There was an abundance of food. Perhaps providing for the village was their way of proving technology did advance. These were no Stone Age cave dwellers with limited abilities. Set up on tables were smaller rounder chunks of breads. Berries and grapes with a wooden gravy boat of honey. She spied eggs, huge and similar to ostrich eggs. On another table sat cheesecake and bees wax. She picked up a small square and took a tentative taste of the cake. It was different but pleasant.

Her suspicion of an ocean nearby was confirmed when she saw large animal skulls filled with oysters and mussels nestled in ice. The ice was saltwater when she ventured a small taste. Clarity wondered if their dwellings were privy to an ice cave lower underground. Shellfish, shrimp, lobster, and crab were surrounded by dried seaweed. Leather pots contained melted savory butter. Greens and wild carrots steamed on small round rock tables with coals beneath to keep them hot. Numerous cooked plants and roots were on similar roundish tables with waiting tongs set aside until the feast began.

Clarity could smell clean air mixing with the aromas. There had to be ventilation shafts somewhere. As long as she could breathe, she guessed it didn't matter where the air was coming from.

Doom came to steer her toward a group of people who were settling onto large furs. There weren't many children. She had seen a few playing, but they appeared sullen. She wondered how long they had been here. All wore the same furs and leathers as their parents but Clarity could tell these children were human. Their bones weren't as dense, their size, like hers, was too small in comparison. Doom's people weren't simply robust, their muscle mass was that of body builders in both man and woman. Their phenomenal power years of testimony to the harshness of the environment.

Gazing at the clan of perhaps thirty, it was undeniable all adults were near the same age, with Doom the youngest. The rest were children, ranging in age from five to twelve. There were no teens or young adults. Clarity felt the bile rise in her throat. If Doom sacrificed children, she would find a way to steal every last one of them and find a way home or die trying.

Oh, the irony of 'die trying'.

Doom stood before his people smiling. He motioned to a man and woman. The couple stood with the small unhappy boy she had spied earlier. The woman appeared happy, the man wary and the boy held charcoal and a strip of birch in his dirty hands. The child was scowling. He gazed up at the woman who had her hands on his shoulders.

"I want to go home now," the child said. "This junk don't make planes. And I need crayons."

"Hush now," the woman whispered.

Clarity's heart sank, the boy wasn't theirs, she was right.

"This isn't paper, it's dumb," the boy grouched, his scowl deepened.

Clarity knew a temper tantrum was inevitable. The boy's back was rigid, his neck reddening. The vest-like shirt he wore made her lean forward for a better look at his exposed arm. He was inoculated. She peered at the other children, they weren't. That had her speculating. Either the other children fell into a sinkhole before mass inoculation started or they weren't from her Earth.

The more she thought on the idea another Earth existed, the more she became positive. The humans Doom spoke of were too docile. Never questioning, never challenging. There were submissive people on her planet but facial features were a dead giveaway when she examined the children closer. Nothing in their faces, subtleties, and nuances. The four other children were apprehensive when the young boy scowled at them as well.

"What have you decided to name your son, Edge?" Doom asked ignoring the boy.

"Flight," the man said and rolled his eyes. Others in the room chuckled.

"My name is Joseph Jay Junior," the boy yelled, turned and stomped his feet. "My daddy's going to fly his plane up your ass."

The woman looked mortified. Doom's eyes widened. The other children shuddered collectively. Clarity placed her hand over her mouth and laughed. Edge growled and, grabbing the boy's shoulders, he swatted the boy's behind making him yelp.

"You can't hit me," the boy raged as tears streamed down his face. "Children's Aid will throw you in jail. My daddy will sue your ass."

Clarity doubted these people would understand the concept of Child Services. Though she admitted at times she didn't either in certain circumstances. As for a lawyer, they might fit in with the raptors.

"The boy will be known as Flight from now on." Doom hunkered down to the boy's level. His gaze was stern. "This is where you live, this is your home. These are your parents. Unless you answer to your name you will be a very hungry little boy."

"I didn't eat all day," the boy whined.

"And unless you answer to Flight you will not eat."

Clarity saw hopelessness seep into the boy's features. "I want my mommy."

The woman scooped him up. "I'm right here, Flight." The boy remained rigid.

Both adults took the boy to another room. Doom faced Clarity. She narrowed her gaze onto him. If he tried to give her another name, she'd taser him. He leaned to grip her hand to pull her to her feet. She stood gazing at the many strange faces before her.

"This is Clarity," Doom began. Clarity sighed with relief. "The first of many in our salvation. There is no need to petition for her, she is staying with me for the duration." Clarity heard groans. Menace had his dark glare fixed onto her. "This human has discovered what we need." Groans turned to gasps.

"She must be placed in seclusion," someone yelled.

"Maybe she should be turned loose," said another.

"No not turned loose, but yes seclusion. She will terrify the others."

Frantic calls continued until Clarity became annoyed. Doom was watching his people, appearing useless. Clarity decided the villagers needed to understand she made her own destiny. She reached into her small bag hanging from the leather rope at her hip.

Doom had seen her use a similar pink object to gloss her lips and he looked confused. She wondered if he could tell this was a different tube. This was her personal taser, disguised in a lipstick tube, and Clarity zapped Doom who fell like a stone twitching. Silence followed. Everyone took a communal step back. Doom was groaning. The shock wasn't high voltage and he was a large man. She was feeling exceptionally smug.

"I'm happy my parents named me Clarity," she said, she placed the cap back on the tube then slipped the taser back into her little sack. She paced a few steps; everyone watched keeping their distance. "Situations become very clear to me quickly. Unless you change what you're doing you'll all be dead, killed by the hybrids. I won't be one of your sacrifices. I just might be your salvation. In any case, if one person tries to hurt me, dispose of me or any other funky thing I'll make you shit your drawers. Understand?"

Doom was stumbling to his feet. Hands braced on his knees he gave Clarity a nasty glare. "I changed my fucking mind. Anyone want to petition for this delightful creature?"

Not a single hand rose.

Chapter Seven

Doom sat watching Clarity eat. After her initial exclamations over the onyx plate given her she hesitantly picked at her food, she questioned everything, sniffed everything. Doom wondered if her small stature was due to the fact she never ate. After the initial taste, she dove into her meal with gusto. Obviously a fan of dark meat, she groaned, eyes closed then sucked juices from her fingers declaring the meat melted in her mouth. Then went on to say words such as "succulent" and "tender".

What was she expecting, raw hide?

She'd eaten with him before but appeared to actually be tasting—everything. Her cocky appearance made him wonder until he tilted her empty cup. He smelled the wine. *She's half drunk.* She was cocky when not inebriated but twice as bad when tipsy. *A fucking nightmare when drunk I bet.* He poured her some water.

Doom gazed around as his people settled with filled plates. All kept Clarity at arm's length or more. Edge and his wife had returned with Flight. The boy dutifully answered to his name—and ate standing up. No doubt his father taught him respect. From the child's demeanor, Doom suspected he'd never in his life been spanked. A catharsis of clarity in a flat, opened hand. Almost all of Earth's children came with an attitude, none as difficult as Flight. Doom's people never beat children, but they did demand compliance. The villagers didn't want the children to fear them. In the world they were dumped in, literally, they needed to listen to survive.

"What is this?" Clarity asked. She held up a hard, small, thin, circular piece of bread with meat pulverized to paste.

"The bread is our version of Earth's crackers, the meat is liver."

"Liver from what?"

"Megaceros or megaloceros."

"I'm guessing either or would feed your village a few meals. Do you have any moose?"

"Moose. The creature has been described. None that I've ever seen. At least not on this part of the planet."

"Is this from the animal hide you have on your bed?"

"No. The animal hide is a mastodon mammoth."

"And this meat?"

"Casteroities, giant beaver. Not all of our animals are hybrids. If it works don't fix it."

"Aren't they like the size of a car?"

Doom blinked at her searching for the word. "Ah yes, things you earthlings ride in. Ve-hic-les with wheels. We also have giant rabbits, some like the beaver adapted but changed. Like your moon-keys."

"Moon-keys?"

"A human once told me Earth has a species considered one and yet the same."

Clarity scrunched her nose while absently chewing. "Monkeys," she declared.

"Yes. Great apes, spider monkeys confuse me though. What an odd hybrid."

She laughed. "Great *apes*, and spider monkeys aren't half-spider or no self-respecting woman would live anywhere near them. And I can pretty much guarantee they'd be number one on the endangered species list." She smiled at him, sucked on applesauce from a wooden spoon, then appeared to have a thought. "So you have your bulwarks you say keep the village safe. Granted they're huge, but what keeps out hybrid mammoths? The strange noise you told me of?"

"The noise keeps out the very large dinosaur and doesn't affect mammals. Our bulwarks aren't only crossed with dire wolves and cave bears. They are also wolverine. The noise doesn't bother them either."

"That'll do it. Wolverines. Nasty little pieces of work. I'm surprised they let anyone near them."

"They're all bred from a long line of hybrids. When the female…"

"Muffin."

"Ugh, really? Really?"

"She looks like a Muffin."

"When *Muffin*," he ground out swallowing the word and making her laugh. "When she goes into heat this year we will breed her with the alpha bulwark. Muffin, is old, almost too old to breed. Once she has her cub-pups we will destroy her and the alpha and raise the babies. Next year we will breed the other female with the beta who will then be the alpha and do the same thing. Only two hybrids, the strongest male and female will be allowed to live from each mother."

Clarity's face had slowly been slipping into a mask of horrified outrage. "That's beyond awful."

"Their sires will kill the others' cub-pups. Even a beta will try to kill the alpha's spawn. The young ones are raised with families who have a child or children. By the time they are too big to house the older bulwarks are dead and the threat is over."

"So for their long years of loyalty you kill them? You don't let the mothers raise their offspring. Muffin is gentle."

"So I saw. Her time is near done. I can't have a muffin for a safeguard."

"Don't you think she'd protect the village anymore?"

"She would protect her offspring first, the village second. Wouldn't you?"

Clarity sat without another word. Doom could see the flicker of her eyes. A quiet Clarity was a dangerous Clarity. For some reason he found the thought to be amusing. Until he realized he was the one stuck with her.

****

"What are you looking for?"

Clarity cast a fast glance at Doom who was trailing her through the jungle-like forest. In a few days everything green had multiplied and enlarged to vast amounts. It was hard to believe she was walking the same forest. Leaves, some as large as her, graced bushes and trees. Rainbow colors filled her sight at each glance. If it wasn't for the dinosaurs, the scene would be paradise.

That and the sacrifice part.

Muffin wasn't too far. The majestic beast followed Clarity, lumbering along, the moment she left the safety of the village but didn't stop her. She knew the beast irked Doom. Muffin occasionally sniffed her hand and Clarity knew she could scent the chocolate she carried in a satchel at her waist. Clarity carried more than chocolate. Doom eyed her when she packed her tasers and mace as well as a few other items. The satchel wasn't large, carrying her purse around would be cumbersome so she settled for a few small bags secured at her hip. As she moved, the smaller bags bounced off her ass and hip leaving her hands free.

"I've been checking out your weapons. Holy Stone Age. I'm surprised you can dress yourself."

"We kill dinosaurs," he reminded her.

"Yes, with something Fred Flintstone might use."

"Who?"

"Never mind, Barney. What I'm looking for are components to create a stronger material. Something that will give you and that tomahawk you wear big girl pants."

"Big girl pants? Why would I wear your pants? Why would a weapon wear clothing?"

"I just mean those Neandersauri have razor claws. You need razor claws. Why the hell hasn't anyone invented a sword?"

"I've heard that word. And boolets."

"Bullets. I can't make a gun but I can make explosives. Sulfur, coal and saltpeter. For bombs. Diamonds as projectiles. Steel, carbon, alloys from iron." She stopped when Doom gazed at her in confusion.

"The humans who have come never mentioned any substance except steel. We tried to make heavy swords with the strongest wood we could find but we can't get within close proximity of the hybrids. We tried to test them on different leather hides but there's no way the wooden swords will penetrate a hybrids flesh. A spear works better for thrusting."

"You can penetrate with steel swords. Once you've knocked the little bastards to their knees, you can decapitate them. Too bad you couldn't make weapons from those unbreakable tusks. Then again, it wouldn't be much good if it was breakable."

An image formed in her mind of a handful of village men racing at a group of hybrids holding a tusk and skewering shish kabob. *Ew*. Clarity began to weave her way through the foliage. At a small clearing, Muffin began to snarl. Huge fangs protruded while her fur puffed. Doom pushed Clarity behind him and held his massive wooded spear ready. Clarity saw nothing while Doom's gaze was fixed on something.

"It's a T-rex," Doom said.

Clarity pressed her chest into Doom's arm. Mace and a taser would be useless. Clarity all but forgot about T-rexes. She looked up, way up, her heart pounding. Her breath came in short pants and sweat beaded her forehead. Foliage began to sway and part. She wondered why they weren't running. Was it true, could T-rex only see a moving object? She guessed she was about to find out. The beast who stepped through the hunter green bushes made Clarity swallow hard, blink and stare.

"I thought you said T-rex was extinct," she whispered. "Is this a baby? Are the parents nearby?"

"No it's full grown. I haven't seen one in years. They were thought to have died out. I heard they used to be massive but their arms were so short they evolved to proportion their body."

The dinosaur was a lot smaller than the museum exhibits she was used to. The beast stood only four feet high, if that, and though it was massively muscled, Clarity was—disappointed. *It's friggin adorable.* An odd thought to be sure, but all the hype deflated as she scratched her head. The mini T-rex opened its mouth and whistled, then cheeped. A cute strange sound she wasn't expecting. The small arms did seem better to accommodate the smaller body. The teeth were decidedly cow-like. The body color matched the pretty greens, reds, and oranges of the lush bush. No wonder she couldn't see it to begin with. There were tufts of feathers making it resemble a badass chicken. All it needed was a do-rag. Clarity chuckled as Bad to The Bone played in her mind.

Doom waved his spear. "Go on, get. Unless you want the business end of my spear."

The beast turned tail and ran. Clarity stood with her mouth gaping. "Well that was—interesting." *Uneventful and lacking luster.* She gazed up at Doom. "No wonder you can fight these things. It looked as dangerous as a cow. A really cute cow."

"Don't kid yourself. There are very dangerous beasts in my world. Some are beautiful, until they're chewing on you."

Clarity cocked her head in the direction of a noise. Muffin continued to growl; her hackles rose. Teeth bared, she was a fierce creature. Clarity was glad she brought chocolate.

"Something else is out there," she whispered.

"Stay behind me and stay close."

Doom pressed her to his back with an arm around her. Muffin crept forward. Beneath her fur powerful muscle rippled as she took each step. The pads of her huge paws left indentations in the soft dirt beneath her feet. Clarity wrinkled her nose. Muffin could produce the same noxious smell of a wolverine. The small open space gave way to dense foliage the deeper they went. Clarity's ill-fitting booties slipped on the few moss covered rocks, her ankles bumped against thick roots. Doom's arm pressed against her was hard and secure. Each muscle undulated mimicking the bulwark.

A small pool of water came into view. An involuntary intake of breath made Clarity cough. The dog lifted his muzzle from the water it was lapping. The tail wagged then stopped when Muffin growled. Clarity slipped from Doom's grasp and shoved the bulwark.

"Clarity, come back." Doom hissed the warning.

"It's only a dog."

"A what?"

"A dog. Looks male. Hey big boy," she crooned.

Normally afraid of large dogs, this one was a glimpse of home. *Cute as hell.* The dog's tail made a tentative motion. He was a big mutt, perhaps Rottweiler crossed with Saint Bernard and maybe even standard poodle. Clarity moved closer. Doom made a grab for her arm but she shrugged him off. As she got nearer she crouched and held out her hand.

"You are a long way from home aren't you? Come here baby."

The dog was on all fours, five feet from her and made a motion to go to her. Clarity screamed when Muffin snatched her by the back of her shirt pulling her back. In the same instance, a monstrous being jumped from the water. A massive mouth opened to reveal rows of sharp teeth, Clarity could see down its throat. The monster struck down and closed over the unsuspecting dog.

The head of the snake-like beast lifted its neck to swallow its prize then stopped. Black eyes on either side of its head blinked, then bulged. The beast opened its mouth and propelled the dog so far and so hard it almost knocked Doom to his knees when it collided with his chest. The beast gave a strangled cry and crashed to the ground bouncing once. The living and dried foliage beneath it settled. The creature lay unmoving.

"Um," Clarity mumbled. "What the hell just happened?"

No one moved as they all gazed at the sight before them. Muffin snuffed and released Clarity who landed on her ass. Doom dropped the dog and strode to her. He gave her a quick check to make certain she wasn't hurt.

"What the hell was that?" she demanded, gripping his arm in a daze. "It looked like a gulper eel got busy with a pound of steroids."

"Just another type of eel we have. These like the bottom of small ponds in summer, and during winter they use small feet to travel over the land to larger bodies of water."

"It looks dead."

Doom inched closer for a better look. "It is dead." He inspected the inside of the beast's open mouth. "Huh."

"What?"

Clarity sidled up to him. Doom pointed in the beast's mouth. Clarity scrunched her nose at the smell. A pile of dog shit sat on its tongue. She glanced back at the dog who sat a small distance from Muffin wagging his tail.

"Scared you shitless eh?" Clarity said and chuckled. She then glanced at Doom. "This dog must be from Earth. I bet Earth toxins killed that creature immediately. Because the dog has been altered over so many thousands of years, his mouth is toxic to this planet."

The dog hunkered down as Clarity approached him. She let him smell her fingers before petting the top of his head. He rolled to his back exposing his belly. Muffin was immediately interested, sniffing him everywhere.

When Doom took Clarity by the arm, the dog jumped up to follow. "Go on," Doom commanded attempting to shoo him away.

"Go where? He has no home. He's alone. I want him. I bet the kids would adore him."

"Clarity, who knows what noxious diseases this thing has. It killed a monster with his shit."

Clarity stooped to pet the dog's head. "Bubble-gum won't be a problem. Will you big boy?"

"Bubble-gum? You want to name the beast Bubble-gum? I have seen a bubble, and I have seen a gummy sticky substance on trees. So in actuality, you want to name your pet Invisible Goo?"

"My grandmother had a mutt named Bubble-gum. Sweet, soft, always wanting to please. It's a perfect name."

Doom shook his head and grumbled under his breath as he strode off. Clarity smiled at the dog who sat on his haunches beside Muffin. An idea began to form in her mind. Not every female wanted an alpha. She then chuckled.

"Match making between a bulwark and a dog."

She trailed after Doom. The sun was rising higher as the morning waned. The scenery, lush foliage, blue skies, pounding waterfalls, were the essence of a gentler time. The dog and bulwark weaved back and forth between the pair making Clarity smile. Doom appeared none too happy. He was watchful and wary. Clarity kept a foot between her and Doom until Clarity heard a distinct whistle. Both she and Doom stopped in their tracks. Goose bumps dotted her flesh, turned icy with dread. She moved to press against him. The animals began snarling, their hides were puffed from neck to ass.

A feeble roar turning to a small chirp sounded and Clarity glanced at Doom. "Should we run or hide?"

The decision was made for her when she heard the unmistakable sound of a child yell. Clarity zipped past Doom. He followed hot on her heels. As they broke through a clearing all became motionless. A young boy of eight was holding a spear swinging at a hybrid. The massive upright creature was obviously amused. To the boy's left was the T-rex they encountered earlier. The beast was roaring, dancing back and forth snapping at the hybrid. Little arms made feeble scratches at the air. The T-rex seemed more vulnerable than the boy. The boy was a whirlwind of motion. His weapon smashed into the hybrid's knees and bounced off. The hybrid swung at the boy and he ducked. The little T-rex moved in closer to offer aid.

Clarity wanted to scream when the child placed himself between the dinosaurs. It occurred to Clarity the boy was defending the T-rex. Bubble-gum had seen enough and raced into the foray teeth bared to aid the boy. Muffin followed. The hybrid was no longer amused, being attacked from all sides. With the added reinforcements, the T-rex developed balls and bit the hybrid's arm. The hybrid snarled, swung, down the T-rex went. The boy bellowed in fury, stabbed the spear into the hybrid's belly, the force of the blow so fierce the stick broke. There was no mark as the weapon toppled to the ground.

Finding her feet, Clarity raced to the boy. The hybrid had an arm raised poised to strike the child. Bubble-gum lunged for the hybrid's throat. Muffin snapped an ankle into her mouth yanking the hybrid down. Doom was bellowing for them to stop the assault. For any hybrid killed they would take the lives of five villagers.

The hybrid shoved his clawed hands at the mouth of the bulwark. The T-rex recovered and bit into the hybrid's back. Doom tossed the dog and regained control over the bulwark. He lifted Clarity off her feet and grabbed the boy by his shoulder, trying to retreat with them. The hybrid was up and glaring. Whistled clicks and arm waving followed and Clarity could see the hybrid was talking, *talking* to them.

"No one needs to die today," Doom insisted.

The hybrid glanced at the T-rex and pointed. The boy screamed in rage.

"You can't have him he's mine."

The hybrid pointed at the boy. Doom pulled him closer. "He's human. We met your quota."

The hybrid's claws were in motion but pulled back. Clarity could see hands beneath the skin and she shivered. A body within a body. He was using his Neanderthal hands to speak with. He wanted to kill the tow-headed boy. Up close Clarity could see the tiny impression of a slight cleft lip on the boys' face, a small nostril in the shape of a heart, the other normal. Deep brown eyes flashed with fury when he gazed back. He was a handsome young man. Emotion dazzled his image. A sturdy lad with a surprising muscular build but there was no doubt he was from Earth, possibly her Earth.

A whiz caught Clarity's attention as an arrow flew by. The arrow slid into the hybrid's face between his nose and mouth. At first, Clarity thought the arrow would fall like the boy's spear, it didn't. The hybrid fell to his knees then to his side. Weak hands pawed the arrow without dislodging it. The beast quieted, the chest stopped rising and falling. Inside the chest she saw movement of the inner skeleton. That motion ceased as well. It was dead. Heart pounding, Clarity turned to see a young girl of perhaps fifteen. The girl was wild. A feral child? She was dressed all in fur, high moccasins, a hide flap around her hips. Her hide vest sported pockets, closed with small pieces of leather threaded through holes. She stood tall, her bow firm in her grasp, another arrow ready. A leather strip of hide held back a tumble of dark hair.

"Set him free," she demanded of the boy.

Not feral, but wild nonetheless.

"He needs to come to the village where it's safer, you have no idea what you've done," Doom said.

"I did what you and your people are too afraid to do. You're all a bunch of filthy cowards. Release my brother. Or you're next." She settled another arrow into her bow and pulled back. Her hand perfectly steady near her cheek strung back the bow with two fingers.

She was definitely familiar with her weapon.

"My village will suffer the consequences or another village once this hybrid is found," Doom yelled.

"Throw the bastard in the falls." Her contempt was palpable.

The boy struggled free of Doom's grasp and ran to the girl, followed by the small dinosaur. The boy stuck his tongue out at Doom, so did the T-rex. The trio took off. Clarity stood gaping. She went to the hybrid and pulled up on the arrow. The arrowhead was crafted from bone. Sharp, large and well made. Squinting, she thought she detected a smear of blue. The shot took skill. After examining the beast, she smiled.

"Well, look at that, a hybrid Achilles' heel, only it's on his face. We won the battle, we may just have figured out how to win the war."

Chapter Eight

"What are you thinking?"

The hybrid was heavy, between Muffin dragging him and Doom, the hybrid was muscled over a cliff into a falls that would hopefully take his body far. If they were lucky, a carnivore would make short work of the carcass. After disposing of the hybrid's body, they returned to Doom's home.

Clarity was sitting on the edge of his bed; Bubble-gum was fed and sleeping after eating as though starved for weeks. Muffin was sent to guard the perimeter. Clarity appeared lost in thought. Her nose scrunched and her fingers tapped at the fur beneath her. Doom's heart was still racing. Killing a hybrid was huge in so many different ways. He was terrified and yet, exhilarated. The hybrids could be killed from a distance with a simple weapon. He wondered if Clarity could make that weapon the girl had. Something told him she could—and then some. Clarity wasn't nearly as rattled as he.

"You saw the menace on the hybrid's face, and for a little boy. I doubt a Neanderthal had so little compassion. They must have at one time possessed empathy. A dinosaur kills to eat. It has no feelings for food; it would be like us mourning broccoli. There was rage on the hybrid's face. Hate. A creature that thinks, strategizes, breeds with an emotional entity must be an emotional roller coaster."

"I wonder how many others are out there, humans, or lone villagers, hiding from us and from the hybrids. If you don't belong to a group that gives into demands, would you be safer?" A *yes* niggled in his mind. Smaller bands of villagers, still-roaming nomads, while Doom's people satisfied *their* quota? Is that why the hybrids wanted more every year? The idea made him furious. Were there others out there having children?

"I got a good look at those children," Clarity said. "They weren't overly filthy. The boy was dirty, but he's a little boy. The girl was comfortable with her bow and arrow."

"Is that what that weapon is? You know of it?"

"Yes of course, and she knew where to strike the beast. Those hybrids have a weakness. Why haven't you capitalized on it? Did you know they had a weakness?"

No.

Doom was feeling frantic. Hope, anger. Scared shitless.

"For every one of us there are fifty of them perhaps more. They won't bother with two or more small children. If we start a war, they'll finish it. Sooner or later, that hybrid will be missed. When they go looking for him, and if they find him, there will be hell to pay."

"Then let's give them hell."

"You can't just walk into my planet and demand action."

"I didn't walk in; I was grabbed, and I sure as hell can when my life is on the line. And those kids. They must know what you do and hide from you."

"Children that young need supervision."

"A little girl kicked a monster's ass and threatened you."

Doom ran a hand over his face. "I take good care of my people."

Clarity rose to stand before him. "*Your* people, yeah. It's time to take care of business."

"That bomb you spoke of, will it really kill as many of the hybrids at once as you say it will?"

"Yes. Doom, you can't let those hybrids get a hold of me. If they are learning by advancing somehow they will understand what I do. It will be your people being bombed. They will figure out space flight. Then they'll bomb *my* planet."

Doom had already thought of that. "The things you look for, can you find them?"

"Yes. I also know of a few distractions."

"Clarity," Doom's mind was racing. "There is one way to keep the hybrids from breeding with you, or taking you, but it may want them to kill you."

"Don't say it." Her gaze narrowed onto him. "I'm not going to get pregnant with you."

"You could choose another."

"I'm not choosing anyone. Before we go jumping to conclusions, we need to try to find out what those hybrids want. We aren't certain what exactly it is they want. They might even want a pregnant human."

"A pregnant woman has never been sacrificed. Then again, no human has ever come here carrying. You could tell me what to look for out there, and I can find the materials you need."

"There are certain components. Look I know you're not stupid, the things I need may be child's play in my world, but not yours. Doom, how is it you saw the T-rex so fast? It was camouflaged in the trees."

"I was called color blind by a human. I see what for you isn't there. All of our leaders are like that."

Clarity nodded. "Menace, too?"

"Yes."

Clarity traced a few of his tattoos. "Maybe one day you can tell me their story."

Doom decided he would. He only hoped he would never be telling another person Clarity's story. He had wished for warriors to save his people, and humans. Here she was—a female. She gave him hope, real hope for the first time in—forever, since Alice was taken. A dangerous female he could lose his heart to—possibly his life.

****

Doom had no choice but to take Clarity out of the safety of the village circle, again. She knew the other warriors frowned on the idea. Humans weren't supposed to go anywhere. Clarity wasn't a sheep or a lamb; she was a tiger, a fighter. Clarity gave him the description of what she needed but sat back waiting, knowing his attempt would be futile. He was colorblind. He had no idea what she needed, compounded with the fact she was evasive and a bit misleading.

A whole lot misleading.

They were in a large cave where Clarity set up a small experiment. She wanted to make certain until all the villagers were on board with her idea to fight back she kept her experiments secret. Doom agreed. He was gazing with curiosity, and some skepticism, rocking from foot to foot. The components to make her distractions when necessary were easy enough in small amounts. All she needed was to capture his attention, then super-size her efforts when it came to the hybrids. That would take teamwork. She set up NH4Cr207 with HgSCN and lit a match. Doom jumped back as small tentacles wormed their way out of the substance, serpent-like.

"Damn, that's amazing." Doom squatted down twisting his neck this way and that. "Creepy, too. Can you imagine the chaos if this was bigger?" Doom stood up fast and gaped at her.

Clarity smiled. "Now you're getting it."

"I think an entire area creeping with this would make me need new pants."

Clarity laughed. "It's simple really. Even small amounts will capture their attention. What we want is for the hybrids to be freaked out. Soon they'll start looking for our distractions, instead of us. That's the time to strike."

"With what?"

"The material I mentioned before. You have what I need for bombs. We only need a few of your people to help bring what I need back in large quantities. If we can find the hybrids' homes in your area we can strike. If they live in caves, we can seal the entrances and exits and cause cave-ins. Next, we need to find or make swords and sharper arrows to penetrate those hides of theirs. We need carbon and alloys of iron."

He looked lost. She knew he didn't understand anything she said. Clarity reached out to hold his hand. There was nothing stupid about Doom. A multitude of emotion flickered across his features.

"I'm sure you and your people can think up distractions," she said. "Have any of your women ever left an egg on too long, had the water evaporate, and the egg explode?"

"Hell, yeah, made one little guy piss himself. Geez, I haven't thought about that in years." He was smiling.

"Why don't we go search that cave you thought I might find other things I need." Using a stick she kicked apart the evidence.

Doom led her out of the small cave, keeping her close. Clarity didn't mind he kept her inches from his side. His world was intriguing and deadly. Bushes rattled, and when the wind whistled she would stop dead in her tracks. Doom never laughed at her, never belittled her fears. To Clarity, that was the intelligence of a real man. Accepting failings with grace. He wasn't a bully or a hypocrite.

At a sweet-smelling tree Doom picked two pieces of fruit, handing her one. The taste was delicious, the juice dribbled from her chin. Doom reached to dry her off. They gazed at one another in silence. The ancient depth of his gaze compelled her to move toward him. Doom let his fruit fall to the ground. He lifted his hands about to place them on her shoulders then stopped.

"You are a dangerous woman," he muttered.

"Perhaps, but I think I see hope in your eyes."

"I've seen more things to give me hope in the last few days than I've seen in my entire life. How can one tiny female change lives so fast? Change my life so fast?"

"I've spent my life being devoted to a task and seeing it through. Life is a journey of battles. The hurdles get higher but the prize is bigger. Never stop believing in hope, Doom. Never surrender to fear."

He gave a curt nod and began walking. She

watched his shoulders straighten. His stride was no longer the movement of a beaten man. Something was going on in that mind of his. When Doom stopped moving, she bumped into him, almost losing her footing. She peered around him and turned cold. The dinosaur was twelve feet tall sporting the fangs of a carnivore. The rush of draining emptiness in her face let her know she had gone white. Goose bumps dotted her arms and she dared not breathe.

Clarity had no idea what kind of hybrid this was. The dinosaur was completely black with white eyes, unblinking. Its head was in proportion with its massive body. The back of its head narrowed to a sharp edge resembling ebony ivory. The body hunched over, standing on two clawed feet. It weaved back and forth sizing them up. Its gaze settled on Clarity. The smaller of the two.

Clawed arms raised for battle, it cocked its head and hissed. Doom's muscles bunched and he used a hand to guide her further behind him, but she had seen what it looked like. It stood erect on three-toed talons for feet. The beast swung around. Doom lifted Clarity into his arms and jumped high, avoiding the tail. Three-inch quills poked from ass to tail tip. The beast split a tree, the trunk exploded and the tree toppled to the ground with a hard *thump.*

In one quick motion, Doom dropped Clarity and sprang forward with his spear as the beast's belly was exposed. Doom watched her the night before trying to lift his weapon of choice; it was the first real smile she had seen. The spear was taller than Doom and almost too heavy for her to lift. The thickness was that of a young tree trunk. Doom hefted it easily; Clarity couldn't get her fingers around it.

The dinosaur attacked. Doom kept the beast between him and her. Clarity realized she was the intended victim. The beast clawed the air, missing Doom by inches. Doom stabbed up and sunk the spear into the underbelly thrusting up with a hard jerk. The beast roared then silenced, crumpling. The sharp end pierced its heart. Doom, with lightning speed, grabbed for the dagger on his belt and slit the animal's throat. Then stepped back. He hadn't broken a sweat.

"Nasty little piece of work these things."

Clarity knew her mouth was open and she was gaping up at him. "Let me get this straight. You can kill King Kong in a heartbeat but can't take out a hybrid?"

"Hybrids know hand to hand combat. They are skilled. Their weapons, all they need, are on their body. They think. The dinosaur looks at you and me and its only thought is, 'oh look, tiny tasty prey'."

"Because we're smaller it thinks we have no defense?"

"Yes. Why would it think anything else? When a feline hunts the mouse, there is no fear, there is no caution."

"You have the element of surprise."

"Perceptive."

"Help."

Both Clarity and Doom started at a man's call. Doom ripped the spear out of the dinosaur and grabbed Clarity's hand pulling her to her feet. His pace was too fast for her and when her foot left the ground, she was yanked farther faster, flying over rough terrain.

Not far from them was a man grappling with Muffin. The bulwark had firmly been told to stay behind, but the desire for treats from Clarity was too much to keep the animal at the village. Her gaze searching Clarity wondered if Bubble-gum was still with Flight. The boy adored the dog, all of the village children did.

"Muffin," Clarity called.

The beast was standing over and on the man. He was unhurt but his face was red when Doom shoved Muffin off. The man jumped to his feet; he was filthy, his clothing torn, his eyes wild. He looked as though he had been running circles of terror. Clarity, seeing the fury on Doom's face, raced over to drape an arm across the beast's shoulders.

"Nice catch, Muffin."

Doom glared at her and the beast. The man was jumping around, all nervous excitement. Clarity could see his pulse pounding in his throat.

"My name is Clarity." She stuck her hand out to the man.

For a second he stared at her, then gripped her hand fast and let it go. "Heath, ma'am."

"Clarity. You call me ma'am again, and I'll let Muffin finish you."

"Where the hell am I?" Heath demanded in a Texas no-nonsense way.

"A planet like Earth might have been if the meteor didn't hit and didn't have an ice age, or volcanoes, or tsunamis, or pretty much all of that other wacky weather crap."

Heath eyed Clarity and then Doom. He was gorgeous, wisps of darkish hair curled at his ears. His brown eyes were expressive. He stood at least six-two. Well built. Decidedly lost as hell. The jeans, boots, and shirt he wore screamed cowboy. All he needed was a Stetson. Clarity grinned wondering if Doom was going to get his hands on the boots, she doubted it. A cowboy and his boots were like a woman and her purse.

"Damned if I didn't see a chicken with a tail. Funny lookin'. Five of 'em. Looked at me as if I might be lunch."

"Compsognathus." Heath stared at Clarity when she spoke. "It's about the size of a chicken. I've seen a few running around. Don't get cornered by a group of them."

"Ya think?" His sarcasm wasn't lost on Clarity. "Death by chicken would be a certain kinda irony. I ate enough of them."

"I think we should get back," Doom said. "Those clothes of his will draw a bigger crowd of curious carnivores. He needs to change and get washed in our own soaps. Humans wear too much perfume and cologne. He smells like he wants a date with a raptor."

Clarity laughed at the man's indignant expression, but Doom had a point. Heath smelled like he was hunting, but she imagined dinosaurs were the furthest thing from his mind. Except he was disheveled. His hair was tousled, his hands filthy as the rest of him. His ride from a sinkhole was no doubt eventful. They followed Doom. Heath stayed beside Clarity, away from Muffin.

"Rough trip?" she asked.

"Holy hell, I've ridden sweeter bulls. Been tossed far enough into the air to think I could fly, but droppin' down the rabbit hole was no trip to wonderland."

"Did you fall straight down or were you pulled in a different direction?"

"Dropped down."

Clarity checked him out as they walked. Was he from her Earth? How could she find out?

"Wait," Doom said, snapping the word. He held his spear ready.

Another creature melted from the bushes in their path with a low growl. This beast was covered in tufts of fur. Scars riddled its body. Fangs dripped saliva from a massive head, a bear mix of sorts it seemed to Clarity, but none she ever imagined. Black soulless eyes took in everyone at once. It was ready for a fight. Muffin's hackles rose and she flipped Clarity down and under her. The underside of a stinky part-wolverine's belly was no place to be. Clarity plugged her nose. She couldn't see anything. She heard enough to make her skin crawl.

Doom was bellowing, Heath added his howls. Muffin swung long claws. They battled more than one it seemed. Something else crashed through the underbrush. Tufts of fur dropped, gray flesh dropped, plopping near her face. Clarity gagged. From ground level she saw moccasins, more bulwark feet, cowboy boots, and dog paws. Bubble-gum was loose and pissed. War was being waged.

A scream sounded, human or dinosaur or beast, she wasn't certain. When the bulwark let Clarity climb out from under her, she stumbled to her feet. Blood was everywhere. Dinosaur limbs littered the ground. The bear creature was on its back, all four legs in the air, its belly ripped open. Doom and Menace were breathing hard as was Edge. Heath was down. The other three bulwarks had come to their aid.

"I don't know how, but that damned dog knew something was up. He bolted into the forest. Flight went after him until I tossed the boy to his mother. That child has no fear," Edge said.

Clarity wasn't certain if his tone was prideful or exasperation, or both. "I promised I'd bring him back. But for cripe's sake can you change the mutt's name? A grown man running through a jungle yelling for invisible goo sounds stupid."

Doom strode forward and grabbed Clarity into his arms. He crushed her against his chest. His eyes were wild as he felt her body checking for hurts.

"I'm fine. No worries. Your little sacrifice will still be able to help you." She was feeling sarcastic as he continued to feel her—everywhere.

Thrust to arm's length Doom gave her a hard look. "Do you really still believe I'd hand you over? Has this week meant nothing to you?"

Her eyes widened in stunned surprise. Passion burned from his gaze. "I, I," she stammered. Doom again wrapped her in his arms. She could feel his heart hammer against her. "I feel your heart pounding," she said. Before, he never broke a sweat. He was shaking. Looking around, Clarity could tell they battled for their lives.

"That's because right now it beats for you."

Her mouth opened wide in dumbfounded disbelief. Except she knew he spoke the truth. Edge scowled and strode off. Doom released her and tossed Heath over a shoulder. A small amount of blood trickled from a head wound. Menace cast a shrewd gaze at Clarity. He moved to stand next to her shoulder.

"Humans have never been allowed out of the village. I knew it would happen sooner or later. Doom has a heart; apparently, he's given it to you."

Clarity continued to gape open-mouthed and trailed after the men. Muffin walked with her head over Clarity's shoulder. She was feeling a little stupid. All week a change had been happening. The more she thought about it, the more realization hit. No man was allowed to say anything negative to her, or Doom bit his head off. The lingering looks, the times she woke with him gazing at her. Each touch was growing bolder.

How could she have been so blind? Doom had grown to care for her. A chill ran down her spine. She had grown to care for him. Had she doomed his people? Her shoulders set; she picked up her pace. The hybrids would die. Determination the likes she never felt before drew her brows together. She never had any intention of dying. Now she had no intention of letting Doom die. Never give anyone hope then snatch it from them.

Chapter Nine

Doom's fingers trembled when he traced her skin from shoulder to cheek. Clarity could see his inner turmoil. He touched her in a way no man ever had. She wanted to talk to him after they returned to his home. A decision shone from his eyes. There would be no going back.

"Sometimes I watch you sleep." He surprised her by saying. "I think you're a dream. Planted in my desire for hope and want. You fill my thoughts and chase away doubts. If I were to die right now without having you, I wouldn't feel cheated. How could I? When I've been able to touch you, see you. Let me taste you and add your lips to my list of growing blessings. The joy of being me is knowing you."

There was something to be said for primitive man. Doom didn't care about her employment; he didn't put his own work before her. He killed dinosaurs and wrestled bulwarks for fun. He looked pained when she sometimes caught his reflection. She was aware he couldn't stand the sight of himself. There were moments he stood still with a hand pressed against his tattoos, his head bowed, lips moving. At times, she watched him at night as well. Doom would swing his legs over the side of the bed, shoulders slouched, and she would hear him sob. The pain of a tortured man was hard to ignore. She wanted to lay her head over his shoulder those nights and tell him there was hope; she didn't think him a monster. Years of watching his family and friends die would take a hard road to finding any salvation.

Knowing his feelings of remorse, Clarity determined to save him from pain. The battle would be long and hard. When he pressed against her for a kiss, the bulge of his outline showed her something else was long and hard.

"May I please kiss you?" he asked. "I've never kissed a woman before except my mother. A gentle pursing of lips, nothing more. I want your mouth, Clarity. There's a hunger inside of me needing to be set free. Free, Clarity. You make me want to be *free*. I can say the word without cringing, without crying. The most elusive word I've ever spoken isn't said with sadness. It fills me with power. I feel the old warrior I know is in me surging and struggling to break these awful bonds of despair."

Doom moved closer, his body shaking. His lips slid across hers, tempting, teasing. Warm breath bathed her face. When his moist mouth met hers in a dance, she melted against him. The strength of the hard-muscled man was phenomenal, but a soft sweet kiss nearly brought her to her knees. Small pants of expelled breath glided down her throat as he strove to keep from devouring her. His commanding arms quivered, his expression of wonder led her to know she was his first; he wasn't lying.

Tenderness flowed from him. She *was* the most important person in the world, his world. If she let him make love to her, there would be no going back. He would sacrifice himself for her and she knew it.

Passion tingled her skin from his fingertips. So many, too many years of need spilled from the depth of his yearning gaze. They had a long hard year ahead of them. A year to save his life. If he perished, she would be sacrificed as well; she knew it. There could be no baby. There could be no flight—only fight. Their kiss broke.

Clarity smiled. "I've still got a lot of fight left in me," she sang in a whisper.

His bemused expression gazed back. Clarity ran her hand over his chest and dipped lower. Doom groaned when she reached his straining manhood, caressing him through his pants. He dropped lower to rest his forehead against hers while his hands cupped the sides of her face, his thumbs stroking her cheeks.

"I will fight, Clarity. I will kill any dinosaur or hybrid to keep you safe. I will not die and leave you alone."

"Those are the most romantic words anyone has ever said to me."

On her tiptoes, she crushed her lips against his. Her hand clung to the back of his neck when he picked her up and cradled her to his chest. The warm furs were piled high, and she sank into them when he set her upon the bed. She sat up as he slipped the revealing hide shirt over her head, tracing his fingertips up over flesh. Spiraling goose bumps to dot her arms. For a moment, he gazed at her breasts. His hand shook when he lifted it to trail his fingers over her curves. The pads of his thumbs grazed her buds as they hardened and strained toward him. Mouth open, he panted then swallowed hard.

"Clarity my insides crave to be a part of you."

He leaned to nuzzle his nose against her cheek. The warmth of his breath tingled her skin. His lips kissed her ear and tugged against a lobe. It was Clarity's turn to shake. His hands roamed her back, searing a path of discovery. When he satisfied himself after touching every inch of her, he began again on her front. His assault was no less lethal to her quivering flesh. Her nipples ached for their turn and she wasn't disappointed when finally his large beautiful hands cupped each breast.

"Your beauty would shame flowers to hide at your approach."

He was killing her with words alone while she remained tongue-tied. With a gentle ease, he guided her to lie back and again he stared at her. His gaze centered on her face. The loving look he cast was almost her undoing. She didn't know a man could make love with his eyes. He was already inside of her. At that moment, she was claimed.

"Doom," she whispered.

For a second his gaze clouded. "I hate that name."

"Don't."

He sighed and attempted a smile. "You're right. Now isn't the time to mention the word hate, because that word is far worse than my name."

Clarity shimmied out of her pants and lay before him. Doom leaned to kiss her belly making a trail downward to stop between her thighs. A gentle nudge was all it took for her to spread her legs and welcome his touch. Coaxing fingers slipped within her folds and he grinned at her when he discovered she was ready for him. She stifled a laugh thinking Niagara Falls would be dry compared to her.

"I didn't know a woman's heat would make my cock jealous of my fingers."

"Make your cock jealous of your tongue."

He cocked a raised eyebrow at her and grinned. Doom dipped his tongue into her wetness and licked at her until she writhed. His tongue was maddening delight. Round her folds he went as he whispered words such as sweet, delicious, beautiful. Her teeth clacked together as her need built.

"Please," she whispered.

When he stood, she wanted to scream at him to get his ass back to her. With slow deliberation he removed his belt, letting it fall to the fur beneath his feet. His pants followed suit. The entire length of him was engorged and thrust forward.

Clarity wanted to impale herself until a fast realization struck. "Damn." Frustrated she jumped from the bed and raced past him. He spun, eyes wide, arms spread wide.

"Am I really that big?"

Clarity was fumbling in the side pocket of her purse. If she didn't have him inside her soon she knew she'd die of longing but this was important. She fumbled with the condom, ripping it from the package and raced back. She jumped on the bed and knelt before him. Doom gripped her hand when she began to roll the rubber onto his cock.

"You want me to wear a coat on my cock? I just took all my clothes off. This is the last thing that needs to be dressed. Isn't it?"

Clarity laughed. "It's a condom. We can't make a baby. Please let go. If that massive appendage of yours isn't inside me soon I might rip my hair out."

Doom frowned but let go of her. Clarity was intrigued by his cock; magnificent was a puny word in comparison. The condom wasn't large enough but it would serve its purpose. She lay back and tugged his hand.

The look on Doom's face was priceless. "Earthlings have clothes for everything. I hear they put clothes on animals. I feel a little silly."

"I'm not looking for style big boy, just action."

Doom swung his hips back and forth. He widened his eyes at her. Clarity had to make him stop before she was consumed with a bout of hysteria. She grabbed his cock and tried to draw him closer. Doom took each of her ankles and pulled her toward him. She let go and he kissed the instep of her feet then each ankle.

His hands moved lower as he crept closer. She breathed a sigh of relief when finally he lay over her. The head of his cock pushed deep inside and she groaned in desire. Every inch of her was on fire. The broad span of his back rose and fell with every thrust. Clarity lifted her legs to wrap around his waist. Doom tested her depth and once realizing she could take all of him, his actions grew eager.

"You are the beauty of the first snowfall. The aroma of the first spring day. Colors of autumn pale in comparison."

"I thought you were color blind."

"I see differently, but I know beauty. I've never seen anything as beautiful as you. I've never touched anyone the way I need to touch you."

Every word he spoke was emphasized with passion—his need to make her believe what was said. He fisted a hand into her hair and forced her to expose

149

her throat. He nipped her and using his other hand gripped an ass cheek, curling her body under him.

Clarity didn't know how to respond. Edward swore a lot when they had sex. *Fuck you're hot, hell you feel so damned good. Rock my world, baby.* Nothing turned her on more than Doom's words. Beautiful, flowing, sunshine words. If Edward had spouted anything else, she'd consider him sickly sweet. Not Doom. He spoke from his heart not lust.

Heart pounding, Clarity wanted to say something back, gift him with something as she was gifted. *Do me hard baby,* didn't seem to capture the moment. Had she ever spoken from the heart during sex? *Never.* What a sad thought. *Now who's the heathen?*

"Doom your name is beautiful. As wonderful as any name, because it's yours. I never knew I had to travel to another world to find you. I'd fall through a dozen sinkholes to get to you."

When he gazed into her eyes she saw tears. "I'm not worthless when I'm with you."

Raw emotion as real as any tore at her chest. The power of the emotion built within her until waves of desire made her whimper his name. He wrapped her in his arms and rocked with a gentle motion until they were both spent. For a while neither moved. Doom shifted.

"Clarity?"

"Hmm?"

"My new coat fell off. It's kinda gross."

****

"Why not just rope the little bastards and shoot 'em? They're animals after all, not like they're human." Heath was showing off his rope technics in the main hall. A bandage was wrapped around his head.

Children were in another room being entertained by the dog and watched by a few women while a discussion took place. Doom wanted his villagers to know his plans. He knew with Clarity the people had a shot at a real life.

"The sacrifices need to continue. The hybrids will slaughter us all," Edge argued.

Doom could see the man was furious the humans knew what was going on and he was afraid of change. They all were. They had every right to be. What he was asking of them went against their survival instincts.

"You've been between her legs and it's stunted your thinking. A man who thinks with his cock has a hard head, and a dumb ass," Edge raged.

Doom smashed him in the face. Edge lay stunned on the ground. No one had ever struck him before. Fists balled Doom jumped up on a table.

"Anyone who thinks I'm weak is welcome to challenge me."

No one moved. The men of the village were hard and powerful. It wasn't Doom's size that gave them pause, it was the burden of the tattoos he wore. His pecs flexed making the tattoos dance to be noticed.

"Doom is right," Menace said. "It's time for a change. We are going to die regardless. Don't you care how or for what you die? I want to spend time in a woman's arms. I want to hold a child born of my flesh and blood."

"I don't think we are capable of giving life," a woman sadly said.

"Because all we do is take lives. No more. Clarity has shown me inventions that will make you believe in her as I do. Edge, get off your ass. You look ridiculous sitting there," Doom said.

Grumbling, Edge climbed to his feet and glared at Clarity. She glared back. In her hand was the taser; no one was stupid enough to go near her. Especially when Heath saw it, threw up his hands, and gave her a wide berth. It was apparent he was familiar with the weapon, but had no idea what a gun was. Alice had known what a gun was. Clarity muttered she'd never heard of a cowboy who didn't know guns. Heath told her tasers and cattle prods were sufficient. Clarity mentioned it might be why the hybrids didn't have weapons. Another reason to keep her doubly safe from the beasts.

"Doom says the hybrids travel in twos," Heath said. He swung the rope around his upper body. "We can herd the buggers into a trap. After a few start to disappear we're gonna have to make a stand."

"When do we start?" Menace asked.

Clarity moved to join Doom. "We need to make sure we have a huge supply of everything we need. And more people. Doom tells me this is the start of your season to gather supplies for the winter. When snow hits and you have your big sleep, we can teach the children how to make pipe bombs." She cast a glance at Heath. "And a few adults. Come spring, we strike before your time to sacrifice. Then once they figure out what's going on, we hit them hard and fast."

"So you plan on saving the world?" Edge was contemptuous.

Clarity smiled sweetly and squeezed Doom's hand when he tensed, ready to pound the man again.

"Yes, I plan to save the world. Maybe not you, though. You're an asshole."

Heath roared with laughter. "Get 'em girl. You better watch it, Edge. She's more ornery than a wasp nest. Cuter, but mean. Any little filly who cuddles with a bulwark and calls her Muffin can ride a bull into the ground."

"So where do we start?" Edge said.

"It's time we go hunting for earthlings. I think Heath is the first of many to come. I want them all, and I want them ready to fight. We're going to make an army," Doom said. "We'll get so many humans the other village tribes will have to join us."

"An army of humans?" Heath let his rope drop. He looked puzzled.

"You know what an army is, don't you?" Clarity asked.

"If it's a posse to get men together to go after rabid bears and such, sure. Army ants was what comes to mind."

"Armies fight in wars."

"What's a war?" Heath asked.

Now Clarity looked confused. "Didn't you have family who fought in World War One and Two? You don't know about guns, but you mentioned you know what swords are."

"Who do you fight in these wars?"

"Other humans."

Heath scratched his head. "Well no ma'am, um, Clarity. On Earth we don't fight humans, we can kill animals, as long as it's humane, but humans don't kill humans. That's some kinda sick and twisted shit."

Doom heard Clarity groan. He realized she wasn't from the same Earth as Heath. Her speculation was just proven. The sinkholes were gathering other humans. A thought nagged him. Clarity said she had been pulled away last second in the sinkhole. Fear shot into his heart. If she was meant to go elsewhere what would happen if the planet who wanted her came looking for her? Doom would have to be ready.

"I want four other men," Menace yelled and jumped up onto the table beside Doom. "Grab your weapons and let's go find salvation."

A number of men cheered, more looked scared to death.

"Now isn't the time to be seen," Clarity warned. "We need a surprise attack."

Menace grinned; Doom had never seen him grin. "I need to hunt. The hybrids understand a need for food."

Doom sighed. Menace had a need to slaughter. The pots would be full tonight.

****

Clarity walked beside Doom. They were looking for the wild children. Since they were prepared to fight, they needed back up and if these were Clarity's Earth children as she suspected they might be, they could prove useful. Clarity insisted Earth children could be badass if needed. The dead hybrid was all the proof he should need. They walked deeper into the forested jungle.

A strange mound almost undetectable came into view. Doom moved with caution. The cave was made up of smaller versions of mammoth tusks covered in hillocks of vegetation. The nest they stumbled across was recently deserted. Except for one dead occupant. The female hybrid's body was crushed. Clarity knelt down and lifted her into her arms. She was so tiny; her features near human.

"How can they do this? Their own kind, and why? She looks so sweet, so innocent," she whispered.

"Sweet and innocent shouldn't describe a hybrid. The males I met tried to kill me and were only a little older," Doom said.

A cold icy finger raced up her spine. Doom was right. Did mixing humans who knew nothing of war cause humanity in the females? Empathy for life would be frowned on.

Glancing around, Clarity saw human footprints, handprints, claws. It was hard to tell if the prints were only human. No traces of bodies were found, but there were other prints. Dinosaurs. She wondered why the little body wasn't taken as well. But she realized the body was still warm. Clarity glanced nervously around. The hair on the nape of her neck stood tall. They were being watched.

When the hybrid appeared, Clarity set the dead baby hybrid down and stood. She was angry. Doom pulled her behind him. He stayed relaxed but clutched his spear tighter.

"DaV-nin."

The hybrid made sharp whistles and hand gestures. Few words were spoken. Clarity caught some of what was said. He was surprised Doom was traveling outside the village with a human. Doom appeared calm but gestured she was safe enough with him. The hybrid eyed Doom, and Clarity could almost make out the hybrid said, *for now*. She was positive it's what DaV-nin said when Doom gripped her hand tighter at the unveiled threat. The hybrid was then questioning Doom about the hybrid the children killed, but he was searching. DaV-nin was asking if Doom had seen any other hybrid wandering around. There was no doubt in her mind they hadn't found the body. Doom simply shook his head and shrugged. DaV-nin stared at Clarity. He pointed and spoke a few more word whistles. Doom tensed. She knew she had been singled out for the next sacrifice. She wanted to shove a bomb up his ass.

The hybrid turned and disappeared back into the foliage, leaving the dead offspring. Clarity started after him, wanting to rail against the inhumanity of worrying over a grown hybrid while a dead hybrid baby female meant nothing. Doom grabbed Clarity's hand and led her away.

"We need to find those children fast." His whispered words were urgent. "If that hybrid is found before the snow falls, they will be hunted and destroyed, so might we be. The hybrids know we would never kill one of theirs for fear of retribution. DaV-nin hinted at the children out there. Maybe they've seen them use weapons different from ours."

"It's time we stalk the hybrid."

Clarity yanked her hand from his and began in the direction DaV-nin went. Doom raced after and tried to stop her.

"Are you crazy?" It was a yelled whisper.

"I want to know where they are and this is the perfect opportunity."

"But," Doom sputtered.

"If he was going to kill us, he would have tried. No worries, I'll protect you."

Doom glared at her but made no move to stop her as she continued on. Finally Doom surged ahead. He was stealthy; she'd give him that. DaV-nin appeared nonchalant about his motion. Cocky, he was arrogant in his stance. If he suspected they were tailing him, he showed no sign. Or didn't care.

They were downwind and Clarity was glad. The foliage grew thicker, easier to hide within. Two younger hybrids raced to DaV-nin when a short while later they came to a high mountain and a clearing. Doom sucked in his breath as they crouched and gazed way up. After a closer look, Clarity could make out round hole openings in the mountain, partly concealed with vast mounds of green foliage. They'd found the hybrids' nesting area.

As they watched, a giant bird circled near DaV-nin. Perhaps to check out the young. The hybrid gazed up while picking up a rock DaV-nin flung with such force the bird squawked and came crashing down. Another hybrid grabbed the bird and bit into it. DaV-nin snarled a warning and the hybrid dropped the meal when two other smaller hybrids raced forward to snatch the meal, ripping into it.

"Shit," she whispered.

"What?"

Clarity swallowed hard. "Look." She pointed to a board hung near a cave opening.

"Those marks are everywhere," Doom said. "It warns us of hybrid territory."

"I thought you couldn't read."

"I can't, it's a simple mark."

"Doom, that's a sign, not a simple mark. It's a word. *Beware*. The hybrids can spell. They must be able to read. Holy shit, that's not good."

Clarity could see the youngsters were hybrid children. Smaller, their faces juvenile, stuffing themselves on the bird. Then something surprised her.

A little one, younger than the others came forward. DaV-nin studied the child. The way the youngster moved, the way the older males shoved each other but never touched the smaller one. When one of the males became too wild, DaV-nin growled at him. The smaller hybrid reached up for DaV-nin.

She's female.

Clarity was certain. So, some of the females were spared. DaV-nin's perhaps. There was something different about the hybrid offspring. Her features were harder than the dead female they found. Her gaze was—evil. He swung the child into his arms. Try as she might, Clarity could see no mother and the thought gave her chills. DaV-nin reached to retrieve a piece of the downed bird and handed it to the female. Soon her mouth was covered in blood.

"With enough explosives we can level the mountain," Clarity said.

"How long will it take?"

"We'll need the year. But we know where they are. We might come up with a better idea later. And did you see the fur the smallest was wearing? It's not a simple loincloth; it's a thick fur. I bet they don't migrate. If this is where they hibernate, we need to start planning."

"We need to find the human children."

Clarity agreed.

Chapter Ten

A deep darkness rose in the sky and Doom gazed up. High above their heads was a murmuration, the dancing-type motion of an entire flock of large birds shifted on a whim. Clarity stood mouth gaping.

"Look at the size of those birds. They're as big as the one DaV-nin killed. Maybe it flew away from the flock," she exclaimed. "They must be two feet high apiece. I've seen less impressive wingspans on gliders. For a second I thought a sinkhole was forming. Black as pitch, all of them. Massive bats?"

The deep inky black was a startling contrast to the sky. When humans asked Doom what it was like to be colorblind, he in return asked them what it was like not to be. He saw what he saw. Who was to say their words were right and his colors were wrong. Nevertheless, the birds were impressive.

"They're herbivores mostly. They will eat small rodents, and we do watch the smaller children. I guess the hybrids watch them around their young, too."

A sharp squeal to his left and Doom grabbed Clarity to him and bounded for a high rock. The birds would leave them alone. What was coming might not. Clarity gasped when the prey came running into the area then slid to a stop on all fours thrusting dirt and sticks in its wake. A massive-type furred horse with claws ducked down then rose up on hind legs to sniff the air.

"Doom?"

"Shh."

Clarity screamed when a massive creature dubbed a hell pig raced through the bush to land on the furred beast. The horse clawed at the pig but the attempt was futile. Massive tusks gored the underbelly as the pig slaughtered the prey. Entrails slipped from a bloody cavity, steam rising. The slaughter was over quickly. Doom took Clarity's hand and led her over the other side of the rocks. They scrambled down and though cautious, they moved at a clipped rate.

They slowed once they put distance between them and the hell pig. At a clearing, Clarity stopped to catch her breath. The tree she leaned against dwarfed her. She started at a huge butterfly half her size. The winged creature fluttered near her curious, hovering, then floated away.

Doom reached into a sack he brought and pulled out two hard tart apples. Clarity dropped to the ground and held hers in her lap. She had agreed to leave her purse behind, but he knew she wore the taser and mace in a smaller pouch around her waist tied by a leather rope. The pouch bulged and he wondered what else she couldn't live without for their search. Her purse was safe enough; his men liked their balls where they were.

Edge had been stupid enough to slide a cocky hand into a compartment on her purse when Clarity wasn't looking. A snap sounded and the huge man danced around with something attached to his fingers. He ripped the device off and Clarity chuckled when she picked it up. She waggled it at Edge.

"Mouse trap," she commented. "Some hotels I

ended up in were a little on the nasty side. Seems I can catch bigger rodents."

Edge wasn't impressed, but refrained from touching her purse after that, they all did. Doom had only chuckled. The device would be handy super-sized.

"Look," she said rousing him from his thoughts, and gestured into the valley below them. A massive bear lumbered. "On my planet the polar bear has mixed with the brown bear, too. Survival, I guess. Holy hell, that bear's huge. Our colder regions are warming. Icebergs are melting. Do you know if yours are?"

"Icebergs? What's an iceberg?"

"A massive amount of ice not separated but all together. They can move."

"My father showed me once large blocks of ice. They always form in the winter. We have caves filled with ice, some near the ocean. Some are salty, some fresh."

"I wondered about that. Icebergs are miles high and long. They can sink ships."

"A ship is something very large you float on water with."

"Yes."

"Your humans, well the others, talk about a cruise with strange upright walking animals your children love. Human children are spoiled outrageously. Our children learn to survive."

"They aren't yours."

"They are loved and treated as our own."

"Yet there are no grown humans in your village besides Heath and me."

"The bane of my existence. The sacrifice of our young adults makes us all bleed. Any child we have we covet. But the rules of the sacrifice are clear. The hybrids know of the offspring in every village. A father of another village offered his life in exchange for his Earth son's life. They took not only the father but hunted the son. They lost both. Do we lose the one or the two? His wife is now without a husband and her son."

"What a sad horrible way to live."

"I thought so, too, but we were alive. Cultivating humans as one would wheat. You don't mourn wheat. My body isn't covered in tattoos of roots or dinosaurs. You are what living is, Clarity. I'm done simply surviving."

Doom sat beside her and took a healthy bite from the apple. After a few bites, he flung the remains of the fruit down near the bear. The bear was startled but was soon sniffing the air. It found the treat and wandered away.

A lock of Clarity's hair slipped over an eye and Doom lifted a finger to tuck the strand behind her ear. She let the apple fall to her side but pulled her knees up to her chest.

"There is danger everywhere out there," she said.

"Yes. You also realize the dinosaurs know my scent and fear my people. At least you should. Even the mammoth mastodons keep their distance. My villagers are skilled hunters."

"But we were attacked."

Doom lifted an eyebrow. "You were attacked."

"Oh." The realization dawned in her eyes.

"The dinosaurs will learn in time to fear your scent—when you're with me. I'm also a skilled hunter."

"I think maybe those children are, too. I want to get

a closer look. Flight, the boy, said his father is a pilot and when I asked him if he knew what a gun was he pointed his fingers at me and went, *boom gotcha with water*. His arm is marked so I wonder. He's young still. Even our world tries to shield our children from harsh realities until they learn on their own. To us, water guns are harmless. I think these wild children might be from my Earth. Heath knew of a cross bow, but he was adamant you killed animals with it for food. Only food. No sport hunting. That girl knew exactly how to kill and didn't blink an eye. When my Earth humans are threatened we react, she must be from my world, her brother, too."

Doom thought they might be but said nothing. It had been a number of years since a child came through a sinkhole speaking of warrior fathers. At least two decades, maybe more. The years blurred after a while. Extra hunters would be a boon, even young ones. Clarity insisted these bombs she spoke of could be tossed by a child.

When the first spatter of rain struck him, Doom was surprised. The weather was always temperamental this time of year. Horrific thunderstorms blew in fast and breezed out as quick. This time of year the land was thirsty for water as life grew in droves.

Clarity hated their rain. The thought was amusing. Why would anyone hate weather? It had no feelings. Nevertheless, she expressed loathing when the storm rumbled in. Gripping her hand he rose to his feet and began racing toward a shelter. Doom knew every inch of his area. The hybrids' home was a surprise to him because he had never ventured near 'their' side. Learning they could read was a surprise, but Doom had never seen a written word before Clarity came. That the hybrids could read was frightening, their thought process was growing. The written signs he thought were marks began a few years back.

Within a tangled mass of overgrown colossal roots were small shelters. The trees grew overtop the boulders. Clarity screamed when the ground heaved up as they passed a line of trees to get to the trees on boulders. Even the trees adapted. The roots of the other trees on the direct ground in this particular area separated. When the wind blew, the ground breathed as would a sleeping giant.

Doom took her higher to the stable trunks, and they slipped through into shelter as the ground gave up its water supply to the sky. On hands and knees Clarity watched with fascination, peering out the small opening they squeezed through. She was breathing heavily and turned to gaze at him.

"Does it snow up, too?"

"Flakes of snow fly where the wind takes them. In a blizzard, does it seem you're attacked by any one direction?"

"Point taken."

Doom, who had been crouching, settled back against the hanging moss on the inside of the shelter. There were mounds of small sticks and dry vegetation surrounding them. The cave was dry, roots hung like tiny stalactites from the ceiling, curling their way round and over each other before pointing down. Clarity continued to peer outside and he knew she watched the breathing ground until she sneezed and coughed and sat beside him. She swiped at her face and Doom could see she had gotten a breath of rain. The moss door fell into place, casting much of the cave into darkness. From her pouch she pulled her flashlight and flicked it on, the cave lit instantly.

From within, Clarity gathered dry kindling after sweeping a circular area clean. She dug out a small indentation in the ground with her hands and using her fire tube she sparked a flame. She called it a lighter. Truth be told, it was a magic light to hold in your hand. She informed him there was liquid inside the tube allowing it to flame when a spark was produced. The fire didn't burn down but up. Another novelty of the mystic.

The first time a human created matches with a substance called sulfur they melted to liquid and rolled the head of small sticks in, Doom was inclined to make them. A simple trick really, but the small shards of wood it was rolled on burned down to your hand. Useful nonetheless. Fire was a necessity of life. With the fire established, Clarity switched off her flashlight, storing it back in her pouch and cuddled up beside him. He draped his arm across her shoulders and leaned her into his chest. The high rise of her beautiful forehead drew him to kiss her. His hand cupped her cheek lifting her face to his.

"Are we safe in here?" she asked.

"Yes. The animals don't like the storms and they dislike fire."

"The hybrids?"

"The hybrids seem to loathe any uncertain weather. They adapt, they cope, but they appear unsettled in storms."

"That could be Neanderthal or dinosaur or both. It was hard for humans to go too far in dangerous weather. Still is but humans are too impatient. We'd rather risk injury, get to where we're going right this very second, than sit and wait it out. Can't tell you how many rainstorms I've driven through and could hardly see out the windshield. Or blizzards."

"Stupidity or fearlessness?" he was teasing and she grinned.

"Both."

Doom sighed when he saw the sky darken further when the long vines blew up then settled, and he took a quick peek. Few rocks were in the cave and he maneuvered a few onto the vines to keep them down. Only a few strands blew in to brighten the fire with life-giving air. He felt a tug on his hand and took the piece of jerky Clarity handed him from a package she had brought, a treasure from her purse. The meat was soft and different from what he was used to.

"Is this meat?"

"Beef."

"Beef from a...?"

"Cow." She held up the package for him to see. The animal was unlike anything he'd ever seen. They wouldn't last long on his planet. He gripped the meat and tugged a bite into his mouth, chewing with contentment.

"Cow is good. Too bad they don't fall into sinkholes."

"As a matter of fact our planet has been losing animals. That only started recently. Normally it's people. Maybe we should keep watch. After all, if Bubble-gum came through, you never know what else might follow."

"True."

Clarity handed him another piece of meat and stored the rest. "We may need this for breakfast. I don't think we're going anywhere for now."

"We'll be fine. I always have a backup in case."

Doom had other foods for them if they were trapped for a little while. It was best to pack a satchel any time he went anywhere. Some humans were hungry when found, some thirsty. He was hoping to persuade the children with food. Clarity nudged him and handed him a brown piece of something. Doom scowled at it. The substance was chunky and unusual.

"Looks like shit."

"It's a part of a chocolate bar with nuts. Try a taste. And ouch, if you're pooping things like this you may want to watch your diet." She snickered and took a bite of the piece she had.

With a tentative gesture Doom lifted the suspicious hunk to his lips. He knew she wouldn't give him something inedible. After his first bite, he was hooked.

"How can this small block of food taste almost as good as you, Clarity?"

"That was incredibly smart." She chuckled.

His saliva glands went into overdrive. Doom closed his mouth and after the food disappeared down his throat the taste lingered. Now he understood why Muffin adored her. He opened his eyes to Clarity's smiling face. Her hair was in wisps and Doom tucked a strand behind a perfect ear. Humans were dainty compared to his village lot. Fine bones, slender and graceful at one time seemed an annoyance. The work they did was less, the loads they carried smaller.

In time, Doom came to realize they made up for physical failings in emotion and intelligence. They loved harder; their words were filled with passion. Their laughter came easy. The tears they cried from loss were many. Something occurred to Doom.

"Why don't you cry?"

"Why should I?" she sounded perplexed.

"No I don't mean at this very moment. I mean when things are frightening or you're upset, you don't cry."

"I learned not to at a young age. I was surrounded by drama and watched and learned after a while people stop listening if you cry at everything. If you cry when you're hurt, such as a broken bone, then as much as when you stub a toe, how do people know when to believe there is a real problem?"

"Either way you are hurt. Shouldn't that be what matters?"

"I suppose for me it's the equivalent of crying wolf. When I cry, I want who I'm with to know I mean it. I need help, or the hurt is too much or the emotion too much."

"I'll remember that."

Doom remembered his tears in front of her. He wondered if she thought him weak. The way she gazed at him, full of sweet tenderness, made him believe otherwise. She melted his heart with a glance. When she lifted her hand to cup the side of his face, he was lost in her eyes. He might not see color the way she did, but he saw desire and want.

For me. Someone wants me.

The explosion of emotion in his chest brought fire to his loins. The raw physical compulsion to be within her was overwhelming and intense. Exquisite wonder lust wreaked havoc and for a moment, a single moment, he wanted to run away, with her. Doom had never run from anything, masked perhaps, ignored, but not run.

"You deserve better than me," Doom said.

Clarity leaned to kiss his lips in a manner so sensual he thought his seed would explode. Her breath seared his skin and he made a fist as he wrapped an arm around her back pulling her closer. Shoulders shaking, his mouth was on fire with a teasing tiny taste of her tongue. She clung tighter, both killing and reviving her victim. When she released her emotional torture, Doom lifted his fingers to his lips.

"They are still there," was said with wonder in his heart. "You captured my essence where I still burn for you. Am I in there, in your heart with you? Because I'm not here anymore. My breath is yours to have or stop. My heart beats for you. But if I am in you, how can you be inside me? Tremors rock my core. Blood pulses in my veins taking your taste to each fingertip. Are you my blood, are you my flesh?"

"You say I deserve better than you. If I am in you, would you want me to go to another?"

Doom felt the rage flood his face. The burning of heated blood didn't creep silently over him. It crashed through him. Anger that another would think to touch someone so obviously made for him sent his insides to war. A revelation washed through him.

I can war.

"I'll take that particular look as a no," she said and sounded cheeky.

"A 'no'?" His words were soft and volatile. "Death would be sweet humanity to any who as much as glance your way."

"Doom, I think I understand this is your first

experience with love, but get a grip."

"I plan on it."

He pounced. Clarity squealed when her clothes were removed with lightning speed. She was on her back and panting as he rose over her. Her gaze was of mixed emotions which added heat to Doom's action. Trembling, he lifted a finger to again push a wayward strand of hair behind her ear.

"Do you understand what it's like to never let another see you feel? Emotions so gripping you want to howl at the moon while your insides die. Every day, Clarity. Every day of my damned doomed life I fought me. Not anymore, not with you. All this time I thought I was someone else and I hated him."

"Don't you dare hate the man I love."

"I can't. I won't. You introduced me to *me*. A real me. Not some personification of death. I want life. I want my soul back and, so help me, I will get every piece before I die."

"Doom, I want you to take every piece of me. But it's spring. I can't give birth in the middle of a war."

She was right. Doom ran a quick hand down his face as he sat up. She motioned toward the sack she brought. Rummaging through it Doom found a square coat holder. He grinned at her as he opened it. Clarity sat up and helped him put it in. Her fingertips were kisses his cock enjoyed while the rest of him groaned in anticipation. Once he was sheathed, she laid back legs spread. With slow deliberation he pressed his flesh against hers.

A strong root was beside him and he gripped it, fingers turning white, when he thrust within her. Power pulsated beneath his hands and he would crush her if he touched her. Teeth gritted, he controlled each motion until sweat dripped from his brow.

"This is conviction, Clarity." He slammed his entire cock to embed within her. He pulled out as quick and named another thrust. "Want. Need. Desire. Fire. Strength. Determination and not last by any means is love."

Clarity thrashed beneath him and his merciless assault. Her legs, wrapped round him, weakened until she laid spread before him. Hands beside her head on either side were curled, her lips were parted as she begged, "again, Doom, please."

"I will have you again."

He thrust slower but kept his rigid control. One hand pulled her wrists together over her head. She cried out and he winced. Arm shaking, he gentled his touch so she could bear his power. Flesh covered over small twig-like bones was warm in his palms. He released the root from his death grip, noting he had come close to crushing the living entity, and he was sorry. But better the tree than Clarity.

"I will no longer be controlled." Doom's words weren't for her but hoped his passion took his conviction to the skies.

Clarity was watching him soundlessly except for an explosion of breath when he thundered into her once last time. Careful of his weight he lowered to press against the length of her. She was shuddering. When he released her arms, she pulled them to her chest and closed her eyes.

"Clarity, are you all right?"

"Now I see how you can kill dinosaurs." The words were a mere whisper. She relaxed completely and Doom knew she slept.

Darkness was falling; shadow light lost their illumination to the farthest tenebrous cracks of their shelter until dusk was no more. The storm continued to rage to match Doom's mood. They were safe, more importantly Clarity was safe. Nary a hybrid would survive if one so much as glanced in her direction. Safe in his arms it was doubtful one would dare. Doom had no idea there was power in love. For a moment, he understood there was power in hate, and that was what consumed the hybrids.

The thought of the hybrids made them much more dangerous when Doom put the reasoning together. An emotion so strong, so powerful and power filled he knew once the battle began only one side would be left standing. Doom had a village to protect. He led innocents to the slaughter to keep his people safe. No more. Safety was now on his terms. The hybrids were going to die. A shiver ran through Doom's body. He cuddled Clarity closer.

I will prove victorious not because of the power of hate but because of love.

A small smile curved his lips and he was grateful. *One day,* he swore, *there will be laughter.*

****

When Clarity roused, she was trapped in Doom's arms. His weight was welcome and she settled her back further into his chest. When she twisted to gaze at his sleeping face, she saw he was smiling. Wiggling, she pressed against his erection and wondered what he was thinking of.

Sex with me, no doubt.

The storm was finished but only miniscule cracks

of sunlight braved their way into the shelter playing peek-a-boo with the dark. Some vines had broken free of the rocks. Clarity wished the sun would rise, she was anxious to find the wild children. She had so many questions. She wondered how they learned to kill the hybrids. More importantly who showed them? Did a human survive the slaughter and collect wayward children?

The idea held merit. One she wanted to explore. Doom shifted and drew her closer. Clarity groaned and he stiffened. With a gentle hand he rolled her underneath him. They had slept naked. The fire died out, but she was warm. An exquisite kiss fell upon her lips. He then rested his forehead against hers.

"Damn," he mumbled when he turned his head.

Clarity turned her head to gaze in the same direction. The sun had risen inches higher, enough for her to make out the chicken-sized dinosaurs bobbing and weaving outside their shelter. Their quick little innocuous actions of scratching the dirt and dipping their heads as though to peck the ground was deceptive, those claws of theirs could rip a human's flesh, as well as their razor sharp teeth beneath their beaks. The buggers were taking quick glances at her. Doom rose and yanked on his pants. A few would be no trouble but by the amount of feet she saw there were a dozen at least.

"Can you get another fire started?" he asked.

"Sure." Clarity scrambled into her own clothes and grabbed his tinder kit and her lighter. She soon had a larger blaze while flames licked twigs, old leaves, and broken pieces of root.

Doom opened a sack at his side and took a bowl

from his pack. He dumped the floury contents from the sack into a bowl and from a bladder poured water. From the pack he removed a stained thick hide, rounded in the shape of a pan. From another hide-covered bladder, he squeezed out a blob of semi-melted fat onto the hide. The sides of the pan were little more than an inch high molded to stay in place.

Taking a few rocks to set under the rounded pan Doom moved heated ashes just below the stones making certain the hide wasn't directly on any flame. The fat heated quickly and sizzled across the pan as he tilted it back and forth to even the contents. Doom handed the floury paste to Clarity along with a wooden spoon.

"Drop the batter in to form patties. Use the tongs and turn them, don't let them burn."

Clarity did as he said. "Caveman bannock," she mumbled.

"Stay here."

Doom took his knife and axe from his rope belt. Clarity peered out and eyes wide watched him in action. There were decidedly more of the critters than she first assumed. The small dinosaurs must have figured their number would give them an easy meal, not so. Without a sound Doom hacked through the neck of one leaping squawker, and it squawked no more. The same fate befell ten more before the bird-like creatures realized their number was sadly diminished.

Using his knife he gutted three of the small birds moving quickly. Guts, feet, and heads went flying in his zealous hurry. Clarity covered her mouth to cut off a scream. The smell of blood attracted a larger dinosaur. Doom grabbed a few sticks, three of the dead dinosaurs he gutted and crashed back into the shelter, rolling under the sheet of heavy moss. He was smiling.

"Do you see what's out there?" her whisper was high pitched. A monster dinosaur was lurking.

"Relax. That old character doesn't want to tangle with me. He'll grab the ones I killed and be happy. He and I have an understanding; he leaves me alone and I don't break a leg."

As Clarity watched the old dinosaur, she did see it limping. The beast tossed one after the other dead dinosaurs into his mouth and seemed content as it chewed. Clarity scooted as far back as she could into the shelter when he dipped his huge head and peered at her with a large eye, its head cocked. Doom was spitting the three small dinosaurs he caught. He turned the patties she made in the pan. Clarity sat back watching as the dinosaur head tried to poke its way into the cave. Inches from Doom were razor sharp teeth. The moss draped the creature's grey head giving it the appearance of hair, comical horror. Doom crouched preparing food as though man's best friend waited for a scrap.

The dinosaur huffed, ruffling Doom's pants. "Go on, these are mine," Doom called. He whacked the tip of the dinosaur nose with the wooden spoon. Clarity knew her eyes were round as saucers at the exchange.

The beast let out a low pleading growl making Doom groan. He lifted a small dough patty from the pan, blew on it, and pitched it out the door through a narrow opening by the dinosaur's head. The dinosaur shifted back and sniffed the bread. Using its tongue he curled it into his mouth. After a while the dinosaur ambled off and Doom handed Clarity a piece of meat, charbroiled on the outside pink in the middle with the bread.

"You're supposed to thoroughly cook chicken," Clarity said.

"Maybe so but this is a dinosaur."

True.

She took a tentative taste. It didn't taste like chicken. It was a bit gamey, but good. Doom had eaten a whole dinosaur before her piece was gone. He handed her more, then he gave her his water bag. The bladder of some largish animal was wrapped in a hide to keep it from leaking.

"Can I ask you something?"

"Sure." Doom munched giving her his undivided attention.

"Your people have a wonderful way with food. But how do you make cheese? I've been thinking on it since I saw it, ate it, you must get milk from somewhere."

"Every other spring there is herd of mammals that would have been hunted to extinction unless we interfered to keep them safe. They are water and land animals. They are covered in long fur and underneath is a heavy layer of blubber. They live far north, but the females come here when the snow has barely melted to give birth to their naked babies. The males I guess desert them. They make the trek in herds. Unprotected when giving birth or heavy with pregnancy, they're easy targets. A gentle animal. Large. I haven't seen any kind of defense. My guess is they were close to extinction.

"Other animals know the creature is vulnerable. The babies are helpless, their mothers exhausted from the journey and giving birth. The young don't develop legs or flippers to move them across the land to the water for three days. During that time the fiercely protective, yet defenseless mothers won't leave their young even if it means their death. My people harvest their milk. They have tons. It literally spills from them. When the beasts found out we wanted the milk and not their babies or them, they allowed our approach. In return we guard them until the babies are ready to make a return trip."

"You harvest milk?"

"Sure why not? Don't humans?"

"Well, yes but…"

There really was no point in continuing. She wondered if Doom and his people had been told about cows and goats. From his Cheshire gaze she imagined he had. A beast almost hunted to extinction until help from another with a means to an end stepped in. Considering it was a win-win situation, they all benefitted. The idea also explained the tasty butter. Clarity accepted another piece of meat and more bannock. The warm roll was roundish and delicious, cooked in the fat. Doom ate no more until she was finished and full. He then polished off the remains.

Doom stood, though slouched under the stalactites, and stomped out the fire. "Now that the storm has stopped this isn't as safe. We need to get moving. Raptors are rare in this area; the hybrids hunt them to give the humans a chance at survival until the sacrifices. There are other dinosaurs as dangerous, but not as cunning. The raptors are smart, they know to stay away, but two humans alone is a tempting target."

When he looked her over, she knew he meant *she* was the tempting target. Clarity rose and took Doom's hand. As her eyes adjusted to the light, she paused. A movement to her right made her turn. There was a young man in the distance. She couldn't tell his age from where she stood. He wore very little. His wiry limbs were thin but his chin was set in a defiant way. Clarity bet there was strength to the child-man. He appeared human and alone. His stance led her to believe he was either born here to humans on this planet, or had been here a long time.

She whispered quietly to Doom and bid him to look in the direction she was gazing. Doom turned. The male vanished. Clarity blinked thinking her eyes were playing tricks but he was gone. There was no puff of smoke, no black hole. He simply disappeared.

"Well, that was odd," she said.

"What's odd is seeing a wild child and others after all this time." Doom's look was thoughtful. "I never in all this time knew they existed. Or how long they've been here. They must be terrified."

The man-child hadn't looked terrified to Clarity; he seemed pissed.

"You said humans weren't allowed to leave the village and yet here I am. Maybe the boy was curious. Could he be from another village?"

"Not a chance."

"I wonder who he is and how long he's been out here," Clarity mused.

"From the glimpse I got, he looked maybe mid-teens. It's the younger children I'm more concerned with. We should start with them. If that kid is that fast, we'll never get him. Who knows how long he's been out here, he could be dangerous. Especially if he's survived with dinosaurs."

Clarity agreed, though as Doom walked away, she stood a moment longer hoping to catch a glimpse of the young man. Reluctantly, she turned and headed after Doom. The scenery never ceased to amaze her. Supersized foliage and large, ripe berries. It wasn't the size, but the sheer amount in single areas. Enough to feed Doom's village for a month. An entire bush the length of a football field was dotted in red.

As they walked past the bush heading in a different direction, Clarity reached her hand out to grab a few in a single swoop. It took only three to fill her palm. She munched on them enjoying their flavor. Mushrooms larger than life were enchanting. There were differences she imagined. If this planet never suffered the ravages of Mother Nature nor the vicious assault from the sky, things would have progressed differently.

Open fields in the distance from their elevated mountain perch showed Clarity where they collected grains of varying kinds. Long fields stretched with oversized elk and mega reindeer. Their numbers were small, including a group of mismatched massive buffalo twice the size of ones on Earth. The buffalo might have been all males, she wasn't sure, but the reindeer had young. Their racks stretched so long it was hard to tell where one antler started and another began.

The high grass reached the underbellies of the beasts. In the far corners, she noted a slinking motion and Clarity wondered if dinosaurs were hunting in a pack. She soon found out when a sabre-toothed tiger lunged onto a full-grown reindeer, sinking its over-a-foot-long fangs deep into the animal's throat. Blood spurted soaking the cat's face and throat. Mass panic ensued.

"They do hunt in packs," she whispered. "I wonder if they're female or male or both."

Smaller cats hung back, younger in appearance, learning the trade. Five large cats targeted the same animal. The next attack was to a leg where it was hamstrung. Each cat went after a different artery and backed off, watching and waiting while the deer bled out. The majestic animal wobbled in no time, the ground soaking up the red offering. When it finally fell, Clarity let out a breath she didn't know she'd been holding. Her heart was pounding in her ears at the savagery. It was hard to believe a bigger threat was the hybrids.

She gazed up at Doom. "How on earth do you survive here?"

Doom grinned. "We also hunt in packs."

Clarity recalled a few of the furs she had seen; many were the same as the large cats below. As she turned, she stifled a scream. A massive sabre was no more than fifteen feet from them, head low, hackles raised. Doom lifted his spear.

"Do you really want to mess with me?"

Rage replaced Doom's cocky grin as he clutched his weapon tight. His defiant stance was rock solid as he stood feet braced. Clarity swallowed hard, if she were the cat she'd turn tail, literally, and run. The cat roared and leapt away. The expression on Doom's face would have made her run, too. Her leather shoe booties would be half way to China before her legs would think to move, he was *that* scary.

Doom turned to take her hand. "Come on."

They remained in the higher mountains as they searched. Clarity was watching the landscape for any sign of not only life but also shelters. The mountain was riddled with crevices and small holes children could hide in. Places where people Doom's size, or the hybrids, could never fit.

The forest was quiet until eerie whistles began to gain in tempo. Left, then right the pitch increased or decreased.

"Hybrids?" Clarity whispered.

"Not unless it's their young. Doubtful. The tone is close, but I can tell the difference. I've only ever seen hybrid offspring once out here alone and not in this area."

An arrow hit the tree next to where Doom stood. He glanced at it then scoured the area. With lightning speed he stopped the next arrow aimed near Clarity. Doom snapped the weapon in half over his knee. Before he could toss it to the ground Clarity stopped him.

"What's that on the arrow tip?"

Doom held it up but refrained from touching the stone end. Clarity pulled it closer for a better inspection and squealed.

"Doom, this is sandstone. The goo is that blue substance you showed me at the beach. Of course! Sandstone. I bet the arrow that killed the hybrid was coated in it, too. I thought it was, but wasn't sure."

"There is a great deal of this rock. I thought it was useless."

"It's perfect." She gazed up toward where the arrow originated and yelled. "I'm human. My name is Clarity and I'm from a planet named Earth. Are any of you from Earth?"

"If you're from Earth you should know if you stay with him you'll be killed. He's a murderer."

The young girl was above them on a ledge. Her gaze was stormy and directed at Doom. A cheep to her left and Clarity saw the young boy wrap his arm around the T-rex's mouth. He was still filthy but healthy enough. Clarity crept from Doom's side to move closer.

"Doom doesn't kill anyone," Clarity said.

"He leads people to their deaths. What's the difference?"

The girl held her bow in her hand with quivers in a leather tube on her back. Clarity wondered if the bottom of the tube held sand. She felt her heart race, ideas formed at a quick rate. There was no fear on the girl's face, only contempt for Doom, and curiosity when she gazed at Clarity.

"What's your name?"

"Kiki. My brother is Luke. And the dinosaur is his."

"How long have you been here?"

"A few years."

Clarity was amazed. "How did you survive? Who taught you?"

"Nick found us, and he taught us how to survive," Kiki replied.

"The young man we saw," Clarity said, turning to Doom. "He looked feral."

"Is he with you?" Doom asked.

"Us or the others," Luke said.

Kiki scowled at him. "Shut your mouth."

"What others?" Clarity asked.

"Why so you can kill them?" Her words were spat, vicious. "Nick didn't come to this planet alone from Earth. He came with an older brother. He watched a village while his brother kept him hidden. His brother knew you weren't as you seemed, he was no sheep, and so he snuck Nick food. Found a place right in your village. Nick watched when you led his brother to the slaughter. He ran after that and hid. His brother was right; you and the other village leaders are killers. Not to be trusted."

"That's impossible," Doom shouted. "We would have found the boy if he was in our village."

"You didn't," was her response. "You killed his brother and left a six-year-old boy alone on this planet."

"Six?" Clarity whispered horrified. "Oh my God, he was little more than a baby."

"I didn't know," Doom said. "How old is the boy now?"

"Sixteen, and he hates you; we all do," Kiki yelled and with a hand motioned to Luke. They both took off into one of the low cave openings.

Chapter Eleven

"No wonder he seemed more feral than wild," Clarity said. "What an awful thing to happen. Six years old. I'm going after them. I need to hear more."

"Wait." Doom grabbed her arm. "They might kill you."

"They could have already."

She yanked her arm from his hand and crept toward the dark opening. There was a small amount of light. Doom climbed in after her but after a while, he couldn't fit further. Clarity stopped, made him a fire, and with her flashlight she continued on. The cavern was tight, but the T-rex was muscular and fit, so with a few crawls and climbs she inched her way deeper.

The further she went the darker it became until her small light wasn't much help. The dead end caught her by surprise. She wondered if a place in the rock moved but when she lifted her palm to press against the hard surface she realized it was the heavy black stiff hide of a mammoth hybrid. She pushed with effort and soon was rewarded with light.

Small dirty wary faces greeted her. A girl of about eight stood near Luke holding a bow, an arrow in her hand was ready. Two young boys of perhaps four, fraternal twins, held slingshots. Wary yes, but deadly no doubt. The room contained the rocks which lit when touched. Numerous furs covered the floor. It was a large room made up of beds. It was cleaner than she would have guessed with so many young children. The children must know too much scent in one area was dangerous.

Over an open fire a haunch of raw meat cooked. Dripping bladders hung, the liquid clear, pooled at the base where a tin can sat. Clarity blinked hard. The can wasn't of this world. It was also rusted. She moved forward a bit to peer inside; leather lined it catching the water. Other weapons sat in various places and stages of creation. On a mound of sand sat five blue balls she remembered dotting the shoreline. These children were thinkers.

"Want her dead?"

Clarity spun and noticed a young girl of maybe thirteen, her small breasts under her hide shirt, the only indication puberty set in. Her wild black hair hung below her shoulders, brown eyes gazed daggers. She reminded Clarity of the young cats. The girl was all legs.

"She claims she's from Earth, Nina," Kiki said.

"The real one or the dumb one?"

A few of the children giggled. Clarity wondered at her statement. She had also wondered at one time if some of the people, the other humans, were from her world. She wondered if these children were from Heath's Earth but doubted it.

"Show me your arm," Kiki demanded.

Clarity knew for certain then. There was a mark the girl wanted to see. Clarity held up her smallpox inoculated scared arm. Kiki grinned at her.

"You're the first adult from our Earth I've seen. Nick doesn't have the mark but he's from our Earth all right. He knows about wars and stuff."

"Then it's true." Clarity slumped on a fur-draped log. She then glanced at the children. Each one were sleeveless, all of them bore the same mark high on their left arm. Mass inoculations in the civilized world. Her mind was racing. Not all Earth's humans bore the mark. She glanced at Kiki.

"Do you lead this group? Are there more?"

"There were more but the other children don't learn like we do. If they haven't got the mark, we know it's a matter of time before something gets them. They don't think like us, they aren't able to kill. They're like human Care Bears."

She went to hop up on a mound of furs. The youngest boys curiously approached Clarity. One touched her arm.

"That's Blue," Kiki said. "The other is Cole. Fraternal twins."

Blue had light red hair and vivid blue eyes. His brother was a little taller, Blue was stockier. Cole's hair was dirty blond. His eyes almost as blue as his brother's. Cole held back and Clarity saw immediately the alpha of the two. The young girl, Nina jumped down from her perch and went to sit with Kiki.

"How long have you all been here?" Clarity asked.

"Too long," Nina grouched.

"Does Nick stay here?"

"Sometimes. He's busy this time of year collecting the kids who get sucked down the holes into this crapper of a place," Kiki said.

A high-pitched cheep caught Clarity's attention and she turned to look at the T-rex. His small tail waved back and forth indicating he was anxious, annoyed, or pissed. Clarity's head was reeling.

"I'm sorry, but a dinosaur as a pet? A T-rex? You children should know what a T-rex is."

"Ha," Kiki scoffed. "We sure know what one doesn't look like now. I never saw *his* kind in a museum."

Clarity agreed.

"He's my friend." The indignation dripped from Luke as he scowled at both his sister and Clarity. He went to drape an arm around the dinosaur. "Rex is my friend. I found him as an egg and raised him."

Figures, a boy and his dog...

"I came to propose an idea," Clarity said.

"We're not going anywhere with you," Kiki said.

"I plan on killing those hybrids."

"So do we," Nina said, and with lightning speed fired off an arrow barely missing Clarity's head.

"The sandstone was genius," Clarity said, un-rattled. "I have found material to make bombs and steel for swords to penetrate the hybrids' thick skin. All I ask is you be ready in the spring. I can show you how to make weapons. Yours are fine but you don't have the firepower. I want the hybrids dead."

"I want Doom dead."

Clarity hadn't seen Nick come in. There must be entrances and exits throughout the mountain. The young man was two feet from her, seething, fists balled. If what Kiki said was true she could understand the boy's hatred. Because of Doom he was alone. She had no idea how he could have survived.

The young man wore a breechclout and nothing else. Nick was tall and gangly, wire thin with muscles. His gaze was ancient. Nick's arms appeared odd at a second glance and a noxious odor caught her attention, wafting toward her, radiating from him. He wasn't exactly dirty but he was smeared with—something. There were scars on him. One long gash on his chest drew her attention. He sauntered closer and she wrinkled her nose.

Holy putrid, he must stink the dinosaurs to death.

"The mark, bad," he began and with a closed fist smacked his chest indicating his scar. "I six. Doom took brother, others in jungle, left, *he left*." Nick's voice rose an octave as he struggled with emotions. "All alone. But we not alone. Monsters come. Big, scared me. Brother taken. He kick, screaming, crying. I try help. Filthy beasts, cruel, angry. I slashed. Blood. Hurts. Brother gone. One day I kill the monsters, for brother. The monster you walk with dies, too."

The other children were eerily silent. His words were clipped as though he struggled to speak. Some words were slurred, juvenile. She wondered if he went for years without speaking to anyone. Her heart ached for the lonely boy he must have been and still looked to be.

"I won't deny Doom has done some horrible things in the name of his people. Like you, all they want is life."

"I want death, his and monsters."

Again, his words were stilted as though he hadn't spoken in a long time. A young Tarzan of the dinosaur age. His unruly mat of hair was past his shoulders and cut in an odd fashion. Piercing eyes, green as emeralds, filled with unshed tears. He was a handsome young man, full of rage. Betrayal. The way the others were staring Clarity imagined he was normally quiet. Kiki

188

rose and went to place a hand on his arm. He shook her off and narrowed his gaze onto Clarity.

"Get out and not come back. Not need you. Not want you." He was pointing and screaming.

Clarity rose and for a second saw something flash on Kiki's face, her eyes were sad.

"Nick, she says she can show us how to make bombs. Bombs are things that can explode and kill lots of hybrids. We can fight," Kiki said.

Nick shoved the girl hard enough to send her onto a mound of furs. The youngest girl began to cry and Nina glared at him. The twins ran and hid. Luke balled his fists. Kiki jumped up, eyes blazing.

"First rule," Nina shouted. "We do not hurt one another."

"Out," Nick screamed and waved a fist.

There would be no reasoning with the young man. Clarity turned and went back through the hide. The inside of the cave had been warm and the cavern temperature dropped. Goosebumps dotted her arms. She was going to have to warn Doom. A bomb in the hands of that young man would be aimed at him. The boy *was* wild. Wild with hate.

****

Doom wanted to pace, but the cave interior was too limited. He couldn't stand and he didn't feel like crawling. The ground was cold under his ass. He flexed his fingers in front of the small fire which did little in the way of warmth. In his odd way, he felt by keeping his shirt removed the sacrifices could see. He knew the idea battled a more pressing inkling, he needed to see the victims to know in some strange way they were safe with him. Rarely was he cold. He wondered if it was worry that drew the goose bumps.

Doom tossed the remainder of his tinder onto the small blaze. There were too many crevices to heat. He was anxious for Clarity. His thoughts wandered to ten years prior. He remembered a young man, just turned a man. A fidgety, creepy, strange man. Doom rubbed at his face. The man—Chris, Chase? No, Chaz, his name was Chaz. They found him almost dead babbling at the end of the cold season. He was nursed back to health, and the villagers were grateful; their quota was met. He'd had little time to make an impression on anyone.

The young man was always creeping around. Things went missing around that time, furs, food, pots and pans. Doom wondered if he had been stealing for the boy. He wondered why the bulwarks never found the child. Then he remembered. The bulwarks were young. Muffin was only just born with a sibling that struggled to live. Her mother was killed during delivery. Her alpha father gone as well. An accident had taken the life of the grown beta male. Only one female bulwark was left, and her pregnancy made her tired. It was little wonder a small boy could be kept secret. Without the aid of the older bulwarks, the hunters needed to go out often. The village women were kept busy as well. Chaz was with them for at least six weeks. He hid his little brother for six weeks, and then his brother watched him being led to the slaughter.

Doom wondered if Nick and Chaz met up in the woods that day. The hybrids would have been in full force. They wouldn't have wanted the boy; he was too small. He would have been chased away, or forced. The idea of the child watching his brother killed, or worse, would have eaten at him. All these years. Doom was amazed he survived. Earth children were a sturdy lot.

"Doom," Clarity yelled.

He jumped up, wary of the low ceiling and was grateful when she stumbled from the crevice into his arms. She was sweaty, and her glance at him was filled with concern.

"The wild child, Nick. He showed up. He's got a hard on for you. He wants you dead in the worst way. I'm worried what will happen if he gets his hands on a bomb. Maybe we shouldn't work with these kids. Maybe we should wait until the hybrids are destroyed, and then try reasoning with him. He leads them, he's saved their lives; they won't listen to us."

Doom pulled her from the cave. He was wondering the same thing. But he wasn't concerned for his wellbeing. If the young man was that angry he might not be rational with strong weapons and could accidently kill himself or others.

"We can discuss this when I have you safely home."

"Wait," came a call.

They turned to look at the young girl as she approached. Kiki was hesitant, spooked and glanced around. She stayed within the cave opening.

"Nick didn't really talk when I first met him," Kiki said and continued to fidget as though she were betraying a trust. "He motioned with his hands and whistled like the dinosaurs and made other weird sounds. He took care of me and my brother. We were so scared. That sinkhole we fell through took our lives away. It took our family and friends. I had no clue how to survive out here. He brought us to the cave, gave us food, and made us new clothes. After a while, he remembered how to speak with a few words. We'd be dead without him."

"I don't expect you to betray him," Clarity said. "We'll think of something after the hybrids are gone. Killing them is our main goal."

"But some of us want to learn," she blurted. Her face went red; it was she who wanted to learn. "If those hybrids get their way, they'll kill everything human, or remotely human." She gazed at Doom. "I don't know why you sacrifice humans, but in a way they aren't, at least not humans from Earth. I don't know if Nick is or not, I know I said he was but he was too young when he landed here, before the mass inoculation was going on. I asked him about wars and stuff when the other children who came didn't have the means to survive. We've lost a few. I made the bow and arrow, and the slingshots. He uses instinct. Nick says he thinks he remembers the things I talk about. But he hits his head when he's frustrated. It's scary. So I stopped asking. Me and Nina have gotten close enough to your village to see people you lead away. None of them have the mark, except Clarity."

Kiki's entire demeanor changed. "Clarity is an Earth human. Whether Nick likes it or not, she's one of us, and we won't sit by while she's slaughtered. In time I know Nick will come around to thinking the same."

Doom knew it was a threat and he'd seen her aim, the threat wasn't idle. She'd pick him off in a heartbeat when the time came.

"Why haven't you or Nick tried to kill me before?"

"Nick's aim is bad. His arms were broken, once when he was attacked by a hybrid trying to defend his brother, and then the year I met him. He's crooked. I know he feels pain. He asked me to kill you last time, but I couldn't. There's so much death."

From her guilty look, Doom knew she had come close. He moved forward and placed his hand on her shoulder. She stood straighter gazing up at him. He could see her strength her character. She was like Clarity.

"We are going to kill these hybrids." He leveled his gaze onto her eyes. She was a pretty little thing. At that moment she was vulnerable. "Once we do, there will be no sacrifices. You will be welcome into the village. You are welcome now, but I know you won't leave until the threat has passed."

"What about Nick?"

"I can't change the past; I can only try to defend the future. You're right about Clarity, she must not die, and I will give my life to save her."

Kiki gaped at him and then glanced at Clarity. "I can get into the hybrids' home. I've done it before. I know where they hibernate. I know a lot about them."

"Do you know what they want humans for?" Clarity asked.

They moved to the mouth of the cave as she spoke. The sunlight was bright and the warmth welcome as they stood. Kiki shuffled her feet for a moment.

"I saw the babies in a nest once." She went pale. "They were eating, at least two of them were. The third hybrid baby was dead. They don't eat their own but I don't know what killed the other."

"What were they eating?" Doom asked.

"A brain, maybe human. My dad was a doctor, so I'd seen pictures of all kinds of anatomy. I thought I'd barf and felt woozy so I ran. I haven't been near a nest since."

A loud sharp whistle sounded and Kiki spun, she gasped and raced off. High on the mountain they saw a young man, fists balled. Doom knew once the threat passed there would be a time of reckoning. He wouldn't kill a child, but he wouldn't let the boy take him from Clarity, or worse, her from him. The idea shot fear into his heart. Doom pulled Clarity behind him. Nick vanished.

****

Mornings were spent making bombs and weapons. The first sword Doom ever held swayed back and forth in his hands, and people gathered with interest. He took a few practice swings after Clarity explained. The sword was made for a man his size. The mold was cast for his needs and his men's size. Clarity felt a smaller sword might be sent flying if swung too hard. A life-size dummy hybrid was set up with a double thick hide. Doom plunged the steel into the hide and gasps followed when he penetrated easier than anyone had ever seen.

Clarity couldn't help the smile that split her face. Everyone saw the implication. *Welcome to the new world order.* After the first demonstration, there were more. The bombs were detonated in controlled areas. They left hide-covered dummies in the protected caves, shut the doors, and waited until the smoke settled. The dummies were in pieces. Clarity assured them the hybrids would suffer the same fate.

A catapult was made after they gathered the multitude of glowing rocks on the sand with sandstone. Strict watch was sent out to make certain no hybrid was watching. Their first attempt was at a woolly rhino. The beast stumbled and lay unmoving after being hit with eight of the glowing stones. It died when Doom and Edge slit its throat. As the villagers stood around watching the animal's lifeblood drain into the ground, they were humbled. After the weapon hit a hybrid, it would need to be dispatched in the same way. The hybrids would see death approach, but their motionless bodies would be unable to tremble in fear. Some were glad.

Each night Doom and Clarity fell into bed exhausted. Both were bruised from battle games. Their fighting done in secret, underground, away from prying eyes. The outside traps were used only on animals and watched closely. As soon as the trap worked, it was dismantled. There were times when Clarity saw Kiki or Nina. There was longing on their faces. Their gazes indicated a desire to belong. She was tempted to hand them firecrackers but knew she had to wait.

Doom adamantly refused the wild children's help. As the days progressed, more outsiders were found. There were no other Earth humans but Clarity determined the planet the people hailed from was exactly like hers in only some ways. These were a gentler people. They had never known war or disease, there was no need to inoculate. A society of bubble-wrapped humans where life for all was pleasant and caring. The idea gave Clarity a better understanding as to why they never questioned Doom's actions. The humans were lambs. They knew nothing of terrorists; none had ever experienced the threat. These humans didn't know what mass destruction was but again never experienced it. The mere idea there were no threats of possible scenarios made their culture complacent. It was as though the sinkholes selected the meek. And the weak, there were a few with deformities, not illness. Failings in their body system made them slower physically.

A frightening thought occurred to Clarity that these people were selected for extinction. Maybe they didn't fit in with a bubble-wrapped society. Heath seemed to have no failings except he was the last man to touch a sword. He seemed guilty when holding it. Doom's people didn't have much to work with in the way of an army, but Clarity vowed to turn them into soldiers.

The only tricky area was involving other villagers' clans. The hybrids wouldn't allow large meetings between others. Only a few at a time for trading. Doom and Menace were always the ones to go, and they traded weapons for simple furs and other items not really needed. To return empty-handed would be suspicious. The guise of furs laden with swords and bombs was met with some resistance by others, but all were interested.

It would take some doing, but by spring the villagers needed to be armed to the teeth. Clarity convinced Doom the best way would be during hibernation. Clarity and other humans could make the trip to nearer villagers and leave weapons and bombs. Once awake, the trading would begin in full force. There would be no suspicion, the hybrids would assume the villagers traded for humans—and they would. Clarity planned on having every human in Doom's care trained. Then distributed to show how the weapons worked. Farther villagers could be reached and so on. By sacrifice time, they would be ready to launch their assault.

****

Clarity hunkered down beside the inky black substance. Doom was decidedly skeptical. His scowl furrowed his brows.

"This is oil," Clarity said.

"Black mess."

"If we can build the containers to hold it, we can boil it and dump it onto the hybrids. It's nasty bad when hot and sticky."

"There are ponds of this," Doom said. "But it smells different."

Clarity rose and stood before him. "I think you mean tar. And yeah, tar is a mess but heavier. I do have an idea for new tar pits. The hybrids I bet have scoured every inch of these forests, but they won't suspect new holes dug filled with tar and covered over. Especially if at the bottom of the pits are sharp spears with metal tips."

"You're a real badass."

Clarity smiled. "That's the general idea of war." She frowned then. "You say you've come across their offspring. When we saw the little ones, I wasn't expecting the way they interacted with DaV-nin. You say they kill the females, but we saw one."

"No doubt she was his and spared."

"Still, we have to wonder what we are going to do with the little ones. They look like dinosaurs and humanoid. Neanderthals were different, they looked different, but I wouldn't want to kill a child of theirs. Or someone helpless."

"All hybrids I've seen are grown males except the three young ones, the young ones I came across who were wild like animals, and the young ones with DaV-nin. Plus the dead females. I don't know how to tell the good from bad if there are any."

"You said you have a big sleep. You hibernate for six weeks?"

"Yes. We store massive amounts of food. During the deepest part of winter we all go into a single room and sleep together. The hybrids might do the same. We need to find Kiki and see what else she knows. Maybe we could trade her something small in return. In our history, there is no mention of any hybrid attacking during the sleeping time. And we are the most vulnerable then."

"Have you ever tried not to sleep?"

"Yes. There were a few, but the experience ages them. In six weeks, if we do not sleep, we will age decades. Normally our hearts give out. The few who stayed awake were exhausted, fighting their bodies' needs. They died shortly after. To age so fast in so little time isn't good for anyone. Why, what are you thinking?"

"Humans don't hibernate."

"I know. It's why they watch the children. We were lucky to find out before human children came that they don't hibernate. If locked in a room with us, they would be dead by the time we awoke. I don't want to imagine a young one pulling on my arms for food or comfort and not understanding why I ignore their needs. It would be a cruel way to die. I'm grateful you came, Clarity. I'm grateful to you for so many things."

With Doom, she never needed to question his motives when he spoke from the heart. He only ever spoke from the heart. An endearing quality. She lifted her hand to cup his face.

"I'm happy to be here with you. Win or lose."

A smile split his face. "Even if we lose, I win. One year of life with you is better than a hundred years without you."

"You realize when you say things like that my insides look like that puddle of oil, right?"

He wrapped her in his arms. Her chin rested on his chest as she gazed up at him. "That oil is dark, I can see dark. You are light. I feel light; it warms my heart and heats my insides. If you mean I make you feel like a puddle of goo, I'll take that as a compliment. I only hope you experience even half of what I do when we touch. My insides melt into vibrant life. There is peace in your arms. I knew I was broken when we met, but I never thought it possible you would fix me. How stupid am I when I didn't think there was a word to replace another in my heart. Love, Clarity. The word 'love' can fix the word 'broken'."

She couldn't help but smile when he lowered to taste her lips; she kissed him hard. The jungle forest was no place for a tryst. They parted, but her insides were warm with want. After a few deep breaths, she became all business.

"We can mold bigger baskets with the strong leather, heat it up, and use smaller baskets, too, for single drops. Near the village, we need to make sure the area is protected. You have children in your village; their safety is paramount. And I noticed something about Flight. He has a mark for an inoculation. When was he found?"

"I found him the same day as you."

"I wonder if he came through a sinkhole on my planet near my home. I've heard him talk of guns."

"There were children in the beginning when the sinkholes opened who behaved as the boy. They spoke of guns and knives."

"All sacrificed?"

Doom nodded; his expression sad. "Not as children, and only after we had no choice. After a time, the children who came through the sinkholes were meeker, gentler."

"I can't help but think there's another force screwing with us, our worlds." The idea grew and nagged.

"I've thought of that. What if you weren't meant to be here? What if whatever wanted you still wants you?"

Clarity grinned at him. "Why do you think I carry the mace and the taser?"

"Badass for sure."

They stood and continued on. Before long, Kiki came into view. Clarity knew she was following them. The young girl was too curious. It appeared Doom was also expecting her. He removed a bomb from his satchel. Clarity gripped his arm.

"This is a weapon of great magnitude," Doom said. "It has the ability to rip through many hybrids especially in an enclosed area."

Kiki licked her lips and tried not to appear too excited, and failed miserably. "What do you want for it?"

"Information."

"About the hybrids?"

"Anything you know that can help."

"I can do better than that; I can get you into their lair."

"There's a condition." Clarity stepped forward.

"That bomb is dangerous; you need to keep it from the little ones. It's also for the enemy. Doom isn't your enemy."

"No, he's not *my* enemy."

"What happened to Nick's brother, Chaz?" Kiki's eyes widened as Doom spoke. "Yes, I know his name and remember him. It was beyond my control. You have lived here; you know what the hybrids are like."

"We choose to fight." Kiki's features turned into a snarl of anger.

"The hybrids don't waste their time with you, you're children. You're ignored and found an amusement. Until you're older, then you'll have to really watch. They hunted my people into the ground. Day after endless day we ran and hid. Do you think a threat from Nick scares me?" Doom was doing some snarling of his own. "What would you do to protect your family, how far would you go? Look at me and these marks long and hard before you judge and say I don't care."

Kiki gazed at the tattoos. She moved forward to study them further. She lifted her hand to trace her finger over the face of a young woman.

"I saw her." Her voice was an awed whisper. "She was young, only a few years older than Nick, maybe his brother's age when he was sacrificed. She ran but it was no use. I tried to call to her, to help, but a hybrid came after me. I was grabbed. I thought I was a goner for sure, but he released me. I swear the monster laughed in my face. God, I was scared to death. I was so helpless."

"So was I."

Doom's features were heavy with his guilt and remorse.

"But you're a grown man," Kiki insisted.

"I was taught to run and hide, not to fight. I can hunt, I can kill, but I know how to think. For every one of the hybrids killed, ten of us, or more were slaughtered. When you face the little dinosaurs in groups do you fight or hide?"

"Hide."

"There are times you know you're outnumbered and you need to retreat."

"Doom is right," Clarity said. "But no more retreating once we're ready. With your help, we can be ready sooner."

Kiki nodded. She led them through the thick foliage toward where Clarity and Doom had seen DaVnin with the younger hybrids. She skirted past the cave openings, rising higher on the mountain. Near the back of the mountain where it sloped straight up there was a small cave. Kiki pulled foliage from the opening and waved them in.

"There's just enough light to take us from cave to cave. But in places there is darkness, so we have to be careful," Kiki said.

Clarity pulled out her flashlight and turning a corner she clicked it on. The walls were a solid grey, depressing.

"I haven't seen a flashlight in years," Kiki said, excitement in her tone. "When we first got here Luke howled for his nightlight. Nick found him a glowing rock but for it to work it needed heat so my brother kept it clutched to his chest every night."

"You must miss your family," Clarity said.

"My mom mostly. Dad worked all the time. They're gone. I wish I had my mother. I have so many questions about becoming a woman. Same with Nina, she's close. We talk but I don't know—much."

Kiki glanced at Doom and went beet red in the soft glow of light. She straightened her shoulders and slipped around another bend. She reached to click the flashlight off.

"We have to be careful. No noise or light."

Clarity could see why when she peeked around the corner. An adult hybrid was alone in the cave with a young male hybrid. They sat on furs. The young male was younger than she thought when she caught his profile in a torch light. Doom stiffened. The young hybrid's features were softer, almost sweet. The brow ridges and dinosaur features would harden as he aged, but for now, he looked half-human. From the way Doom was shaking it was apparent he recognized the child.

"Hers," Kiki whispered and Clarity turned to see the girl trace a tattoo on Doom's chest. He immediately gripped her fingers and squeezed his eyes closed. Doom grabbed them both and dragged them from the cave and into the light. His breathing was rapid, ragged.

"How?" He started to cry out then lowered his voice. It wasn't enough; Clarity could tell he was devastated.

Further he dragged them into the foliage to escape detection. Clarity's mind was racing. The boy had human features and Kiki was right he was the spitting image of the young woman tattooed on Doom's chest. When Doom finally stopped he pulled Clarity close.

"How?" he raged. "They can't mate."

"We don't know what their offspring look like when born, or hatched. How big they are. Human bones won't support the dinosaur weight or height," Clarity said.

"I've seen both live births and eggs," Kiki said.

Doom dropped Clarity's arms and spun on Kiki. "When?"

"After the harvest. I think the offspring are born in the safety of the cave soon after the harvest. I don't know. They're taken to a nest where they're watched. I stay away. I only happened to see the young after this harvest." She seemed thoughtful, then scared. "I think Nick knows. He won't say what he knows, only to stay away from the beasts."

"Will he tell us, me?" Clarity asked.

"I don't know. Maybe. I can ask, but then he'll know I've been helping you. He might be mad."

"Risk it," Doom said.

Chapter Twelve

Clarity could see the tension on Doom as he paced the fur. Clenching and unclenching his fists he stopped stared into space then paced again.

"We'll figure out what they're doing," Clarity said.

"I don't know if I want to know." Doom's whisper was racked with desolation. He spun to face her and pointed at the young woman tattooed on his chest. "That hybrid's face is hers. How can that be?"

"I don't know. Our human structure is smaller than yours. Maybe it's a mix of human, Neanderthal, and dinosaur. I don't understand either. Our bone mass is no good if yours wasn't. All I can think of is there must be a hybrid—hybrid."

"A hybrid mix?"

"Maybe not all of the males born are mixing with humans in some way. They can't have sex, it would be impossible."

"I need to find out what Nick knows."

Clarity went to him. She ran her finger down his cheek. "I can go…" But he stopped her words.

"I did this."

"The hybrids did this. Deep down, I think Nick knows this. He saw you lead his brother from the safety of the village but that's all. The hybrids are the killers. You had no choice, but you do now. The other humans here aren't like me. I know war and terrorists. I've seen fear, but my fear can be fought. You didn't know how."

"I need to learn better. I need you to make me into a weapon." His hands on her shoulders tightened and she winced.

Pain assaulted her being. Everything she loved about him could change. She knew the dangers when bringing new technology into a struggling environment would have disastrous repercussions. But to change a gentle giant into a killer…

"I will teach you to become skilled."

Perhaps he saw the sadness in her gaze, or the way her shoulders now slumped, Doom lifted a hand and caressed her cheek with tenderness.

"I will learn to be skilled. I'm sorry for my words. You don't make love to a bomb, or a sword, an axe or any weapon. You love a man. Skills are far better."

Clarity smiled and kissed his palm. "You have skills all right."

"Do you have any coats left?"

"I think I can find one or a few."

Doom placed his hands on her ass to pull her against his growing erection. He hardened under her and his length grew to press higher on her belly.

"You have the perfect cock."

Doom gave her a mischievous gaze. "Are there imperfect cocks? Cocks that don't urinate? Come? Grow?"

"Let's just say you function with perfection."

"I'm a well-oiled machine."

Clarity burst out laughing. "How do you know what a machine is?"

"I hear humans talk. They think you're a drill sergeant."

"Do they? What else do they say?"

Clarity went to her purse and opened a small square. She snapped the rubber in her hands. Doom grinned and backed up until he flopped onto the bed.

"Heath thinks you're hot. Menace is fascinated by you, and Edge, well he'd like to spank your pretty ass."

"I'd like to taser his."

"That's why he keeps his distance and his comments to himself."

"He's smarter than he looks."

"Flight adores you, so do the other children. They love Bubble-gum. The dog seems happy to play with them and he loves Muffin." Doom rolled his eyes.

"Why do you give the children new names?"

"New parents, new home, new planet. Seems sensible. Some of the children here have forgotten they lived somewhere else. They can't cling to the hope of returning. This *will* be home; it needs to be home. Parents name their children."

"I suppose."

Clarity dropped her clothes as she approached him. She wanted to think of no one but Doom. None of the interior lights were lit. The small, enclosed fire burned for warmth in the cool depths of the home. Doom slipped from his pants. She stood admiring his beauty. The tattoos, and what they represented, told a story. For Doom, the story was pain but to Clarity not all of their tales were sad. Some faces on his body smiled. Doom mentioned the humans were coveted for a year, they had been happy the entire time, perhaps missing family, but they were wanted.

As she approached, she had a thought that made her laugh and cringe. Doom gazed at her in an odd way.

207

"What?" he asked.

"It's pretty morbid."

"My cock?"

"Yes and no. I was thinking if I did somehow get taken, would my face be tattooed on your…"

"Don't say it," he warned. "I'd spend every second crying and alternately caressing you."

"Okay you upped my morbid."

"My up is coming down."

"I can fix that."

Clarity placed the rubber off to the side, wanting to taste him. Doom lay back with his legs spread and his feet touching the floor. His muscular thighs were a magnet. Power, masculine, rugged. She traced her fingers up those perfect thighs to her main goal. The sheer length of him made her quiver with want. The way he gazed at her filled her with tenderness. Lust and love, there was no fine line, the two were separate. And yet, she burned for him while she ached for his soul to need hers.

"You take my breath away," she said and caressed his hard swollen length.

"You are my breath."

Clarity poised over him and took his appendage into both hands. She blew on the tip of his erection loving how he jumped under her flesh. Her tongue laved down his long length and he shuddered. Clarity squealed when he grabbed her and flipped them. She was under him, his cock near her mouth. When his tongue explored her lower lips she gasped. His heat lit her fire. There was no smoking ember; she was melting.

"You run through my veins," she heard him mumble.

She didn't reply but respond. There was no more waiting. Her lips opened to suck as much of him as she could deep within her throat. The muscles on his legs rippled. Harder deeper he went while she cupped his stallion-sized balls. She damned nature for not allowing all of him to fit. Doom's fingers spread her to lick her insides while she writhed.

There was no holding back when she gave herself to him. Her body shook and she gripped his base with a harder squeeze. He groaned and tried to pull from her but she wouldn't allow him to leave.

"Clarity." His word was strangled. He was going to come, and she knew it.

His seed exploded into her and Clarity thrashed wanting him but never having allowed a man to do that before she was surprised with the force. He pulled from her and she gasped in ragged amounts of air. Her hand dragged across her mouth before she gripped his neck and pulled him to a breast. Doom sucked hard, drawing her into his mouth. His hand roughly kneaded her other breast making her whimper.

Doom broke contact, lifted her and threw her higher onto the bed. His fingers dug into her thighs as he rubbed her flesh. He leaned to taste her warmth. It wasn't long before he was hard again, having years to make up for with his loss. He rolled the condom over his cock and plunged into her heat. Clarity screamed from the power he used. A rock solid brick wall was hammering between her spread thighs. His hand pinned her wrists over her head.

"The only time your face will be on my cock is when you're sucking it." The words were snarled, a heated promise.

That was a fine idea to Clarity, but she couldn't speak. Each thunderclap against her grew more demanding until sweat poured from them, mingling. Her wrists tugged on his hand, but he kept her prisoner. Higher she lifted her legs, demanding every inch. The fur beneath them began to bunch as they rocked. She used her fingers to steady her against the headboard. Clarity gasped and watched as firelight flickered beautifully against the stones. The headboard seemed on fire. Clarity was on fire with need.

"Doom," she cried out as she came and as he thrust a final time and shuddered before rolling from her onto his back. He groaned.

"Clarity?"

"Hmm."

"Your coats don't work worth shit."

****

When Doom and Clarity exited his home they saw all of his villagers gaping with awe. Clarity knew why soon. Kiki and the other children were there. On the outskirts of the village they waited. Doom and Clarity strode forward. There were tears in Kiki's eyes. The twins were sobbing. Little Cole was in Nina's arms, Blue in Kiki's.

"Nick wants to see you." She was gazing at Doom.

"Why have you come?"

"I told Nick what you want and he told me to take the children to you, well Clarity really. He wants us to learn to defend ourselves. Whether you win or lose, we will all grow up and the hybrids will pick us off one by one. The age difference is too great. I told Nick that, I figured out what you meant about us being only children and of no use. They will want me soon. They'll go after Nick soon, maybe as soon as next year. Then me, then Nina. Em and Luke will be left alone with the twins and any other child Nick finds before he's killed."

"I'll find Nick," Doom stated and began to walk away.

Clarity grabbed his arm. "I'm coming."

Doom gripped her shoulders and gazed into her eyes. "He wants me dead. I won't take chances with you."

"Doom," a voice bellowed.

Menace and a few village men came forward. There were five human men and three human females with them. Menace carried a young woman in his arms. Clarity raced to him. The woman was unconscious. Clarity's heart began to pound.

"Doom, look." She pointed at her arm. "The vaccine. She's from my Earth." Both gave each other open-mouthed stares.

****

Doom told Clarity to stay with Menace and wait for the woman to wake up. Clarity was hesitant but he promised her he would be fine. Nick knew of his existence for years, he could have killed him. Doom didn't mention he noticed Kiki no longer had the bomb. Clarity would figure it out fast so he had to hurry.

The mountain where the children lived was close and Doom was moving fast. He wanted the confrontation over with. Clarity would worry the entire time he was gone. He knew he was being watched; he could feel it. He wanted answers and he was positive Nick knew something.

Nick stalked Doom. Undaunted Doom spun in a slow circle watching the teen as he moved above him from rock to rock. In his hand he held the bomb Kiki received for information. The other hand held a match. He only needed one. Nick chuckled when Doom eyed the weapon.

"No worries," Nick said. "This for my safety. We face after hybrids dead. I want you pass message to Clarity."

"What message?"

"DaV-nin wants her. He wants eggs, whatever that mean. He want taste her brain. He thinks there be harvest, is good. Your battle, Kiki told me, is go."

"What else do you know?"

"Hybrids sleep, wake when you do. Not like too cold. Some go to heat. Not all. Vul-ner-able under nose. Only five females of own they breed. Don't know how breed, but see human female's guts ripped open, low on belly like they look for something. She alive when they do it. Female's death horrible."

Doom knew he was being taunted. The words were short but understandable. Nick had a vile smirk on his face. The boy wanted him to suffer. The young man wasn't done. Doom already wanted to vomit with the images. Hate ruled the boy-man before him.

"They pin woman down, slice claw in belly, pull something out. Then she killed for brain. Your fault, *Doom*."

"The hybrids do the killing."

"You give victims. You bad. Cruel. Hate you. *Hate you*."

Nick jumped down the side of the cliff and was gone. Doom's heart was racing. The hybrids held the humans for a month. Maybe it took them that long for the hunt. Doom wondered if they waited for a certain time when their females were fertile. Clarity and the other human females had a bleeding time each month. The village women no longer did but Doom wasn't so naive he didn't know the bleeding was associated with sex and babies. Anything was possible. He raced back to Clarity and found her in Menace's home. The female had yet to wake.

"When she wakes take her to the main hall," Doom commanded. He wasted no time grabbing Clarity's hand and taking her to his home and told her what Nick had said.

"My ovaries? My brain? What are they, hybrid zombies?" Clarity asked. "Unless they figured out a way to…shit, that's gross. If they take my ovaries and mix them with their sperm and put it back into a host's body, but that's crazy." She slumped onto the bed.

"No, it's not crazy." Doom gazed into space before sitting next to her. "When Alice came she spoke of being with a man and they couldn't have children. They did something she said a test tube, maybe."

"Do you think DaV-nin could be a result of that?"

"Maybe, somehow. But if they consume brains, she would have been dead before her ovaries were harvested."

"Damn, stem cell memories. I guess it depends on how fast their stem cell memories work. If it's instantaneous then there might have been time. Didn't you say it took a month for the tattoos to appear?"

"Yes."

"Maybe it's not their females but humans they wait for. There is a certain time when a woman ovulates in a month. Holy hell, what if they wait for a human female to ovulate—the best time to try for a child? How old are the humans when they come here?"

"The males are of all ages, the females are thirty and under mostly but not all. I think you're right. They are looking for knowledge. They are breeding."

"If the ovaries are used and a host, the bones might be as strong. If the hybrids use cell memory that fast, the baby within might be conditioned to grow strong. From necessity. Dinosaur DNA to adapt to grow and thrive. Shit. Every harvest they are getting smarter. Heath said they were on the verge of space flight. Soon the hybrids will have all the information they'll need. Even without me. The hybrids need to be destroyed. We need to get busy."

"Come on."

Doom took her hand and they raced to the main room where everyone was gathered and arguing. Luke had his arms wrapped around Rex. It was clear the villagers weren't impressed with the dinosaur in their midst. Bubble-gum was snapping at the dinosaur. Flight was outraged the dinosaur was upsetting the dog. Luke was ready to kill anyone who came near. Doom jumped up on the long table and held his hands up for quiet. He was happy to see Menace, and the female recently found was nestled into his arms. Many new faces stared at him, he guessed the arguing stemmed from them being brought up to speed. It made his job easier.

"We know what the hybrids are after," Doom shouted. As he expected there were calls of questions. He held his hands splayed for silence. When the room settled he began again. "The hybrids are taking the human females' ovaries and somehow impregnating their females with them. They then eat the brains of the humans for their memories."

The female in Menace's arms swayed and he pulled her tighter to his chest. Doom motioned to her.

"You, what's your name?"

"She's Solace. And we determined she's from Clarity's Earth," Menace said.

"Well damn, does she have a taser, too?" Edge grumbled.

"What happened to you?" Clarity asked.

"I work at a daycare," Solace said, she placed a hand to her head. "We, a few children and me, were sitting and playing. There was a commotion. A sinkhole above the children dropped strange toys. Before I could stop them, the children threw some of their toys up into the blackness. Then, one boy stood up. The blackness began to fall and before I could grab the child, he reached up. The second his fingers touched the darkness, he was sucked in. Then we all were. I tried to hold onto them all but was yanked away in the dark. I lost them. How could I lose them? I was responsible for them. Two and three year olds, gone. They aren't here. Menace said no children came through the sinkhole with me or the other people. I don't know any of these other people. I feel so alone."

Solace began to sob, and Menace comforted her. Clarity stood beside Doom, and they clutched hands. Doom could see the sadness in Clarity's eyes; he could also see the determination grow.

"We need to think bigger faster, if we're going to save all three of our planets," Clarity said. "Every second we have between now and the next sacrifice matters. We need to break up into groups. Solace, do you know anything about weapons?"

She dried her tears with the back of her hand.

"Sure, I'm an army brat."

Clarity's smile beamed letting Doom know Solace being a self-proclaimed brat was a good thing.

"Gather together," Doom shouted. "This is what we're going to do."

****

The long process of making fertilizer mixed with coal dust, molasses, and oil was tedious and Clarity had to make certain of safe storage. The shelter, constructed away from the underground homes, was difficult to reach during the high snow and impossible during a blizzard. Nothing could be made unless Clarity and others could remove their work from the main hall. The last thing she wanted was an explosion. Solace helped make crossbows from wood, the metal tips of arrows rolled in the light blue substance. Solace informed them her father had a fondness for making wooden gun barrels that he shared with her on numerous occasions as she was growing up. Solace was an only child and her father was indulgent, teaching her everything he felt a young woman needed to know in this world to survive. The information was put to good use. They lined the barrels with sandstone to shoot small pieces of debilitating blue matter separated by sandstone and rolled by sandstone.

The long process of making glass was difficult but Clarity wanted glass tips and boxes. An idea formed in her mind the first time she heard of what the blue stones could do and how she could harvest their power. The glass needed to be strong enough to not break with simple use but to shatter when dropped.

Baking soda and vinegar were easy staples and though Doom wouldn't like it, she planned on using many of her condoms for a surprise on the hybrids. Balloon bombs shot with an arrow over an intended target. She planned to fill a few condoms with a noxious substance, hoping to blind their enemy.

"Flight?" Clarity said bending down hands on her knees.

The boy came running over with the dog. Bubblegum was taller than the boy. He loved all of the children but held a fondness for a little boy who always seemed left out. It didn't help his expressions were laughed at, though the words weren't meant to be unkind. When Flight mentioned to Ada his mother used to tell him she loved him with all her heart, the woman scoffed and asked the boy how you love with that particular organ. She went on to say you don't love with your kidneys or intestines.

Clarity was relieved the other children, her Earth children, took to him easily. Flight managed to smile a little more when he was understood. He wasn't ignored by Luke when they wanted to tussle. The other children knew nothing of hands-on play.

She put her hands on his shoulders. "How would you like to help me make paper for balloons?"

His face lit up like a Christmas tree. "Oh, boy would I ever. Can I use some?"

"Sure. We're going to need pulp and water and make a screen. Later I can show you how to make grass paper."

Flight was practically tap dancing. Clarity taught all of the children to make firecrackers. Village women taught human females how to make baskets for the oil they would heat. Steel was melted in droves. Tomahawks were given hooked ends, deadly for slitting hamstrings. The humans they found beside Solace were squeamish and timid but when informed of their fate worked with a vengeance. Using a long soft hide and charcoal, Doom and Clarity mapped out the areas they would set traps. The hybrid home was underlined. They would strike there first. Clarity was forming her own plan in her mind. The big sleep would be a big boon.

They all worked hard and were starving by the end of the day. Clarity made an iron pan and seared a hunk of meat from a giant reindeer on all sides, using the flavored butter, salt, and herbs to season. She dowsed the meat often with the wooden spoon scooping up the juice. Doom declared the meat delicious. Fast rolls were made. Sleepy children were carried to beds in their own homes. Bubble-gum followed Flight. Clarity knew Muffin slept outside the child's door. The bulwark was smitten with the dog.

Soon after dinner it was time to retire for the night. The children from Kiki's group plus one T-rex were placed in a home of their own. Clarity watched Luke clutch a small stone of light to his chest as his sister pulled a fur over him. She glanced up at Doom.

"They're all so young," she whispered.

"They're smart."

"They're strong. They don't want to be on this planet. I wish we could get them home."

Doom placed his hand on her shoulder to guide her to their home. "I think the girls are happy to be around you."

She knew he was right. It didn't stop her from wishing. "I wonder if there's any hope of returning them."

Doom took her in his arms as the door slid back.

"Do you want to leave?" His sadness crashed over his features.

Clarity cupped his cheek with her palm. "I am exactly where I want to be."

"Even though I drool in my sleep?"

"Meh, what's a little spit?" Doom grinned as she sauntered toward the bed. She sat and patted the fur beside her. "Besides it's your farting that really kills me."

Doom stood with his mouth open and Clarity laughed. He then tossed his head back and laughed, too. The sound was as surprising as it was pleasing. Even on this Earth the word fart was a mood breaker. Doom was breathtaking when he laughed. He was still chuckling as he dropped his belt and pants.

Chapter Thirteen

As the weather began to change, Clarity loved the massive falls Doom brought her to. Water teemed over to fall and break new-forming ice. Crystalized ice glistened over rocks. Nearby, green pine needles dripped water from the round wet tips as ice melted. At night, winter was dominant; during the day, the sun lazily claimed back parts of its domain. Clarity could almost envision the sultry cheeky smile of Mother Nature as she taunted the elements.

It was Doom's idea they get away for quiet time. Every waking moment was spent making bombs and planning strategies. Menace and others smuggled the new weapons to the closer villages who in turn smuggled them to farther villages. Knowledge was shared about the planning. Excitement was growing and villagers had to remember to walk with caution if confronted with a hybrid. One small slip and disaster would strike if a hybrid decided to make a meal of a villager, rare but known to happen.

"In movies, it always seems danger lurks around every corner," Clarity said.

"It does here, but dinosaurs have a certain respect for me and my men. We hunt well."

Doom was never without his spear. He had a new weapon hidden in a sheath at his rope belt. A knife, the blade steel, the handle bone. All the villagers wore one, including the children. All villagers were becoming skilled in hand-to-hand combat with Solace's training. She proved a huge boon to their cause. For now, the swords remained hidden, their number growing in all homes.

"I think Menace is falling in love with Solace," Clarity said.

Doom snorted. "Falling? He falls any harder and he'll be his own sinkhole."

"I loaned her a few coats for precaution."

"Well damn not too many I hope."

"No, not too many. I need a few for another reason I'll tell you about later. It's a good thing I bought a box before I fell down the rabbit hole."

"You're ready for anything, well at least your purse is. Now you have the other women making purses."

"Mine comes in handy, but it's easier to carry what I need in few smaller sacks at my hip. Out here you have to ready for anything."

"Be ready to be amazed."

As they slipped through the foliage, Clarity sucked in her breath to see massive long necked dinosaurs. They were high enough they could look down on them. Between their feet were smaller dinosaurs, all herbivores, quiet and calm. In her mind, she wondered if T-rex were still huge if he'd come crashing through the serenity and scatter everything. The blood would follow. This planet was growing on her. Few dinosaurs ventured near her when Doom was around.

"Your planet is dangerous but calmer than I would have imagined for a place filled with dinosaurs."

"Years ago, it wasn't as calm. The hybrids were out of control. Death was rampant. One human changed their thought process." Doom slipped his hand into hers. "I can see how that's possible."

On tiptoes, she kissed him. Her arms snaked up around his neck as the kiss deepened. A slight movement to her right and she jumped back howling. A massive cave hyena was watching them. Doom gripped his spear and took aim. A flurry of activity was in their wake in seconds. Kiki was in front of him with her arms held splayed.

"No, wait, Bongo is my friend. His mother was dead and I picked him up and refused to part with him. Nick would only let me keep him a year in our cave. Besides he grew too big." Kiki raced to ruff up the cave hyena's mane and place herself between man and beast.

Doom shook his head then cocked it sideways. "Are all children full of this many surprises?"

Clarity chuckled. "More."

"There is no way that beast is coming into my village."

Kiki smiled. "He doesn't need to. He just wants to check on me from time to time. He'll stay away from the village. He wouldn't like Muffin."

Doom was grumbling. "Muffin, Bubble-gum, and Bongo. Do you females ever pick decent names?"

The hyena ambled away after a few more pats and scratches. Clarity wondered how often Kiki followed them.

"Are they still kissen?" A voice called. Kiki groaned.

"Luke, I told you to be quiet."

Luke came lumbering out of the foliage with his hands stuck in the pockets of his tanned pants. Rex followed. The dinosaur gave the boy's hair a playful chomp until he was pushed away.

"I ain't no snack," Luke grouched.

"Where are the other children?" Clarity asked.

"Blue and Cole like Solace, she plays cool games, for babies," Luke said. "Nina is crazy, every time Menace says anything she giggles and sighs. Oh, Menace, that's wonderful; you're so smart." He tittered rolling his eyes.

Clarity hid a laugh behind her hand. "The others?"

"Em's hanging out with the kid named Flight," Kiki said, she seemed sad.

"What is it honey?" Clarity asked.

"Em's afraid to talk to the other kids, the other human kids that aren't our human. She made friends with a boy last year; he was ten. He was killed. She refuses to like the others, afraid they'll die, too."

"They always do," Luke said and again rolled his eyes. "They don't have the good sense to run when they need to. I always tell them find your damned feet."

"Luke."

"Well, it's what Nick says."

"All right, back we go to the village," Doom said while Luke protested. "Back, let's go."

"Geez. You gonna kiss her again?"

"Luke," Kiki yelled again.

"None of your business, and stop following us," Doom said.

"Kissy kissy," Luke said swaggering. Doom swatted his ass.

****

The first snowfall was met with delight and dread. Within the safety of the village, the children could play when not making weapons. It was common to see

Muffin and Bubble-gum roughhousing, and it was also plain to see in the coming months a new mixture including dog would be born. Doom showed no anxiety, he was happy to let the bulwark have her pups. They would be kept safe in the area made for the new children who slept together with Muffin, the dog, a T-rex, and occasionally one huge hyena.

Damned hyena.

It was impossible for him to tell Kiki no. Doom never before allowed himself to get too close to children, but Kiki and Luke were starved for attention. He decided, until the hybrids were defeated, the children would keep their names and be given to no one. They had taken care of each other for a long time. Things would stay the same unless the children gravitated to a certain couple. All couples had their eyes on the twins. Since the boys adored Solace, Menace kept the others away.

The time of the big sleep was still a ways away. Doom spent every waking hour with a sword until Clarity dragged him outside. The snow was only ankle high. Doom was shirtless. The cold wouldn't affect him until the season deepened. He didn't like wearing shirts regardless. A wad of snow hit him in the belly. Clarity stood laughing. She wore fur from head to toe.

Doom gazed down at his bellybutton full of snow. "You realize this means war." His eyebrow lifted.

He was hit in the chest from another direction.

Doom, quick as lightning, scooped snow and began to throw in a mad frenzy. The children squealed, Bubble-gum spun and using his paws sent snow everywhere. Muffin followed suit until Rex was buried to his chin. The dinosaur groaned and shook his head in annoyance. The twenty humans who had been found joined the fun, and the village became a mass of flurried action.

Clarity flopped onto her back to make a snow angel. When she was done, she pulled Doom over to look.

"We call these snow angels."

"What's an angel?" Doom asked.

"What's an angel?" Luke yelled in mock outrage. "Geez Louise." He flopped back and made his own while Clarity chuckled.

"Earth humans say there are angels who watch over us," Clarity said.

"I never heard of such a thing," Heath said.

"Do you have religion on your planet?" Clarity asked.

"I don't know what the word religion means," Heath said. Other humans nodded in agreement.

"That actually explains a lot," Clarity said.

Doom had no idea what she meant, and the others looked as confused. The humans from the other Earth were sweet and calm. It was hard teaching them to fight. Doom knew Clarity grew frustrated with them. Only Solace understood the drive behind Clarity. Doom could see the differences between Clarity and the other humans he'd known. He and Menace spoke often of the determination in the two females.

The villagers took to fighting like fish to water when they began to understand there was hope in their actions. As he gazed at his people playing with the humans and animals, his own hope surged. Doom was going to win his life back.

****

"Try and stay out of trouble," Doom said as his thumb caressed Clarity's cheek.

The room for hibernation was prepared. Menace was kissing Solace. For six weeks Doom's people would sleep. The humans were left to take care of everything. Clarity admitted she was excited.

"Everything will be fine," Clarity promised.

"Don't let that damned dinosaur eat everything," Edge said snarling.

Clarity laughed when Rex took off with a string of sausage in his mouth, Bubble-gum trailing fast on his heels. The bulwarks were already settled in their own sleeping chamber. The hyena was nowhere to be found.

"We'll make sure everything is ready," Clarity said.

"I won't lock the door from the inside," Doom said.

"You can," Clarity said.

"I want you to sleep with me at night, please?"

Clarity rose on tiptoe to kiss his lips. "That's going to kill me."

"Just make sure you have about a dozen coats when I wake up."

"They're all gone, at least they will be. I need the ones I have for our secret attack. I split some of them with Solace, too. Seems like Menace is as sexy as you."

"To her I hope, not you."

"I'm kinda crazy about you."

Doom smiled. The villagers gathered in the room where massive amounts of furs were strewn. An intense heat from dozens of rocks warmed the room. There was little in the way of ventilation except enough air to keep them alive. Clarity would need to open the vents further if she were to stay in here at night. It wouldn't matter, the vent could be almost sealed when she left, and she could touch the rocks to heat them.

Clarity sat near Doom as he burrowed under furs. He wore his own furs now that the weather had changed. She was surprised how cold it got. They were safe underground, but above ground was a winter wonderland. They were snowed in.

As everyone settled, the humans left. Doom reached to hug Clarity one last time. He yawned, lay back and stopped moving. He could be woken in an emergency he informed her, but he would be groggy and not very responsive. Clarity kissed his forehead and tucked the covers high under his chin. She rose, gazed at the others and left, sliding the door closed behind her. It was time to get moving.

Clarity gathered everyone into the main hall and stood on a table. She held snowshoes in her hand.

"I've had you all make a pair of these for a reason. These are snowshoes. They strap onto your feet so we can walk on top of the snow out there. We're not as trapped as Doom thinks we are. We have a lot to do."

"Woot," Luke yelled.

"Luke, you and the other younger children need to stay here and help guard the home front."

"Aw, man."

Flight jumped off his chair, arms outstretched and every so often pretended to be firing a machine gun. Soon Luke, Em, and the twins were returning fire. Nina flopped onto a fur, clutching at her chest.

"You got me." Nina in her drama queen fashion twitched and kicked her legs, once, twice, and lay with her tongue lolling out.

"Well aren't *your* Earth kids a wee strange," Heath drawled.

Clarity grinned at him. "If you only knew."

"I'd like to go with you," Kiki said. "I can help."

"Yes, of course you'll be a huge help and bring your arrows and the knife Doom made you. Everyone, I want you armed to the teeth."

"Uh, how in the blazes do you arm your teeth?" Heath said.

"Our Earth expression." Solace leaned in and whispered. "It's time we got badass."

"Well, geez, Clarity already scares the crap outta me."

"I think it's safe to travel with the weapons we trained with. The hybrids should be sleeping, but we're not sure what we'll run into. If they're awake, I want enough bombs to seal them in, and keep them sealed in, although I doubt they are awake," Clarity said.

"If they aren't asleep?" Heath asked.

"We're going to have to crawl out of here; do you really think if they're awake or haven't migrated they'll be wandering in all that snow? They may wear furs but they're animals. I don't think Neanderthals hibernated, but during winter when it was dark I bet they slept for hours."

"She has a point," Solace said.

"But what if some have humans in them. More geared to our kind?" Heath asked.

Clarity shoved a sword into his hands. "Let's go find out."

"You're lucky you're so cute, because you sure are bossy," Heath said and winked at her.

"I also have my tasers and mace."

Heath rocked on the balls of his feet in his high booties. "We better git then."

The snow was so high they had to shovel their way out the door. The air was crisp and clear. Everything asleep as far as the eye could see. They stood for a moment admiring the white snow blanket where before almost everything was green. The trees were heavy with the weight, snow bowing the branches.

Heath whistled low in his throat as he gazed around; there was no one awake from the village to whack at him.

"It's like Old Man Winter suddenly jumped on Mother Nature and she wouldn't get busy, so he flies into a rage of frozen anger because he can't get laid. Then spring will come in a few months, just like Mother Nature will finally let him come to make him mellow. That old bat keeps that man on his toes."

On snowshoes, they trekked to the hybrid mountain wary of the sabretooth cats. Doom was positive only the animals left in the area were the ones that hibernated, but they carried a barrage of bombs and swords on sleighs that skimmed over the snow easily. The mountain was easy to get to with the foliage almost completely buried everywhere. Once inside the nearest sheltered cave, they removed their snowshoes and crept within the larger cavern.

A few sucked in their breaths when the first cave they stumbled in was the hybrid sleeping chamber.

"They're all asleep. We should kill as many as we can."

"These ones yes." Clarity stood over a group of hybrids. All males, with young ones half their size in the mix. The young were all male as well. The furs under them left their nude bodies exposed. She paused for a moment noticing three who looked familiar. DaVnin's children. They were twice the size of what they were a few short months ago. Almost full grown.

"Do you think they'll wake if they smell blood?" Solace asked.

"Maybe." Clarity replied.

The idea gave her pause. Killing them now was a perfect opportunity, but when they woke everyone would have to be ready, even the other villages. Clarity exhaled loudly, her breath spiraled around her face. There had to be a better solution. There were also unexplored caves. They might risk being detected if this wasn't the entire lot. She didn't want to wage war this very moment.

"It's freezing in here, do any of you notice that?" she asked. "There's frost on their bodies. Doom's people are huddled up and warm. These hybrids look like they froze to death."

Clarity moved toward the closest male and leaned down. His eyes snapped open and Clarity stumbled back trying not to shriek, landing hard on her ass. The hybrid's body was motionless. Solace helped her up and together they made their way toward him again. The hybrids eyes remained open.

"I can't see a pulse or his chest rise and fall," Solace whispered.

"On Earth there are frogs that hibernate. They stop breathing, their heart stops beating. Maybe the dinosaur hybrid has a few more quirks than we thought," Clarity said.

"Maybe," Solace whispered.

"We should look around first," Clarity said. "See if

it's feasible to kill all of them in the mountain and leave no trace."

The group began to make their way through the intricate caverns. There were storage areas which surprised Clarity. Baskets of wheat such as Doom's people collected. She wondered if the Neanderthal structure within needed the roughage and vegetables. The closer she examined the food the more merit the idea possessed. There were roots and dried fruits.

"I have an idea," Clarity said. The others stopped. "We poison the food. If they do what Doom's people do, wake and gorge, then we could get a lot of them before they even leave the cave. We can risk coming back. There won't be any trace of us or blood if we were to miss any."

"Can we get the idea to the other villagers?" Heath asked.

"We probably could but the others need to know where their hybrids are hibernating."

"I know where there are four caves," Kiki said. "But what do we use?"

"I can make something tasteless and without a scent. We'll need to use gloves to handle it. After they've woken for the first time we can come back and set traps. I want everyone in this cave dead. There are so many caves here, but so far this is the only storage place we've found. After we poison them we can come back with swords and kill any who are alive. The traps are for added caution."

"We better get back. It takes a while and we need enough poison for the other caves," Heath said.

"Kiki, how long will it take you?" Clarity asked.

"Not long."

"How many do you need to go?"

"Just me. I'll find Nick; he'll help. The two of us have a better chance of not being detected. Nick knows every escape route possible. I'll be fine."

Clarity thought about it for a moment. The girl knew more about the area and with Nick's help they would be faster. She wasn't concerned about giving Nick poison. He already had a bomb. She wasn't Kiki's mother, though she had grown to care for the girl.

"All right, let's move out."

They filed out of the cave, strapped on their snowshoes and began the long trek back.

Chapter Fourteen

The weeks dragged after Clarity and a few others went back to poison the hybrid food. The trek back to the cave was done by only a handful. The poison was administered to every last bite of food the dinosaur hybrids would eat. A large freezer of frozen meat was discovered, and Clarity had gazed over the finding in shocked awe. Dinosaurs of all sizes were frozen, as well as mammals, heads and bodies intact, innards removed. Her heart palpated as she glanced from raptor to giant hamsters, all solid. Lifelike in death. The meat was poisoned through the open cavities. They were quick, efficient, and left as soon as the task was done.

At home, time was spent honing skills. The twins were too young for weapons but were given wooden swords. Clarity watched Luke spin and swing his weapon. He was becoming proficient for a boy his age. Em returned the swing with her sword and they clashed sending sparks.

"That's good," Nina said, Clarity agreed.

Again they bided their time waiting for Doom and his people to wake. When they did, they stumbled from their furs bleary eyed, starving, zombie style minus the gore. None spoke a word. They were frightening to watch. The villagers, including Doom gazed through everyone acknowledging no one. They gorged without stopping for hours. Shoveling food down their throats in a manner she was surprised they didn't choke. Vast amounts of beverages disappeared in a single serving.

"They're spooky," Luke whispered.

Clarity turned to look at the boy. Startled, she took a step back. Luke stood beside Rex. The dinosaur was wearing a shower cap, lipstick and eye shadow. Her lace shawl was tied around his neck. When she continued to stare Rex groaned and shook his head.

"Luke have you been in my purse?"

Flight shoved the hand holding her eye liner behind his back. The twins were also covered in make-up.

"I only wanted war paint."

Rex waggled his claws and groaned again. The pink nail polish on the dinosaur was the same Em now sported. The children took off followed by the T-rex. Clarity was glad her dangerous items were always carried on her. She should have known *her* Earth children would get into things they weren't supposed to.

The zombie villagers continued to eat, oblivious to anything. Clarity worried they would eat everything, but they had planned for the extra mouths. Silently, the villagers stumbled back to their furs. Once sleeping and covered, tucked safely away for the remainder of their slumber, Clarity nodded to the others. They would head for the hybrids first light.

Their second trek back consisted of any who could wield a weapon; they discovered the freezer empty and all food eaten. It was hard to tell if the hybrids were dead. Each was dispatched quickly, a sword stabbed into their face between the nose and mouth.

Traps were set, spiked logs triggered to smash at two heights; one set at the offspring height the other the adult males. A nagging feeling bothered Clarity. There was no sign of DaV-nin, but his offspring were dead. Word had come back with Kiki the other hybrid caves were found. Plans of action went into effect.

****

When Doom woke, he noticed Clarity curled up beside him. He was refreshed from his long sleep. He picked her up and headed for his own room where he lay her down as she woke.

"I missed you," he said.

She smiled and traced his face with her finger. "Back at you."

"I want to love you."

"Spring is coming."

"I know, I can smell it. The season will change fast."

"I noticed. Every season I've witnessed so far comes in fast with a vengeance as though it shoves the last season out of its way for a chance at life."

"When the time comes, we will kill for ours."

"We kicked ass while you were sleeping."

Doom was confused by her cocky gaze. "What did you do?"

"We poisoned the hybrids while they slept, then went in and killed them. We set traps too. Not every hybrid on your planet is dead, but we took out a lot to help even the odds."

"That was dangerous."

"They were sleeping. It was sad to kill off their young, their faces are more human. It hurt my heart."

Doom kissed her. He then settled beside her and held her. "They would have grown up and killed. If they're left all alone it would be worse. Waking to find their families dead would have been cruel. We'd have a planet full of Nick's. Revenge is a scary thing when it eats your guts. You did the right thing."

"I know, but it was hard. Solace and I had to do it. The others couldn't. Heath cried. Poor man blubbered like a baby. I don't blame him. There are some images I wish I could erase."

"My images will never be erased." Doom wiped a hand across his chest after taking off his furs and shirt. "This mark is a tool we use to cure hides. The man who loved to use it was funny. He told jokes, every time he said 'knock-knock' we cringed. The knitting needles here are from a female who could make something from any kind of fur or fiber. She was sweet and caring and loving."

The tears in his eyes began to pool and drip from his face. Clarity was quick to stop them. She wiped them away as gently as she could and though he could see the moisture in her gaze, she swallowed hard and kissed him. He only wanted to let her know she wasn't alone in her grief.

Small kisses were trailed over his tattoos. In a way, he felt she eased the sorrow of many with a kind touch. She nestled her face into his throat where her warm breath bathed him.

"I wish you had more coats," Doom said.

"We don't need them anymore. We will battle for our lives in the next few weeks. We should love as though there will be many tomorrows, with many hopes and many children. Don't ever enter a battle thinking you might lose. Perceptive and heart are everything. We *are* going to win. There is no other option."

Doom gathered her closer, loving the feel of her

warmth pressed against him. If his seed started a child he would be responsible for him or her forever. Unless the village men were as sterile as their females. He realized it wouldn't matter; he was responsible for Clarity. They should love, not as though there would be no tomorrow, but as she said, there will be many tomorrows.

She sat up and with slow deliberation he slid her fur from her shoulders. Her breasts high and round were as perfect as he remembered. Not one mark blemished her body. There was no hint of a tan line, but her cheeks were rosy. He cupped her face to kiss her lips, her cheeks and eyelids. Down to her shoulders he went sucking and tasting, running his tongue in small circles across flesh that quivered.

The furs covering her ass were hip hugging and he slid them down over her thighs until she lay exposed beneath him in only the fur shoes she called booties. Doom still didn't know what booties were, but her tone was wry or derogatory when she used the word. These ones had finally formed to her feet. When he lay over her, the tip of his hard cock tasted her warmth and he plunged while her back arched. Clarity moaned accepting all of him.

"Oh, it's been too long," she whispered.

Doom silently agreed. She was tight but wet. He spun with her and she settled over him. Her hips rose and fell in a gentle motion. Doom savored her, his hands kneading her breasts, alternating to her ass, while she made little gasping sounds. Wanting every inch of her, he flipped them again. Doom stretched over her, keeping her tucked under him. His pace increased until they were breathless.

Clarity cried out his name and for once he didn't cringe. She made his name sound sexy and safe. She called to him, wanting him, needing him. Her mouth fastened onto his flesh, searing him. Small teeth nipped, her tongue soothed. Clarity screamed as she came under him, his release rocked his core.

Spent he lay unmoving. "I love you, Clarity. Whatever happens I will die loving you."

"You're not allowed to die. If we made a little you, I can imagine the size of the diapers that will need to be changed, and you are getting your share."

"I'll remember that when I face off with a hybrid."

"You bail on me, and I'll kill you myself."

Doom chuckled. "All right, no bailing. I'm starving. Is there any food left?"

"Some. Solace and I went hunting with Muffin and Bubble-gum. Like you said, the beasts woke early. Luke has Rex trained to help him hunt those chicken dinosaurs. So we have a feast waiting. There's still snow but not much."

Clarity rose to dress and Doom sat gaping at her.

"Well come on," she said and slapped him with her shirt. "The only thing you'll catch naked and gaping is a cold."

"Yes ma'am."

Clarity punched his arm. "You ain't wearing a Stetson, bootie boy."

****

"It's time."

Doom was standing on the table with Clarity in their main room. She looked everyone over. The sacrifice was to begin. The hybrids would find war awaited. By now, Clarity felt the hybrids knew something was amiss. If they discovered their dead, they would be watching. The oil and tar traps had killed a few more. It was time to launch the battle.

"Is everyone armed?" Doom shouted.

A cheer resounded and swords raised. The only ones not attending were the youngest children except Luke. Kiki wanted him where she could see him. She knew if he was left alone he would follow. Nina, Em, and the twins hid in the hibernating room with the others, and a very protesting Flight, the door locked from the inside. The bulwarks were used to watching the village but Muffin was locked in with Bubble-gum and the children. One troublesome and mischievous T-rex nipped tails.

"Move out."

They left in pairs and groups of three, all racing from different parts of the village to meet later. Doom and Clarity set more traps around the village. Heavy containers of oil hung from the trees, fire roared nearby with simple torches. The oil was easy to heat in small containers but if the hybrids tripped the wire, they could be set to flames once doused. Kiki and Luke settled near the oil in trees with smaller fires below. A fiery arrow could be sent flying. The metal could penetrate the hybrids' hides. Clarity and the others knew from testing the metal on the hybrids they dispatched.

Clarity set her other experiments up in massive quantities. It wasn't long before the hybrids attacked.

"DaV-nin," Doom whispered and pointed.

"We're ready for him."

"Are you ready?"

Clarity smiled. "I was born ready." The song "Eye of the Tiger" raced through her head as she stood up from her hiding position. As the words played out, she began to sing. DaV-nin locked his gaze on her. The words died on her lips.

"You murdered my children. I smelled you on them," DaV-nin growled in a whistle of heated words.

"Your kind murders your own children."

She walked with confidence around the village, her gaze intense, she had no fear. Doom kept her in his sights at all times. Clarity saw him, sword ready waiting to pounce. DaV-nin threw back his head and howled at her. As he raced forward in a rage followed by two more hybrids, the oil trap tripped and one hybrid was doused. Within seconds, he was in flames. Kiki's arrow was true to the mark, hitting the creature's back. Another arrow fired by Luke engulfed the hybrid from the knees up.

DaV-nin and the other hybrid stood for a moment. Clarity saw the confusion on their faces. The glass coating covered the arrows that were dipped in the blue substance. They would shatter on impact rendering the hybrid immobile. The glass case kept the ones shooting arrows safe from accidently cutting themselves when an arrow was removed from the tubed container held on their backs. It worked, the burning hybrid dropped like a stone. The hybrid closer tried to slap out the fire, but the oil soon covered him. Another arrow sailed hitting its mark. With one hybrid down and the other flailing for only a second before falling and twitching, and both on fire, DaV-nin raced for Clarity. The other hybrid ceased to move, burning to death paralyzed. With DaV-nin's back to the children, Clarity saw another arrow hit his ass. DaV-nin roared as he slid to a stop. He yanked the arrow out and stared.

The hybrid glanced back to the trees as he held the freed arrow and snapped it in half. Clarity groaned, either Luke forgot to coat the arrow head in the freezing gel or it had no effect, or the glass hadn't shattered. The children were in danger. A bomb exploded in the distance as well as one close to DaV-nin. He was tossed into the air and came crashing down with a hard thump. Doom raced from his hiding place, he had his sword drawn, raised high. The two engaged in a battle for their lives.

DaV-nin's razor sharp claws skidded along the length of the sword drawing sparks. A fast jab and cut to his leg surprised him. DaV-nin was bleeding. Clarity pulled her sword to aid Doom, but more hybrids appeared from the foliage and instead, she taunted them to follow her. Leaving Doom and DaV-nin to battle, Clarity ran for her life while the hybrids chased her.

Deep in the heart of the jungle where the foliage was wakening, the ground was soft and wet under her leathered feet. *I will not die in booties,* became her newest mantra. All around, ground bombs were exploding, people screamed as trees toppled. The forest filled with humans of all kinds and hybrids in numbers she didn't think possible. A battalion of grouped balloons formed in areas tied high in trees were numerous hybrids prepared to attack. The balloons were popped by arrows; one by one the bombs exploded killing mass amounts of hybrids. Others roared blinded by the assault.

Firecrackers tossed under hybrid feet confused many. Younger hybrids fled. The hybrids weren't used to humans attacking; it didn't fit in their natural order. Humans were supposed to be docile and easy marks.

Their once indestructible bodies were succumbing to weapons never seen before, a knowledge that would have been theirs. Body parts were strewn, the dead or dying hybrids, the killers, were being killed. Clarity's plan was working, but if she didn't run faster she'd be dead before she could celebrate. The hybrids on her tail were catching up, and Clarity was cut off from any bombs they hid and stored. She had to do something drastic.

Clarity reached the end of the mountain and began running downhill. The grass wasn't high enough to mask any dangers from her vision. She skidded along a huge downed trunk with slippery moss and hit the bottom, her sword went flying. She flipped in a tight circle, arms pinwheeling. Her feet hit the ground and she landed running. Startled dinosaurs reared and pawed the ground. When the raptor spied her, Clarity knew it was time for a fast getaway. Having lost the hybrids in her tumble, she raced again. The open grass turned into a jungle of growing foliage.

Racing further into the woods, her chest heaving, she gasped for air but dared not stop. The single raptor was hot on her heels. Clarity came to a long slope of wet rock and debris. The rock she jumped on, landing on her hip, spiraled her down as the raptor snapped at her. Clarity bellowed as the rock sped up smashing into smaller rocks, upsetting foliage. The raptor was left behind, blasting a loud cheep, but she faced a new danger. The cliff she was fast approaching made her suck in her breath, she knew where it led. There were two separate sides to the hill she raced down. A huge drop off to the one she was headed for would kill her if she didn't act fast. Clarity, balancing precariously on hands and feet, jumped and grabbed a small tree. Her weight was too much for the tree to bear. Both she and the slab of rock careened over different sides of the cliff where she dove into the water as the rock slab went airborne smashing into pieces on other boulders.

Clarity mermaid swam up into the fast current, floundering when she burst the surface hungry for air. Animal carcasses, logs floated by. A huge piece of flat wood bumped into her shoulder. Struggling she yanked her tired body up, tried to stand and groaned. Arms out at her sides, knees wobbling, she surfed with the current. Debris from all corners assaulted her small safe haven and staying upright was her mission. The noise of the racing water bombarded her ears. The foliage before her dipped and spun and Clarity realized if she didn't get to land she'd die. The trees dipped downward on either side of the racing river, crashing together, splintering as the chasm narrowed. Groaning, she noticed the end blocked by a huge mountain base. The water formed twenty foot tidal waves, and when faced with a dead end and nowhere to go, crashed the water back onto itself.

Don't puke, don't puke.

The wood she was semi standing on was suddenly cracked into by another piece of tree trunk tossing her closer to the water's edge, almost upsetting her precarious balance. With relief she jumped before hitting the whirlpooling dead end and swung from a tree. Her drenched hands slipped, and she fell into an open running tunnel, landing in another downward slope. Light dirt beneath her feet in the open tunnel kept her from being able to find a solid grip. Her legs jelly, Clarity fought the urge to collapse, knowing she'd somersault to wherever the tunnel ended up.

As Clarity's feet raced forward, sliding, against her will she tried to steady herself by waving her arms backward. Walls high on either side showed no end in sight, and she swallowed hard when she saw the dinosaurs set a trap of their own. A small mountain of rocks was triggered in a rock slide when she tripped a vine.

Fuck me, what human taught them that?

More disturbing, a hybrid waited ahead of her in the tunnel. Clarity looked ahead and behind, her momentum speeding up. Trapped. The rocks gained on her, a few small ones rolling past, a hybrid before her, its long legs able to jump from the trap. And he was grinning. Clarity dropped and slid under the legs of the hybrid that swung for her. Yelping when the razor claws caught a tuft of hair, Clarity jerked her head to look back behind her.

Catching air instead of its intended victim, the hybrid started to run but a mad rush of racing rocks smashed into it at waist height. The hybrid stopped the flow of many, some rolling up and over his head, before he dragged his body and battered form over the tunnel's edge, muscles rippling with effort. The numerous tiny rolling stones and slick dirt under her ass and hip ached as Clarity raced faster around a wide corner, slightly rolling to a hip. Clarity screamed as she flew under the legs of another hybrid that pounced last second and missed. She sucked in her breath as she gazed behind her. Clarity wondered if her clothing was similar to what protected a motorcyclist skidding on pavement.

Holy fucking sledding. Leather, who knew?

The hybrid jumped too late and the cascade of

rocks had a similar effect, crashing into him, slamming him at his knees then thighs before he could escape. Clarity spied a bigger threat. Nowhere left to run, or slide. Clarity saw the dead end wall; the tumbling rocks a hairsbreadth behind. Her body wouldn't be able to bear the brunt of so many. Screaming, she planted her feet hard, rolled up, and jumped as high as she could trying to reach the surface. A hand and arm lowered over the edge followed by a face, and Doom was there, reaching down last second to grab her hand. Just as the rocks hit and smashed. They both went flying. Shards of rocks exploded, casting small stones over them. Doom pulled her under him.

"Holy hell." Clarity gasped.

"I can't leave you alone for five minutes."

"Where's DaV-nin?"

"Wounded and regrouping. So are we."

Doom yanked Clarity to her feet. She looked at her clothes. "Damn, I bet the people on bikes would love this material. I'm not shredded, but my ass and thighs throb, my entire body is killing me."

"It'll have to kill you later."

Gripping her hand they ran. Everywhere, humans and hybrids were fighting within the forest.

"So much for regrouping," Clarity said as they came to a halt.

Mass anarchy everywhere she looked, Clarity winced when she saw a human hit the ground. Not only were the hybrids attacking humans, but they were fending off other dinosaurs. The war had turned into a free-for-all. Death assaulted each corner, blood smeared trees, rocks, humans, and animals. Muffin ripped into a hybrid downed by Luke and an arrow under its nose.

"Don't kill the dead ones, you dummy," Luke yelled.

"Damn, if Muffin is out here, the younger children might be, too. Oh my God, there's the dog," Clarity cried out filling with horror.

Kiki was behind Luke watching her brother's back. Bubble-gum grabbed the ankle of a hybrid and would have been slashed if Muffin hadn't leaped to bite the wrist of the swinging claw. Rex hid behind Luke peeking around the boy as he fired arrow after arrow. Clarity could see the arrows he shot had brilliantly blue-topped heads under the glass shining in the high sun. Clarity wanted to panic. Night would soon be on them. The kids had reloaded. From the corner of her eye, she watched Nina pitch a bomb. Three hybrids were dispatched, limbs flying. The girl was too close, a twig sliced across her arm and she went down to crawl across the ground, trying to get away.

Solace and Menace stood back to back. Terrified, Clarity watched as the youngest children from the village spilled into the midst of the battleground. Solace and Menace raced to them, tossing the twins high into the air at a tree base and yelling for them to climb. Em followed but Flight shook loose from everyone. The boy held a small wooden sword in his hands. Clarity could see his terror.

"Run," she screamed when a hybrid went for Flight.

Solace was the first to reach the boy. Menace attacked while she grabbed Flight to run. There was nowhere safe. Without further aid, the twins could climb no higher. When Cole fell to the ground his brother jumped after him. Solace pulled the boys along with her and Flight. Everything was out in the open as they spilled into the grassed area. Raptors slunk in and grabbed the fallen. DaV-nin and Doom faced off once again. Bombs exploded while the two males engaged in heated battle. Clarity could tell there would be no regrouping. The fight would be to the bitter end.

Nina, arm bloodied slipped into Clarity's line of vision. The girl was done fighting. Weaponless she looked for shelter. Clarity took her by her good arm and raced them both to a hollowed out trunk. Nina pressed as far back against the trunk as possible.

"What do we do?" Nina asked as tears slipped down her face.

"I'm going to catch my breath. I need to catch my breath. See those knobs of wood in here? You use them to climb. Stay in here and hide. I'll help you but then I have to get back out there and help Solace."

When the ground shifted beneath her feet Clarity screamed and clung tight to a root as the dirt became an inky black hole. Nina screamed and reached for her, but Clarity pushed her back. The sides of the dirt were rolling into the ground. But Clarity could see a light and a bottom to the hole. She was sucked into a tube, a cover closed overhead; she was trapped. Her fists pounded against the hard container.

The humming of a machine hurt Clarity's head. The chamber she found herself in was a large tube swinging low in the ground. It appeared to be following a route. The motion stopped slowly. The door swung open and she crept out, blinking against the sudden light. Heart pounding, Clarity took a few small steps.

"You needn't be frightened. You're finally safe."

Clarity gazed at a tall man, his black robe hung

covering his head to the floor or perhaps he hovered over the ground. He was shadowed, broad. His voice was deep.

"Who are you?"

"Telk."

"What am I doing here?"

"You were supposed to be here last year but my colleges and I wanted to see what would play out on Earth Twelve."

"Earth Twelve?"

"Yes. There are twenty Earths in all. Each different yet the same. We control all."

"Twenty Earths? Dimensions?"

"Not at all. Each Earth is real. All different. We sent the meteor to change the course of history on Earth Six. Your Earth, Clarity. The hybrids on Earth Twelve are breeding, genetically selecting the biggest, smartest. Like humans breed dogs, but with that comes complications, disease. While the humans are disease free on Earth Twelve, they have no clue how old they are, it was to even the playing field. The hybrids die out and can only breed every year so the process of a genetic change took longer."

Clarity crept closer, her heart racing, she quivered. She always knew something more was going on. On a massive wall and surrounding them were blue balls of planets, except one, one was black. She pointed.

"Is that an Earth?"

"Yes, the oldest, Earth One. It's almost dead. Trillions of years old it advanced such as your Earth. There are no humans left. They killed one another. It was sad to watch but a learning experience, so we decided to intervene and open the sinkholes when we found your Earth on the same destructive path. We draw hope from the disaster. Before Earth One died there were too many survivors to house everyone. Every corner of the planet was inhabited. If you place caged animals together, they will fight, they need room.

"Don't you think there is a reason the world has become so overpopulated so fast? Everyone who has ever been born returns. Earth One dying and another, Earth Two in the stages of death are sending millions of souls to *your* planet. It's up to us to distribute them accordingly, but we must be careful. If not dead, some humans lack the ability to fit in with their new environment." He made a flourish with his hands indicating every planet.

Clarity took that to mean all people everywhere were privy to the almost dead planet and its deceased occupants.

"You steal people. Souls."

"When we approached your government, we gave them information of technology in return for individuals who could populate new planets. There are some humans from your Earth who are selected. It's a great honor."

"But you have killed others."

"Collateral damage, to a small degree in essence. Some sinkholes didn't open on the other side fast enough."

Clarity felt ill. "That fall I took, if it abruptly ended, it would have been like a freight train hit my body."

Telk was silent for a moment. "It would have been far worse but quick."

"Are those the people only returning to Earth after

being gone two years?"

"Yes. It was unfortunate. The sinkhole between destinations is a stasis of sorts. There is no time. For us, the problem was instantaneous, for earthlings it was two years. We thought the least we could do was offer families closure."

"Closure? They suddenly showed up. *Dead.*"

"It's necessary to thin a herd, souls are easier to distribute. We are not about barbarity, but obligation. War, terrorists, cruelty have run amok on your Earth. We had no idea our technology would be accepted so fast by your people. The government began building sinkholes, with help from us to take people to different worlds. Even the elderly embrace their new situation. Some with difficulty; others prove to be far superior. Hence the problem. There is a mark certain genders of your people wear who were off limits. The government was too afraid of amalgamation, thinking they couldn't handle change. A study was necessary.

"Those humans do handle some situations depending on the age and gender. Some have become multimillionaires on different planets, some leaders. In order to take the single person we want, they get lost in a crowd, and can't be identified. Their records are expunged. Your world is anarchy. It will settle once half the population has been removed to their destinations. Once removed from your world, in death, they are returned to the last place of origin. Our worlds. They can begin again, new, and each world will grow. Unfortunately, other alien races have discovered humans. We are not impressed with their interference. These are *our* humans. Not only are they disposing their undesirables onto other planets including yours, but the aliens are stealing humans. We will get them back."

His tone was that of annoyance, perhaps anger. Clarity remembered the frightening sinkholes other aliens climbed from. Her mind was in a tailspin.

"But my Earth inoculated again."

"The inoculation was given before the aliens discovered Earth. A strain of virus on the planet you should be on appeared. Nasty little bug. Space viruses are so unpredictable and can mutate from planet to planet. You refer to them as super bugs. The virus has been defeated; we can't take the chance with you if it returns in a different form. Not all humans were given the same inoculation. Only your Earth. You are protected from all diseases known to us."

Clarity was fuming as she absently fingered the bump on her arm. "You say you'll get the humans back. You do have a device in us."

"We tried. Not all are willing to have the shot."

"What about Doom's world? Why is he tattooed after the sacrifices?"

"That is unfortunate, but a necessity. The tattoos he and a few others bear are necessary to ensure we keep tabs on the humans. Those humans never needed to be inoculated. Their world is peaceful and disease free. Boring really. We have discovered a breed of aliens steal souls. When Doom finally succumbs, we will sort out the humans and their new locations."

"You keep a record of kills on a man's body for reference?"

"Each image is triggered by Doom's or the other leaders' memories of those people. Each object or face is his way of sharing their loss. Haunting, and yet the images help them heal. The images aren't meant to be cruel but to help him and the others cope. He is a sensitive man. I take full responsibility. The hybrids were never to evolve in such a manner as to achieve space flight. The first human they encountered changed their fate. She was a mistake. The hybrids would have been content to kill the humanoids over the next millennia and take over the planet. It was their destiny. Now they seek knowledge.

"We had no choice but to send humans. DaV-nin struck a deal with the humans. He never would have done such a thing, but again our mistake. If we sent no more humans, the villagers would have been slaughtered faster. We have enough dead and dying to attend to now. We needed to bide some time. A wave of that magnitude would interfere with us finding and relocating the humans stolen. Those aliens must not be allowed to breed with any human. The universe, the galaxies will be forever changed. We can't take a half human soul; you can't split a child, one half for us one half for the aliens.

"We tried to aid the villagers by sending your Earth children at first with adults from another Earth. The children were too young for war, but your kind of people are programmed for dominance. The battle would continue at a slow pace. The hybrids would learn no more about space flight. The other Earth is merely developing the infancy of space flight. It's time to stop sending any human to Doom's planet. We had no idea the villagers would ever hand over the human children they loved and coveted after they reached adulthood. We hadn't counted on the deep bond of the race, their loyalty to one another. The hybrids' intelligence took another leap after the slaughter. I'm sure you've guessed your Earth mind thinks differently than the others. Instead, we send the infirm or those with no concept of killing from another planet.

"But there are Earth Six children on Doom's planet."

"Again, there are casualties. It is unfortunate, but they will not last much longer."

"Unfortunate?" Her rage was building.

"Those children have no knowledge of how to create space flight. They were and are too young. We're trying to weed out the violence in these creatures. Their females began to possess too much compassion. Humans from Earth Five have no concept of killing. They are from a gentler Earth. The hybrids killed off most of their own females, unless they could scent savagery. You see why we can't send you back? By simply being there, you have changed the course of the war. The hybrids cannot have you, the stem cell memories you possess from ancestors alone are too valuable. DaV-nin will learn more than space flight. They will kill other planets. Worse, they will join with other aliens."

"Stem cell memories?"

"Not only can the knowledge you have learned be found in your brain cells. When you were a child you had three blood transfusions, each was from a scientist to help bring further knowledge to your new planet. When you were ill after your inoculation, you were brought here and infused with more stem cell memories. Some of mine included. The institution you work for is run by a college. You must remain with us until we can transport you to your new planet."

"So what are you saying? What about Doom and

the villagers?"

"Doom's world is—doomed."

"But we are fighting back. We have Solace to help."

"Solace is not meant to be in that world. With the situation here being volatile, one or two tend to run amok. We only noticed her missing. Her information, if caught, would be as detrimental as yours."

"But she's there," Clarity stressed. "Just like I was there."

"It's unfortunate this has gone on as long as it has. We have you and we will have Solace."

"Doom's people are not doomed if they have us."

"They are. You are not part of the deal. You belong to destiny."

"The hell I do."

Clarity dipped her hands into pockets she sewed in to her pants. The being howled when doused with mace. He disappeared and reappeared healed behind her. Clarity stumbled as he tried to grab her. He was close. Clarity zapped him with her taser and fled, dropping the weapon. The machine was humming and the alien disappeared again while twitching. Instinct told her he would return healed. She needed to move fast. Clarity raced to the tube and slid the rounded door closed. A flash of light, the tube zipped down, up, around and she was again inside the massive tree trunk. Nina was gone. Dazed she climbed out as the top opened. She managed to roll from the tree trunk as the tube was sucked back down.

All hell was breaking loose. The battle for supremacy was fierce. Nick had found a sword and was battling a hybrid. Hatred plain on his face; Clarity knew he battled rage. A slice of claws and the young man went down. Blood flowed from a gaping wound. Below them, a line running across the field opened a huge hole in the ground. Clarity screamed. The earth shook beneath their feet sending all spiraling to their knees. She was terrified the alien she encountered would take the many for the ones it wanted—her and Solace. She needed to warn Solace.

A roaring sound from underground rattled Clarity's teeth. The hole was massive and black to stare down into. The roaring grew in intensity while her heart thundered in her chest. Something was coming. A plane emerged, swooping, wings spinning top-like. The vessel shot from the ground sending those trying to regain their balance crashing down again.

Whoever the pilot was, he or she was in a battle. The plane slowed, spun lazily once, then twice before leveling off and Clarity rose to shaky feet. She lifted a hand across her brow to shield her eyes from the glare of the sun.

"That's my daddy's plane," Flight screamed.

The pilot was weaving, no doubt struggling to get the craft righted. The wings teetered banking left then right before the nose of the plane could settle into a straight line. Clarity gazed around her. The plane was headed to the hybrid mammoth stampede, where the ground was trampled. The only open area in sight. The wheels hit the ground and Clarity wanted to cover her eyes. The plane bounced.

Solace had the boy in her arms racing to the plane. She was screaming for Menace to follow her. Doom and Menace were back to back swinging their swords. Hybrids were falling, finally falling in droves. DaV-nin was joined by another.

"Menace," Solace screamed.

"Go. I swear on my life I will be with you soon, help the children," Menace bellowed.

The plane only had room for eight. The twins were small and considered half a person weight wise. Doom yelled for Clarity to run. Instead, she helped to physically throw the children into the craft. Solace and Kiki dragged Nick's battered body onto the vessel. The little ones went after, Solace stood back. The village children were eager to leave. The plane loaded quickly. Nina and Em were crouched near the back trying to look smaller. Kiki and Luke refused to run. The planet had been their home for three years. Clarity knew they thought their parents were dead; Kiki was certain she'd seen them fall into another sinkhole different from her and her brothers. Clarity and Doom were the closest they had to family. With Nick needing medical aid, it was the right choice to send him. The little dinosaur gazed at Luke sorrowfully. The eight year old went to stand with his pet.

"I'm staying," Solace said. "I can't leave Menace."

Solace was yelling over the confusion and noise of the plane. The children were shouting. Clarity and she clutched hands. Clarity tried to yell her worries over the noise.

"Aliens," Clarity screamed at Solace.

"What?"

As Solace stepped away from the plane a man grabbed her back, her hand ripping from Clarity's clasp. Solace screamed for Menace. Amidst the foray Menace heard her call. He raced for her. Solace was shoved into a seat, the door slammed closed and the plane began to take off. Menace was pumping his legs faster, faster. The plane hit a bump and was airborne.

"I will find you," Menace screamed. "No matter where you go I will come for you."

Solace had her face pressed to a window, tears streamed in rivers down her face. She mouthed the words *I love you,* hands splayed against the glass. Menace, head in his hands dropped to his knees.

"I will find you," he whispered.

"Menace," Clarity screamed.

A hybrid was creeping up on him. Menace slammed his sword behind him into the hybrids belly. He stood, spun and yanked the weapon free to slam it into the hybrids face. The hybrid went down.

The plane soared higher, up into the heavens then dropped straight down where the hole remained, shrinking. The craft turned on its side and through it went. The hole closed. They were gone. Where, Clarity had no clue, but from the look on Menace's face she knew he would be leaving soon. He would find a way; no matter what, he would be finding Solace.

Menace bellowed and Clarity spun. DaV-nin was too close to her and gaining fast, clawed fist raised in fury, one heated blow would be her demise. With no sword or spear left to use for fighting Clarity had one chance. She pulled the small bottle of hairspray from her pocket and her lighter. She held the lighter to the spray and aimed for his face. DaV-nin, caught off-guard, howled in agony clawing at his eyes. Pools of blackened soot dripped down his cheeks leaving scorch marks in their wake, as his eyes melted leaving hollowed sockets. DaV-nin threw his head back and roared to the sky. Clarity was thrown back, away from imminent danger as Doom attacked.

For the moment, Doom had the upper hand. His broadsword smashed into DaV-nin's arm. DaV-nin, blinded, took the hit hard. DaV-nin spiraled back and stood still, a calm washed over his demeanor making Clarity catch her breath. Clarity screamed when his body jerked and the image of a face pressed hard to DaV-nin's high upper chest, from within, bulging out from his torso. Side to side, the face pressed against inner flesh as though seeking escape. From within, she could make out the features of the human cheeks, jaw and eye sockets.

DaV-nin took two claws and ripped high into his flesh, two horizontal slits where the sockets were slowly exposed, a trail of blood dripping, allowing the opening for the eyes underneath. The two eyes blinked, cleared, and stared at Clarity with fury. DaV-nin thundered an ominous laugh, raising the goose bumps on her arms. She thought she might vomit.

The hybrid could see using his skeletal humanoid Neanderthal eyes, weapons. Leaping, DaV-nin landed onto Doom slicing at his flesh. Slashing tattoos. Long talons and claws ripped into him mercilessly. Doom faltered, tried to swing his sword and missed, the weapon clattered to the ground when DaV-nin sliced across his back. With his last act of war, Doom grabbed his knife and hamstrung DaV-nin. Clarity grabbed Doom's sword and rammed it in one of the exposed eyes. DaV-nin bellowed in agony. Clarity ripped the sword out and plunged again. DaV-nin went down. He stayed down.

Clarity dropped the weapon and staggered to Doom. She threw back her head and screamed as

Doom's blood soaked the ground beneath her. She couldn't feel a pulse. Clarity staggered to her feet, screaming, her vocal chords straining as she stormed a circle around his battered body.

"You did this!" Her fury was aimed at the Heavens. "You let this happen. You had no right. Fix him. Fix him, do you hear me? So help me God I'll find you if you don't, and when I do I will slaughter all of you. Every last one of you. I know you can hear me. I found your tracking device in my arm, you fuckers. Did you think to pull me away once he's dead? I'll use it to find *you*. You know I'm smart enough. You will die. I hate all of you. Fix him or kill me before I get to you."

The tall dark shrouded alien appeared a few feet away from Clarity. She leveled an intense gaze so filled with fury onto him it reflected back at her in his dark eyes, and he retreated a step.

"Perhaps you are too primitive for our advanced culture."

"I'll show you primitive, you fucking piece of crap."

Clarity lunged at him. She knew he would disappear, but she was ready. She had already reached for her leather square, the sand glued to each side of the surface. The blue rock lying at her feet spilling out of the broken glass case was snatched up. He returned a few feet to her left and Clarity let her stone fly. The glowing rock hit his midriff and the surprised shock on his face gave her satisfaction. He was paralyzed in seconds from the waist down. The being was large, she knew it would take more than one stone to collapse him but she needed him to speak. He was on his knees. Clarity raced to Doom, grabbed his knife and went for the alien, she placed the knife at his throat.

"You have three seconds," she bellowed.

"I am paralyzed."

"Your friends aren't. I know they can see what's happening." The knife nicked his flesh.

"This should prove to be an interesting new turn for the planet."

Doom's body spasmed and lifted off the ground. Blood dripped from his wounds. Then stopped. The claw lines raced backward to close the gaping wounds. He coughed and gasped in air. Doom's eyes opened. His body floated higher until he stood upright hovering over the ground. He was healed. The tattoos adorning him began to slip from his body as though wind were sending them to freedom. One by one, they vanished until the reminders of his pain were gone.

The alien in her grasp melted from her arms, disappearing after the tattoos. Clarity screamed when the small pink mole on her flesh began to burn. The skin peeled back high on her left arm to reveal a microchip. It was ripped from her skin by an unseen force. Blood oozed between her fingers where the small mark had been. She knew she would never see these aliens again, even if they did continue to watch this planet. They wouldn't steal her away. She was too dangerous.

"Clarity?"

Wide-eyed and open-mouthed Doom gazed at his flesh, his hands trailing over his body as his feet settled onto the ground. His knees buckled and he dropped. "My shame, it's gone."

"It was never yours to begin with. You were never at fault. The sacrifices weren't your mistakes. The only thing you're guilty of is loving your people."

She raced to him and dropped to the ground as he struggled to stand. She wrapped her arms around him as tight as was humanly possible, and sobbed into his chest. Great heaving noises were torn from her and Doom tilted her face.

"You *can* cry."

She snorted a laugh. "Of course I cry moron."

"You're beautiful."

"My nose is running."

"It runs well."

"I'm glad you like it because it's running all over your chest."

She wiped at his chest until he stopped her. Doom pulled her tight to his flesh and stood. Cradled against him she felt small, but not alone. The sun in the distance was lowering and they watched as it crested on some other part of the planet, gracing the earth in brilliant reds and oranges. A slight breeze ruffled her hair. It had been a long year.

"I don't understand what's happened," Doom said.

He gazed at the hybrid bodies strewn along the forest floor.

"We won. At least for now. And boy do I have a story to tell you."

"Our future is out there," Doom said.

"Do you think Menace will find Solace?"

"Yes. Or die trying."

Doom began walking. "You can put me down now."

He grinned and kept going. "You are my clarity. I think I'll keep you next to my heart for a while longer."

Clarity placed her head against his chest where his

heart thumped. Their work wasn't over. In droves over the horizon, Clarity saw villagers from other tribes walking toward Doom's home.

My home.

There would be no more sacrifices, no more sinkholes. As she watched, Heath reached to hold the hand of the woman beside him. More hands clasped with neighbors. The remaining children were smiling. Kiki took the hand of her brother and walked with the other villagers. Rex took a playful snap at Muffin's tail until she and the dinosaur and dog were soon in a free-for-all.

Clarity wrapped her arms tighter around Doom's neck. Doom's skin was warm against her face. There would be other battles, but not now, not this very moment. The second they reached home she knew what she wanted, she would show him beyond a shadow of a doubt he was Clarity's Doom. There had never been a more beautiful name than his.

About the Author

I love to write about everything and can't wait for an idea that gripes me and sends me to a new place. Between worlds keeps me busy, that and chasing after my children and grandchildren. Plus one ornery 116 pound mastiff who thinks he's a lap dog. Welcome into my adventures, and hang on!

~*~

Visit C.L. at

http://clscholey.com

~*~

To chat with C.L. Scholey and other Wild Rose Press authors of erotic romance, join us at

www.groups.yahoo.com/group/thewilderroses.

Also Available

Universe Hunters: Taken

by

C.L. Scholey

https://amzn.com/B01CV4KEMG

Being lost in the forest is the least of Cali's worries when she's attacked by a flesh-eating creature not of this world. She is rescued by a scorching alien light that kills the creature but inadvertently burns her. Cali wakes to find her body healed but her sanity in question. She can't really be zipping through space on a vessel manned by two light beings who have taken the form of human men—two sexy as hell human men calling themselves…Universe Hunters.

Two male beings, one human female. Life as Cali knows it changes in the blink of an eye, or in her case, a flicker of light.

Also Read

Captive Heat

by

Susanna Eastman

https://amzn.com/B015JPRND2

Captured by slave traders, Mia Townes fears for her freedom, her life, and worse. Drugged by her captors, her body is not her own. When she's rescued by Jaden Zoma, the rugged space trader becomes her only hope of sexual relief for light years in any direction. Then he goes into heat.

With the sexual time bomb on a short clock sabotaging Mia's self-control and Jaden's need to mate, can these virtual strangers from a different species trust each other enough to meet the erotic demands of survival?